DAHLIAS, SAPPHIRES, AND COOL AUTUMN DARK

A City of Secrets, A Girl Who Won't Stay Lost

THE NEWPORT DIARIES BOOK 2

REBECCA ROYCE

Dahlias, Sapphires, and Cool Autumn Dark: A City of Secrets, A Girl Who Won't Stay Lost

Ebook 978-1-960447-25-8

Paperback Print 979-8-90122-000-9

Hardback Print

Copyright @ 2025 by Rebecca Royce

Cover art by Mibliart Designs

Print Cover Art by Mibliart Designs

Content Editing: Virginia Nelson

Copy Editing: Jennifer Jones at Bookends Editing

Final Proof Editing: Viv Jackson

Formatting: Ripley Proserpina

forbidden without the written permission of the publisher.

Published by Rebecca Royce

www.rebeccaroyce.com

"You snagged your favorite spot today," Jeremy said as he slumped down in the chair next to me, earning a glare from a woman typing on a computer at the table nearby. Her expression gave a clear message—she was working, so we needed to stay quiet. I might have shot her some attitude if we weren't in a library.

Instead, I smiled at him, happy he decided to surprise me with a visit. I offered my hand, pleased when he slipped his fingers through mine—*will the novelty of it ever wear off?* Aloud, I said, "You hate the library."

Julian loved the library, but his twin wasn't as much of a fan. It was kind of epic—I got to see what parts of Manhattan each of the four Lent brothers loved, and so far, I found them surprisingly revealing about their personalities. Over the last two months while we explored the city and each other, real life hardly touched us. I'd been dumped here five months earlier—exiled by my aunt in Chicago, who accused me of trying to seduce her boyfriend before throwing me out. I read that he managed to make bail, but he still faced charges for rape in Maryland. Not seeing my family for months didn't make me sad in the least.

I won't be upset if I never see any of them again. I doubted I would manage that feat, though. Since my mother's death, I'd been passed around among relatives. First, Uncle Shane and Aunt Susan got custody, then Aunt Amelia, until they finally stuck me with Aunt Tricia and Uncle Matt. He was never around, and the last time I saw Aunt Amelia was in the Hamptons when she had come in specifically from Chicago to try to ruin my life. Since then, I'd called the Lent brothers' gorgeous Park Avenue apartment in Lenox Hill home. I'd moved in after their mother—slipping into a slight break from reality, seeing conspiracies in every corner—threw me out of their Hamptons house. All of it would sound so unbelievable, except it happened to *me*—I lived through all of it.

Jeremy squeezed my cold fingers. "Were you waiting for Jules? He made several of the guys swim laps for getting lazy over the summer. Something about *not being in polo shape*."

I shook my head. "I knew you guys were busy today, though. I just came to read and think."

"Couldn't do that at home?" He lifted an eyebrow. Jeremy recognized hiding, and I knew it. Then again, I didn't turn off the Wi-Fi on my phone, which meant I knew they could see my location, like I could theirs. They added me to the app that tracked each other after my phone got destroyed when I was shipped away from the Hamptons. Being unable to reach me scared all of them, made worse when they couldn't find me, so the tracking gave them a level of security... so long as I wanted to be found and didn't turn off the Wi-Fi.

I hadn't—so far. Honestly, I absolutely loved knowing I could find them and they cared about my location and safety.

I wasn't tracking anyone while reading *The Secret History* by Donna Tartt, though. Hence how Jeremy was able to surprise me. Julian had handed me the book, claiming it would help prepare me for Pullman. Tomorrow, we would begin school there together—me for the first time. I loved the book so far and wouldn't complain if it set the mood for the school. It was dark, but it suited my vibe. In response, I gave him *Jane Eyre*, finding it crazy that he'd never read it for school. I didn't know if it would be his thing. I hoped he would love it. Since getting back to Manhattan, we traded books almost weekly, as his favorite spot was also mine.

Jeremy and Julian started water polo practice weeks ago, despite school not having begun yet. Apparently, it was traditional for Pullman to kick off their season two days after Labor Day. They both seemed so busy and often tired, but then they were team captains. Pullman wanted to win, so even though they both secretly hated the sport, they did their best to get everyone ready. Before they'd met me, they'd spent most of the spring swimming in a club for off-season.

Everyone stayed in shape for the start of their UIL season. They started swimming laps—a lot of them—three weeks before the team even got back together. Exhaustion pulled at Jeremy's handsome features even as his gaze adored me in the main branch of the New York Public Library.

I still haven't answered his question, I realized. "There's a task I don't want to do, and I couldn't bring myself to do it, so I diverted myself here instead."

He leaned forward. "What don't you want to do, Princess?"

I loved when he called me Princess. Over time, they'd each given me pet names. For Jeremy, I became Princess, even if I remained both secretly and not secretly the *Poor Relation* to the rest of the world—in more than fiction.

Julian called me Baby. Sometimes I shivered hearing it. I belonged to him, or that's how it felt, like he'd given that name to *only* me.

Barrett—who started at Columbia the next day—made

me his Sweetheart. If I had my way, the whole world would be sweet to Barrett. Despite no one understanding him outside of his family, he had proved to have the most open and biggest heart out of them all.

Even inside his family, I wasn't convinced their dads really understood Barrett.

Phoenix just called me Red, the simplest name, because of my long red hair. But when he said it, it sounded like his favorite color, though I couldn't explain why.

Then again, maybe I read too much into everything?

Whatever. Their nontraditional family core, which had begun long ago, continued when Rosalind secretly married four men. In public, they all called Kit *Dad*, but they varied biologically. Barrett was Daniel's, the twins were Stephen's, and Eric was Phoenix's dad. The nontraditional family setup didn't *start* with their generation, though. Their grandmother, Dina, married four husbands—Nathaniel, Robert, Victor, and Ed. All of them died in a car accident before my guys were born. And Dina hadn't been the first either. It had been going on for generations, and I didn't know if even they knew when it started.

Their family existed in the social limelight of wealth, yet they managed to hide their secret lives in plain sight. Apparently, nontraditional families were more common than I ever guessed, with a whole area of Louisiana populated with families like theirs. No one in New York knew the truth. I would keep their secret; in return, they kept mine. Normally, everything went into my work, since I was the writer and creator of *Gretchen, the Poor Relation*. My stream got popular, though I created it to keep my soul alive despite the hell of my everyday life at the time. They were the only people in the world who knew about it.

"Shouldn't you be at practice?" I asked as I released his hand. In public, there could only be cautious affection. If someone saw me romantically connected with all four of them, questions would be asked, which was too much attention. So instead, we lived with a certain amount of caution.

A man walked by wearing a pair of torn sneakers. They appeared otherwise new, save for the hole, which hit my radar. I couldn't make him out, so I surreptitiously took another peek. *What does it mean?* Usually, I could tell a lot about a person by their shoes, although the Lents defied my sneaker logic. *I should reconsider my system.*

"Redirecting me?" Jeremy shook his head. "I'm not distracted. I should be at practice, but my shoulder hurts. Besides, Julian is having them swim, so I left." He shrugged, but it didn't look like his shoulder hurt.

I lifted an eyebrow. "Really?"

"Okay." He sighed. "I just *left*. They could throw me off the team, if they wanted. I probably would thank them."

Despite beginning their senior year, the twins seemed altogether done with school. They would have to go to college, so I hoped they were sick of Pullman, not just done with school. A junior, like Phoenix, I knew I wasn't nearly ready for the real world yet.

"I need to pick up my Pullman uniform from Aunt Tricia's. It got delivered to the home of my legal guardian." I shrugged, pretending a casualness I didn't actually have, since I constantly feared it would all be taken away from me. "Technically, I'm supposed to be living there. I hope she didn't do something to my uniform. Do you think she would do something like that?"

He frowned. "I wish you'd said something sooner. No way you're going over there alone."

They had so much on their plates—school, the bombshell Kit had dropped on them about their mother's family, and the possibility it all linked to Phoenix's kidnapping. Come to think of it, Phoenix wasn't anywhere near sober for over a week. He alternated between ADHD meds—prescribed, though his brothers thought inappropriately—and living in a K-hole.

I couldn't fathom how he got through school. Then again, I would soon see firsthand.

Regardless, I didn't want to add another problem to their pile. "I can do it. Don't worry about it. I'm actually going now."

He squeezed my hand again, and I smelled the faintest scent of chlorine. They always carried a bit of the scent lately. His blond hair hung dry around his handsome face, but he likely hadn't showered yet. Like everything else about the four Lent Brothers, I already loved the smell. So. . .*them*.

I hated letting go of his hand. The summer meant we were alone in New York City, but as school approached, the rich and powerful returned in droves from their summer homes. The Hamptons. Martha's Vineyard. Nantucket. Europe. Asia. The brothers recognized someone everywhere, which meant we had to be more careful.

We remained completely non-compliant about the rules in the Hamptons, but their father Stephen had read them the riot act over Zoom about it the week before. If we were going to make our relationship work, we had to adopt the same carefulness as the rest of the family. Sure, people asked questions. . . *Why does Kit, technically Rosalind's husband, live with his wife and three brothers all together?* Generally, people thought they were just too close—making them an odd but acceptable level of weirdness.

Phoenix said people thought Stephen was gay and hid it, Eric kept a woman in the Village who he couldn't marry, and Daniel still pined for a long lost love. I didn't know where people came up with those stories, and neither did they. Regardless, no rumors claimed they all loved Rosalind, meaning they kept the world fooled.

We would have to manage something similar, if things worked, and if we stayed together. *If they don't get tired of me. If I don't get sent away.*

He smiled, undeterred. "I'll come with you. You can't carry all of it yourself."

He wasn't wrong, but I planned for that. "I'm getting a car."

I hated using my aunt's credit card, but some things were necessary. To attend school, I needed my clothes, so a car apparently fell on that list. I used my subway pass from Barrett sparingly, but I still wasn't one hundred percent certain I knew my way around well enough. And it was going to be too much for me to carry right now.

They preferred it if I didn't travel alone at night, but it would happen out of necessity eventually.

"Smart, but I'm still tagging along for moral support. She might not be home, so you can grab your clothes and get out without her even noticing."

In my wildest dreams. "What if she is?"

"Then we deal." He shook his head. "Where did Barrett and Phoenix go, anyway? I didn't recognize their locations when I looked for you."

"Barrett is getting a haircut," I said and smiled. "While Phoenix is...doing what Phoenix does once a week."

He knew I meant buying drugs, though we never spoke about it outright. He only returned to his brothers after they agreed to let him live with his choices, leaving it the constant elephant in the room. No one got to discuss it except Phoenix. He knew we worried and wanted him healthy, but until he wanted that too. . .

Until then, I just love him. Judging him would fix nothing. Loving him might help him someday fix himself.

"Right." Jeremy nodded. "Well, let's get this done. We can drop in on Granny, too. Jules checked on her yesterday, but it'll be good to see her. If everyone is back, we'll go out to eat. A final hurrah before tomorrow."

I loved the idea. "Thanks for giving me something to look forward to today. All I've been thinking about is the apartment, Tricia, my family, and then Pullman."

He winced. "All bad stuff. No wonder that look is back on your face."

I shook my head. "What look?"

"The *world might blow up* look. You lost it after we got back from the Hamptons, once we chased you back to the city. You stopped looking like the end was near, and instead you've been beautifully happy." He pointed to my eyes. "Now your brown eyes are hurting again. I hate it. I want to fix it. Let me." He lowered his voice. "I love you."

He was so good about saying it. Out of all four of them, he was the only one who did. I wanted to say it back, to proclaim it to all of them. I loved them.

But if I said it, and *then* everything blew up? It might kill me.

He smiled. "I know you love me, but you're still scared. The day you say it, I'll know you feel safe."

We ordered a car, and no sooner were we inside and moving than Jeremy leaned over and kissed me. Hard. A claiming, so I held on, letting him. I kissed and kissed him until we arrived at my aunt's building. I should try to think about it as their granny's building, as Dina's building since she lived there too. It would be less negative of a connotation.

We both panted, my body buzzed, his eyes glazed, and he laughed, throwing his head back. "Shit. Okay."

We'd only kissed and snuggled so far, none of us going further despite the temptation. I feared sharing so much with them and, like love, trying to survive once it inevitably ended.

I hoped they were right. I hoped time would solve everything.

Dina caught sight of us as she exited the building and we got out of our rideshare.

"Darlings!" She rushed over to hug us together tightly. "I love you. This is such a gift. What are you doing here? I have a meeting. We will get the East River cleaned up this year, even if we have to clean it ourselves."

Was it very dirty?

If any person could handle this, it would be the glamorous, full of secrets, beautiful seventy-something year old Dina Lent, the matriarch of the family. I loved her. My summer project started with typing up her journals, something I intended to return to once she gave me permission again. In her words, she wanted me to enjoy the summer rather than working.

I did.

"I have to grab my Pullman uniform from upstairs."

She smirked. "Tricia runs from me when we see each other. I think she's afraid I might treat her like someone did Ted." Her eyes twinkled. "Excellently handled with style, I heard."

Kit. We were all but sure he set the cops on Ted after Ted and Aunt Amelia pulled a stunt at the Lents' Hamptons house.

"Well, we are three ships crossing, so to speak. I love you."

Jeremy kissed her cheek. "I love you. Any news we don't have?"

Her smile dimmed. "Your mom is getting better. Kit and Daniel will be back this week. Stephen, the next. Eric is on leave until Mom is better. His partners aren't happy with him —he is the biggest earner in their practice—but they know the deal if they want to work with the most sought-after plastic surgeon in Manhattan. He keeps his own schedule. He'll stay at the lake with Mom and come back with her, but you know all this. You want to know about the other part. Phoenix's kidnappers. Alatheia's family secrets. Unfortunately, the answers remain no. What is hidden, for now, remains hidden."

She waved her hand in the way she did when she was done with a topic. "I am going to go hold kittens tonight. Oh, Alatheia, I think it's time. Our project? Start back up."

I nodded. "I will."

A taxi pulled up behind us as Jeremy shook his head. "The one that she won't tell us about."

"Yes, that." Dina grinned. "Oh, look, it's Barrett."

As he got out of a stopped taxi, he kissed his granny then she rushed away. *To clean the East River.* I grinned. She ran more charities than I could count.

"I was going home, but I saw you guys on the app, so I diverted the taxi a block. Were you visiting Granny, or are we here for something less desirable?"

Jeremy frowned. "We have to get her Pullman uniforms from her aunt."

Barrett winced. "Well, then, let's do it. You okay, Sweetheart?"

I nodded and then shook my head. They would know if I tried to lie or pretend I was okay.

The doorman opened the door for us. He was new, which meant that Barrett didn't know him. He stopped to introduce himself, letting him know Dina was their granny and that my aunt lived upstairs. By the end, Barrett knew just about everything about the guy, a skill I both admired and feared.

Barrett loved music and conversation and could play the piano like a professional. Even though he wanted to open music clubs, support musicians, and teach, he studied law instead. For the moment, anyway, because it was what his family wanted from him.

We entered the elevator, so I steeled my back. Gravity

intensified, my every step heavier as we approached Aunt Tricia's door.

"Got your key?" Barrett leaned over and quickly planted a sneaky kiss on my neck.

I breathed, eased by his touch. "I do." I pulled it out of my bag.

"I hate that you're going to Pullman without me." Barrett frowned.

"Me too." I also hated thinking about the beautiful coeds he might prefer over me at Columbia, but that could happen anywhere.

Jeremy sighed. "I'll be there."

"Yes, but you and Jules will be in the senior hallway, separate from the rest of the school. You'll never see her."

That means what? No one told me. The elevator dinged and opened.

With a groan, Jeremy hit Barrett's arm. "You just made her *more* nervous."

"You didn't mention that yet, dipshit?"

"No," he shouted back but then shrugged with one careless shoulder. "I'll find a way to see her. Julian will find a way, too. Phoenix will be with her constantly. They even have a class together, first one every day."

He wasn't wrong. I stepped toward the door. Due to being placed in remedial study skills class together, we would have one class together. I snorted to myself, thinking we both fit there, since it was where they put any students they feared might not be able to keep up with their studies due to past academic performance. Apparently, it was his fourth time in the class, though it would be my first. People graduated out of it, but not Phoenix. He didn't give a shit, in his words. I probably wouldn't get out of it, either. In addition to being dyslexic, I honestly wasn't very smart when it came to school stuff.

After I turned my key in the lock, the grandfather clock ticked in welcome.

No one greeted us, and I took a deep breath in relief. *Maybe we can just get in and out.*

"Alatheia," my aunt said, making ice skate through my veins and freeze me like a statue. "I wondered when you would get around to gracing my doorstep. I see you brought the Lents with you. Two of them? You're home, so do you intend to ruin lives here again?"

A martini glass clinked with ice in her hand, and she took a gulp as if the noise reminded her she held the drink. I bit my lip, since *of course a martini in the middle of the day. Why not?*

"Aunt Tricia." I kept my gaze down, my head slightly bowed. It went better for me when I pretended obedience and subservience, at least. "How have you been? I came home to get my uniforms, if you don't mind me picking them up."

"Where *exactly* will you be taking them?" She sloshed some of her gin onto the floor, gesturing as she spoke, then taking another hearty gulp. I could smell it from across the room, the scent biting at my nose with memories.

I cleared my throat, trying to resist the bile rising there with my anxiety. "I'll be staying elsewhere."

"Oh *no*, dear. No, you are not." She laughed. "You are *mine* to deal with. You'll be staying here. You live with me, your legal guardian."

I think my heart stopped, since all of my fears came true in that moment.

"No, Tricia, she's actually not." Barrett strode past me toward my bedroom as if he belonged there. "Unless you want me to get my granny up here? If you would like, we can have her explain to you all the reasons you're going to do exactly what we told you to do. She is coming home with us, as per the plan. You're going to continue to pay for her credit card, which she hardly uses anyway, and provide anything else she needs to ask you for. If you don't agree, we can look into things a bit closer. . ." He paused. "We wouldn't want that, would we?"

Barrett used to be polite to her, but apparently those days were over. My family had tried to ruin me in his home. Rumors would likely circulate due to her sister's actions at that party. Maybe the people who heard them would know Ted was an accused serial rapist before they heard my aunt's other version—where I seduced her boyfriend.

But rumors still would persist.

My aunt's face twisted, derision not pretty on her features, so like my mother's. "You Lents. You think you control everything? You don't. I've got news for you. She is here by my good graces alone. You have *no* idea how much worse things could've been for her." She almost sounded hysterical. "The second I can, she'll be sent to boarding school—a far kinder fate than my sister wanted for her."

She shouted the words, and half the remaining martini ended up covering my shirt. I didn't drink it myself, and the smell brought back memories so fast and hard, I finally unfroze. I shouted in surprise, and Barrett turned around quickly to protect me. I obeyed my reflex, tugging the fabric away from my body and trying to squeeze it out as if the chill burned.

Way too dramatic. I forced myself to calm, adjusting my shirt back as best as I could. *She's not going for death by martini.*

"I'm okay." I said for my sake as much as Barrett's, since his laser focus on me when I gasped seemed to be awaiting a target.

Jeremy wasn't deterred at all. As Barrett rushed into my bedroom, Jeremy stormed past my aunt into the kitchen and returned with a soft blue towel. He began patting at the martini covered fabric, his voice intentionally calming as he said, "Let's get you dried off."

"You let him touch you like that? On your breasts!" she shrieked. "You little slut."

Whack. I didn't anticipate her slap, so I didn't see it coming. I cried out, bending over in shock.

"Hey, don't you touch her." Jeremy's voice became frighteningly low. He yanked her arm back, jerking her two steps away from me. "Back off. You *never* touch her again, do you hear me? Your daughter in London? Does she like her life? Her husband works for a subsidiary of a company my uncle owns. Do you understand what I'm telling you? Alatheia is *with us* now. And if I'm being totally honest, if you weren't a woman, you'd be on the ground right now for what you just did."

Barrett rushed out of the room, carrying hangers. "Did she just *hit* her?"

I turned away from them all, facing the wall, because I couldn't resist the urge to cry. I couldn't stop myself, even though I hadn't been hit since Chicago. I never saw it coming then, either, but I should have expected it. Violence hung in the air of the apartment from the day they moved me into it. I always knew, it was only a matter of time.

Is it going to leave a mark? I didn't want to start school with a black eye, but I once had one last for almost a month after a PI accidentally punched me.

Fuck. I put my fist in my mouth, trying to keep the tears at bay. I bit down hard, the pain a sharp distraction from the way my face throbbed and my memories crashed into one another.

"Take these." Barrett said to Jeremy, passing him the clothing. "I'll grab the rest. You're going to regret that, lady."

I couldn't turn around, couldn't help them, and couldn't do anything other than bite down on my fist and breathe. I blinked fast, trying to keep tears from falling. Jeremy pressed a hand on my back, so I let him lead me away from the closest living relative to my late mother. Her twin. Identical. Identical to my mother, who I missed so much my chest hurt with it.

I shouted, spinning on my heel and releasing my fist from my mouth. "Why do you hate me?" I kept my eyes closed, tears pouring out despite my attempts. I couldn't control any of it anymore. "Why?" I couldn't look at her, so I just waited, my heartbeat sounding too loud and too fast in comparison to the tick of the clock.

She didn't answer me. Instead, a distant door slammed.

"Let me look at you, Princess. Look at me." When I blinked open my still tearing eyes, Jeremy held four pairs of skirts in his hands. Despite that, he examined my wounded face with his gaze. "Bet that hurts. I'm so sorry, but you're going to be okay. I...I want her dead. I mean *actually* dead."

"Can we go? As soon as Barrett comes back out." As if I called him into being, he appeared, carrying more clothing. "Can we go now?"

"Are you okay?" He sounded frantic. "I can't believe that just happened."

I could. *It is always a matter of time.*

⚜

"No RED MARK." Phoenix ran his fingers through my hair, and I laid my head on his lap. His gaze might be a bit more vacant than I liked, but he wasn't lost, which meant a lot. He stroked my hair over and over, seemingly enchanted by the repeated motion. "They let her live. They have so much more restraint than I do."

I once thought he might strike the PI with his skateboard, and the guy didn't even mean to hit me. He didn't though, not turning to violence when his temper got hot. Phoenix might be impulsive, but he wasn't stupid. He might talk a big game, but I knew he wouldn't have hurt my aunt, either.

I sniffed. "I feel like such a big baby. I got slapped, so what? I need to get over it. I've had worse."

He met my gaze. "I hate knowing that even more. Still, I'm glad they both threatened her. I'm also glad she knows our position now, too. Kit knew they had some idea the power we wielded, but not all of it. Barrett probably emailed him." I'm not sure why that made him laugh, but it did. "Got to cover our bases. Anyway, you're staying and that's the bottom line. Sorry I wasn't there."

I took a long breath. "Are you going to be okay tomorrow?"

"No. I'm never okay in school. But I'll be. . .alert? If that's what you're asking me. Right now, everything is beautifully blurry, but even I know I can't get away with it at school. I hate school."

I remembered getting to see the video game he was creating when we were alone a few weeks before, and I couldn't help finding him utterly talented and brilliant. In his game, he made the zombies the good guys, and humans were the ones who didn't understand. Humans tried to kill them, when they just tried to keep their community safe. A muted game, but he intended it to have very little noise as a finished product. Just breathing, while they tried to explain to a world that wouldn't listen.

The project reminded me of the man, a reflection while a creation at the same time.

I hated how pain chased him constantly, as real and visible as a ghost that lingered behind him in shadow form.

I understood the drugs, even if they scared me—he avoided his pain with them. He hated using them, but he didn't know another way.

I hated that he thought it made him a zombie.

If he ever did anything with the game, it would sell a billion copies. Despite my easy acknowledgment of his gift, his imposter syndrome was loud, so for some reason, he couldn't see it.

He stroked my hair again, his gaze as peaceful as it ever became. "But it will be better this year. You'll be there, and that will make it much better." He smiled, a wistful expression. "Julian suggested you be his girlfriend, with him as the public face, the way Kit is for Mom. He intended to tell everyone at lunch tomorrow. He told us last night after you fell asleep."

Wow. I used to wake up at the slightest noise, but apparently, they shared conversations while I was out. *I really do sleep better with them here.*

"And?" I wasn't sure why he decided to tell me, especially if they all decided already.

Phoenix's lips curled into a devious grin. "I told him if he did that, I would kiss you on the steps of Pullman at opening bell. That way, everyone would know you actually belonged to me."

I lifted my head, heat flooding my cheeks as my heart beat faster. "Oh, I...see. So, you didn't like that idea?"

"No. You're *mine* in public or you're no one's. Jeremy said, if I intended to do that, then he would post on social media everywhere, telling the world you are his girlfriend."

Double wow. All of this while I was sleeping? "This is complicated?"

Phoenix nodded, still stroking my hair calmly. "Barrett pointed out it would be best to just say you were his, since he's not there. Besides, as the eldest, someday you'll be his wife, legally. Traditionally, the oldest male marries the wife legally. Things kind of dissolved at that point, so we had to move to text to avoid yelling at each other."

I put my head back down, chin hitting my neck with a snap. "Have we made a terrible mistake?"

His thumb stroked across my forehead. "No, Red. We're good. I think. . .I think ultimately we will do what you want. When you figure out what that is, you'll tell us."

What I want? I barely understood how the relationship could work. Honestly, I still wobbled between feeling insanely lucky and like I was being terrifically greedy by keeping them all to myself. But I got off his lap, leaning over to kiss him before I got up totally. He touched my un-slapped cheek with his thumb.

"What I want is for everybody to be happy. Do you think

that's even possible?" I whispered, staring into his eyes for the truth. "Can you be happy?"

He blinked. "I am happy with you. I am happy with us. It's everything else that I'm still struggling with, if I'm entirely honest. If I could lock us all up in here and never leave, I would be great." But even as he said it, I knew he didn't fool himself with the thought of holding time still. He wanted more—wanted to grow, to become the man he was meant to be. "So, yes, I can be happy. Alatheia. . ." But he trailed off, as if he left something unsaid.

I waited then eventually asked, "What?"

He smiled, amused that I noticed. "I don't know. Never mind."

I kissed him again, my lips unable to say things my heart felt. "We're going to eat soon. I don't know what. When Julian gets back, we'll eat."

"Sounds good."

I called over my shoulder as I headed into the living room. "I need a few minutes to do something for your granny."

If I didn't tell them, they would read over my shoulder. I loved their curiosity, their infatuation with me. Craved it, actually. But my work had to be private, as per their grand-mother's orders.

"Yep," Barrett answered. He tapped one ear, showing he only listened to music through one earbud. Jeremy lay out cold on the couch, face down, his arm dangling over the side. He snored, the sound muffled by the pillows where he planted his face. At least we knew he could still breathe.

I sighed. *The early morning swims are getting to him.*

At the desk, I opened my laptop to type while I read. I'd missed Dina's journals over the past few months, and the way she saw the world at eighteen. It gave me hope, knowing she

made it past all of it to the present. She remained a light in my sometimes very dark world.

❧

DECEMBER 1ST 1966

Dear Future Reader,

Well, I'm here! Lac Vieux, Louisiana. Growing up where I did, I never heard of or imagined such a place. Cool foggy weather permeates the chilly, fifty-degree air. It lends itself to the eeriness of the region, and perhaps to their mythology. I feel bad saying it, since Mrs. Lent and her friends and family have been so kind to me.

Reserved and untrusting...but kind.

I guess I should explain myself here rather than being vague. A remote exiled place, it seems to exist almost outside of time itself. People indeed lived the kind of lives the guys told me about—like their mother, with her five husbands. It was a common yet secretive practice on the two lakes that made up the town.

On the surface, it looked lovely. One big lake with a smaller one less than half a mile away, perfect for summery fun and wintery ruminations. We drove around the length of the town the day before, seeing all the waterfront houses. Getting anywhere away from the water took half an hour at least. The rural nature of the area didn't make it foreboding— maybe not all of Sabine Parish itself—was surrounded by the largest pine trees I've ever seen. Apparently, there used to be more. A lot more, but it still seemed like a rather dense forest to me.

Their fathers made their money from logging, a dreadfully long and boring story and eventually the cause of their demise via shipping of the logs. On the larger lake, where

Mrs. Lent lived, everyone seemed wealthy. Beyond living comfortably, their fathers had left an inheritance substantial enough for her children to open department stores in Manhattan—stores now left untended because I needed time with their family.

Which was pointed out to me quite plainly by Mrs. Lent, not that I blame her for being honest. I'm upending their plans, and I never even considered it or them when I made my demands. I'm a selfish, difficult girl.

Maybe my uncle could just see it better than most people. He knew, but it took others longer to notice.

The other lake—or the other side of the lake, as they called it, though it was really a whole different lake—was poor. Tattered children ran barefoot along little more than a dirt road, their scrubby clothes streaked with dust, their faces and hands unwashed. The adults moved differently too, slipping about with an almost predatory air, The whole atmosphere carried a very different rhythm.

The guys definitely prefer their side of the lake. They rushed past the other lake in a hurry, not saying much and then quickly changing the subject. Despite their hesitancy to share, I'll ask them more about it soon. Still, they wanted me to see how their neighbors lived, pointed out a lot of things were just traditions.

On the porch swing with Nathanial the night before, we rocked and looked at the stars together. He admitted he thought when they moved away, they would leave the Life— that's how they referred to it, to leaving behind their tradition. They would each have a wife of their own, live more standardly normal lives.

Then they met me, and they knew they wanted me together, the way they were raised.

When we leave, I'll want to meet the other families in NY. How do they manage it? Here, people leave them alone.

They pass their houses on, or buy them from each other, keeping the outside world out.

Nearby, they're clearing land for a dam that will become a reservoir, but otherwise modernity hasn't made it onto Sabine Parish.

"You wanted to leave it," I told him. "You wanted out."

"I still do," he whispered back. "I love my mother. I have good memories, but I always knew I wasn't made for here, for this town."

Could we have all of it?

I need to leave. Mrs. Lent wants to teach me how to cook the catfish Robert caught out of the lake. (?!?!) They do something with cornmeal, or so I understand.

More soon. How could there *not* be?

D

৩ৈৡৄঌ৻

I ALWAYS FELT out of it after I read Dina's journals. I remembered her words from June—*there's always the other side of the lake.* I wondered what she meant, especially now that she gave me a peek at the other side. I knew that better than most how fickle happiness, money, and joy could really be, easily popped like a soap bubble in a heartbeat. I spent my first eleven years in trailers—I probably looked a lot like the barefoot, dirty faced children on the other side of the lake at one point. But why didn't Dina and her Lents like it on the other side?

Dina wasn't a snob. Well, no more of a snob than any other rich person, I guess would be more accurate. I knew she loved her family, seemed to love me, was kind and cared about people, and that had to count for something.

Phoenix—who was lost and blurred at the moment— might have been kidnapped by someone from Rosalind's family, who lived on the other side of the lake. The second oldest of eight, Rosalind's kids didn't even know the older sister existed until they were told recently she was murdered when their mother was a kid.

We need answers. Due to the private nature of that town, though, I wasn't sure how to go about getting them.

Or even if it was my place to try. In a few months, I could be off at boarding school, far away from all of it. *The kinder option.* What did that even mean?

I put away the journal, deciding that was sufficient for my first day back to work. Julian tore through the door, making my timing perfect, his hair still wet.

"Are you okay?" He didn't give me a chance to answer, just kissed me. I closed my eyes and let him, his kisses made me feel a little drunk on the taste of him. From the couch, Jeremy snored while Barrett listened to music. Phoenix hung out alone in his room—everything so perfectly normal. Dinner would be soon.

Meanwhile, Julian's lips slid across mine, his tongue tangling with me until my breathless gasps had his lips trailing down my throat. It still baffled me—to be touched by one of them while the others were still so close, but he stroked a hand up my side, making me groan in need.

Julian kissed me like he might lose me, claiming my very soul with his mouth.

With a sigh, he dragged his mouth away, leaving me trembling. "I'm sorry. I don't check my phone when I'm in the pool."

"It's okay." I kissed his chin. "I'm okay, other than I'm starving."

"Me too." He released me with a sad sigh then shook Jeremy's arm. "She's starving. Let's go eat."

Jer lifted his blond head, blinking in surprise. "Okay." He

got up, blinking his equally pale lashes blearily. "How long was I out?"

"An hour," Barrett said as he rose. "I have class at eight, so it's good if we go now. We all have to be up tomorrow." He shot a glance toward Phoenix's room. "Is he awake?"

"Last time I saw him." I headed to check as Phoenix strolled out of his room.

"Did we pick a place?" He rocked back on his feet, stroking his hands up and down my arms.

Picking dinner might be the hardest decision of our lives lately. Everyone always wanted the other person to pick, until inevitably someone didn't want to eat what another person finally did pick.

"How about the Italian place where Julian took me for our first date?" I didn't usually suggest anything, since I was still learning the neighborhood, but I wanted pizza—theirs was great.

They actually liked my idea. I snorted, remembering how Phoenix said they just did what I wanted. Could they be happy *because* I suggested it?

⚜

MY STOMACH WAS TOO full to care about big things. I slipped into my pajamas and crawled into bed with a yawn. It was Julian's turn with me, and Phoenix always had one side of me since he couldn't sleep alone. Everyone completed all their getting ready for school preparations.

"Do you two want to sleep in your own rooms?" I asked Barrett and Jeremy. "Jer, I worry because you're exhausted. Barrett, you have a huge new day tomorrow."

Their refusals rang out in unison as Barrett shut off the light from his phone and stretched out onto the mattress on the floor—the one they rotated on and off, depending on who was with me. Two of them crammed into the room with us.

"I'm exhausted, too," Julian admitted then yawned next to me.

Phoenix lifted his hand as if voting. "I'm always tired."

I sighed. "You should probably *all* go to your bedrooms, and I'll sleep on the couch. If you're not getting enough sleep because of me, we should figure something else out."

"We are." Julian rolled to face me on his side. "We're just water poloing, so this is always how the season begins for us. Barrett isn't exhausted. And Phoenix—well, dude, you know what you're doing."

It earned a laugh from his younger brother. I sighed, deciding it wasn't on me if they thought they were fine. The twins would have to practice before school every day, getting up at five starting tomorrow. Phoenix wasn't likely to rouse at that hour even if they got dressed on top of him. Barrett probably wouldn't, either.

I got slapped. How bizarrely awful is that.

Quiet pressed over the room, a heavy sort of sacredness like a blanket when they started to fall asleep. I would never want to share the very private moment with anyone but them. They trusted me with their most vulnerable times, and I did the same. Sometimes they had nightmares or morning wood. Sometimes kissing sessions happened with one or two of them while the others slept.

I didn't know how I'd lived without them, and I didn't know how I would when I had to again. I sighed. *Why do those thoughts always find their way in?*

Jeremy fell back asleep, his nap obviously not enough from earlier. His snores soon sounded slow and steady. Barrett conked out, too. Phoenix's hand rested on my stomach, his usual pose as he fell asleep. I could feel his fingers twitch sometimes, especially when he dreamed. He tucked his forehead against my neck, so I could feel him breathing, and I was grateful for it. My mother died in her sleep from a drug overdose, so I absolutely loved being able to feel him breathe and know he lived.

Julian wasn't asleep, though. I turned my head to regard him, practically feeling his alertness. "You okay?" I asked him.

"I finished my play during our break this morning. It terrifies me, but I would love if you would read it. I think...I *think* it might be good?"

I wasn't sure if I'd ever heard him sound insecure before, so it took me a second to recognize the differences. My heart clenched and I kissed his nose. "Yes. Tomorrow. Give it to me."

"Thank you. Tell me if it's bad, you can be honest. I trust you. The stuff you do with the *Poor Relation*? You're talented is what I'm trying to say. I might not be."

I shook my head. "I can do *one* thing. I've never written a play."

"You're talented, Baby." He smiled, his teeth glinting in the darkness. "Are you okay about tomorrow? I wish I could walk you to school, but Phoenix will be with you. I'll find a way to see you during the day. Plus, you're going to come to our scrimmage tomorrow, despite the fact we'll lose. The teams from Dallas always eat us for dinner. But who knows, though? Maybe we *are* better this year. That's how we'll find out."

I nodded. "I'll be there."

"Good." He kissed me gently. "You're sure you're okay after today?"

"I'm never *really* okay. You know that. Today...it's not harder or worse than other times, but when your brothers were with me, it made it...survivable."

He didn't speak for a long second. "If I was there, I would've lost it."

I could believe that. Jeremy often got painted as the more volatile of the twins, but when it came to me, Julian lost his cool if I was hurt in any way.

"Oh," he added then sighed. "Don't let Phoenix kiss you on the steps of Pullman, okay?"

I laughed gently, which made Phoenix mutter something and shift his hips, his body pressed more fully against mine. He didn't really sleep for years before I came into his life, but now he was convinced I was the reason he could finally rest. I sometimes wondered if it was less about me and more about the peace he found in surrendering to the idea of staying with his family. I mentioned the theory to him, and he didn't agree, but did it really matter so long as he got rest?

It was so much better to have a rested Phoenix than a not-rested Phoenix.

"I love you," Julian whispered, tucking me a bit closer to his body. "I know you don't say it yet, but I love you. I want you to know that, to hear it and believe it."

I ran my finger over his nose. "I'm just afraid."

"I know. We'll be okay. Soon, things will be normal, or our version of it. You'll be able to trust it."

I hoped he was right, even though I kind of doubted such a thing was possible.

❧ 3 ❧

I felt Julian get out of bed but didn't rouse entirely when he awoke. It was more like the absence of the sound of his breathing that caught my attention. I'd gotten used to how he and Jeremy snored, and I liked the sounds. The noise told me they were in the room, nearby, and that was what I wanted every night. All of them in my room.

I would give it up if they needed it, but I wanted it just the same.

I drifted back to sleep, still wrapped up in Phoenix and grateful that they had their alarms on their watches, which softly woke them, so we didn't all have to be on water polo schedules. I never heard Barrett get up, but I smelled the coffee he brewed in the other room sometime around six-thirty in the morning. He would leave in half an hour, which was technically when Phoenix and I should get up to be at school at eight.

Phoenix agreed to that time.

I opened my eyes to find him actually awake already. He smiled at me, a soft look, lit by the morning starting to stream through the bottom of the shade on the window.

"Little did they know all they ever had to do to get me up was to brew coffee," he whispered, and I grinned.

We brewed coffee lots of times and it had absolutely not awoken Phoenix, but it was a cute thought.

As with other mornings—actually, most mornings—he was hard against me. We'd never discussed morning wood, and I could feel it against me, but alone, with just the two of us, I felt brave.

"Does it hurt?" I'd never brought it up before. Not once.

He didn't pretend to misunderstand me. "Yes, an ache. But I love it because I know I'm here with you. I know what it means, and I know what some day it can mean. I know that it means I'm alive."

I swallowed. "I love that you're alive."

"You do, don't you?" He closed his eyes, pressing our foreheads together before he kissed me. "And I love you. I wanted to say it before today." He sighed. "And I just want to stay in this bed with you. Awake. Not sleeping. Wrapped up like this. Smelling you. Talking to you. Forever."

I wiped his hair off his forehead. "We could have done that this summer."

"I know and I'm an ass for not thinking about it. Who needs food when there is Alatheia in my bed?" He frowned. "Guess we have to get up."

"We do. I'll bring you some of that coffee."

Phoenix flopped on his back. "Okay. We'll take turns. You do today. I'll do tomorrow."

I doubted I would get him up as easily tomorrow, but I agreed just the same. I swung my legs over and headed into the living room. The AC in their apartment was inconsistent, some rooms cold, others warmer, despite their efforts to fix it. Each room had a radiator system supposed to heat and cool them, but the building was old and some of the rooms needed separate units. The living room was always cold, probably because the windows were so big and maybe, Jeremy said, gave a slight draft. The kitchen, by contrast, was hot so I was glad that I wore my tiny gra y shorts and black tank top. They told me I would appreciate the heat in the kitchen when winter came.

I loved the thought that I could be there for winter.

I lived three years in San Francisco and two years in Chicago, though. There was no real sense of permanence for me.

Barrett wore a pair of dark tailored jeans and a white t-shirt under a navy cashmere crewneck sweater. The silver watch he always wore, because his granny gave it to him for graduation, was on his left wrist. She engraved it with the words *Remember who you are—Granny*. It was vintage and expensive. I didn't know about men's watches, but I could tell that much. His soft-looking black satchel sat on the counter. And on his feet—because I always checked—were chocolate brown lace up boots. They said *I'm rich but I hardly notice it.* I grinned. *Yep, that is Barrett.*

He smiled and opened his arms. I walked into them. "Aren't you dying of the heat in here in that?"

"No." He kissed my head and then left his nose there on my scalp. "I'm used to it in here. Coffee?"

"Yes. Please. I have to bring one to Phoenix, too."

He laughed, a low sound. "He's conscious?"

"Actually, yes."

Barrett didn't know how handsome he was. How gorgeous, really. *Strong. Fit. Put together.* I never wanted to leave his arms. It might sound ridiculous, but it was how I felt.

"So, let's make sure I have it right, so I can picture you all day." I pulled back to look at him. "At eight, you have Introduction to Constitutional Law for an hour and fifteen minutes. Then, at 10:30, you have Philosophical Foundations of Justice. That's also an hour and fifteen minutes, then you're done with class for the day."

He nodded. "Yes, I have your schedule in my phone, so I can picture you, too." He let go of me to fix me coffee, which he handed me before he made Phoenix's. I'll meet you at the scrimmage tonight, and I'll miss you all day, so please text in the hallway when you can, because you can't in class."

"I will."

His smile was small. "I thought I wanted to go to college because I wanted to get away from my family. That's still true. I wanted to because I didn't know how we'd ever have a life that I could be a part of. Like, how would we meet the girl who was going to do this life with us? It seemed preposterous. But here you are, so now I just wish it had all been a year earlier, so I could go to school with you, too."

I set down my coffee and hugged him again, tighter. "When you say things like that, I believe you."

He would know—because he was Barrett—what I meant.

He had to leave to be on time—which for Barrett meant being early—so I brought Phoenix his coffee. He sat up in bed, and if I had to guess from experience, he'd already popped his ADHD pill. I set the coffee next to him and he smiled. "Thanks. Barrett gone?"

"Just. I'm going to shower."

He rose, taking his coffee with him. "I will, too. In my bathroom. See you in a minute."

They had the best water pressure in this building. But then again, I'd thought that at Tricia's, too. Maybe it was a New York thing, or maybe the water pressure at Amelia's in Chicago had just been particularly bad. I showered quickly and then blow dried my hair. I'd added it to my routine and tried to get better at it lately. I actually watched a video of a girl with similar hair to mine, and hers looked great. I tried to copy her work, which I had not attempted before—probably a stupid choice for my first day—but I took a curling iron and tried to make waves. In the end, it wasn't horrible. *Not going-to-turn-heads great but presentable.*

I'd bought some makeup, so I did my eyes and my lips. I was trying hard for me, but not because I cared what the Pullman people thought. I didn't want the Lents to become ashamed of me. The more I was insulted, the more they were bound to change their minds. They had to live in the wealthy world. Further, they needed to fit in, so no one questioned anything about them. I needed to blend in enough that I was only moderately a problem and not a huge one.

I wished I loved myself more.

I used to think about leaving, about my future on my own, because maybe I could love myself then, but I wanted to stay since I met them. I still needed to figure out how to be okay there.

The uniform was kind of awful, but it would be awful on just about everyone. The green and red, with some blue inter-woven into the plaid skirt fell beneath my knees. *Shapeless and drab.* Underneath, we had to wear nude pantyhose, and I had an extra pair in my bag in case they ran during the day. The top was a sweatshirt, which we even had to wear on hot days. I asked.

But Jeremy told me some of the girls wore white t-shirts underneath instead when it got really hot. Mostly, the teachers didn't comment, but they could if they were *extra.*

His words.

I put on the white t-shirt that said Pullman in green letters across the chest. I stared at my reflection with frustra-tion. It was the best it was going to get. Finally, I slipped into my new Mary Janes. As had been the case in Chicago, only our shoes were allowed to be individual.

I thought the outfit said *I'm blending, leave me alone.* Before I left, I put on the pink freshwater pearls Jeremy had bought me. They said that he thought I was strong—Alatheia strong —so I loved them.

So much.

Phoenix waited for me in the hall dressed in the same color scheme. . .sort of. In his case, it meant khaki pants and a red and blue striped tie to go with his green blazer with its embroidered P. Under the blazer, he was supposed to wear a dress shirt, but instead he chose a white t-shirt. I honestly didn't blame him since it was just too hot for how they wanted us to dress.

He stared at me, his gaze moving slowly up and down my body. "Fuck, you look sexy in that. I've never thought school uniforms were sexy, but it is on you. Come here." He pulled me to him and kissed me thoroughly, so I left some of my lipstick on his bottom lip. I quickly wiped it away then laughed when I fixed mine.

"Thanks?" I shrugged. "I hoped for good enough to make no waves and maybe, just maybe, make one friend."

He tilted his head before he took my hand. "Friends? Yes, you should have friends."

I held up one finger. "I only want that many. I've never had any. Not so easy for the poor relation." I shrugged as if it didn't matter.

"Hmm. You'll have as many friends as you want. Tell me who you want for your friends, and I'll see to it."

I leaned on his arm as we walked toward the elevator. "Phoenix, you can't *tell* people to be my friends. That's not how it works. I wouldn't want that anyway."

"Hmm." His noncommittal noise didn't really inspire confidence.

We strolled to school together, but about halfway there, he released my hand. *Yep, now I can't be with him that way. Now I'm just his friend.* I knew I would hate it, and I did.

Pullman was on East 84th between Park and Madison

Avenues, and only a fifteen-minute walk, when the weather allowed. Phoenix said we would be driven if it snowed.

Then again, if it snowed, he might just skip. I knew I wouldn't be doing that, and I raised my chin primly at the thought.

On his own, he would ride his skateboard to school. Escorting me, he walked. Though I'd ridden on the back of his skateboard before, I didn't think I could do it in my school uniform.

The building loomed ahead of us, a converted mansion in the middle of the city—the old Daven place. I didn't know who the Davens were, but evidently an old money family who once lived on half the side of a street block. Their home towered old and beautiful looking.

And totally intimidating.

Kids milled around on the street, drinking coffee and calling out hellos. The twins were there somewhere, somewhere in the crowd after showering after practice.

I caught my breath, biting my lip. *This is awful.* The first days in new places always were the worst for me, though.

"On god, if you say you want to keep walking, I will gladly go with you." Phoenix then shook his head. "I mean right the fuck now."

I almost said yes, but I searched for courage. *How bad can it be?*

"Lent," a voice shouted to him.

He turned around, a smile cracking his face. "Raz."

I blew out a breath, ready to face the fire.

It helped that Phoenix and I shared Remedial Study Skills together for our first period so I didn't get lost. He wasn't in any hurry to get there, meandering along, so my nervous energy made me want to scream. I wanted to be in my seat, looking down, and bothering no one when the bell rang. Still, I forced my face serene and got myself into the zone to say nothing to anyone. Instead, I watched their shoes and let myself sink into the invisible role I'd perfected before Julian spotted me outside his granny's in June.

The halls were narrow, so everyone crowded their way through the space, the noise at ungodly levels.

Which was about all I could manage to process.

Inside the classroom, I followed Phoenix to a seat near the middle. He liked to sit by the window, so I picked the desk to his left, shifting miserably in the uncomfortable seat. *The least they could do is make classrooms tolerable for the students*, I thought grimly. I slid my laptop, the only thing the school allowed us to carry, onto my desk. The school sent some software about a week ago that I downloaded to be part of their system. The security or "nanny" features would keep me out of my regular desktop during the day when I was in the zone of their Wi-Fi. Phoenix added a VPN to mine, so I could get back to my own stuff if I wanted without the school knowing, so long as I didn't get caught.

He leaned over to me when I pulled out the computer. "This teacher—Collins? She is the worst person on the planet."

"What?" *Why didn't he mention that before?*

He didn't answer me, instead catching the eye of a girl next to me. "Oh, hey, Tiffany, this is Alatheia. She's new. Alatheia, this is Tiffany Roth. She's smart like you, and an artist. You two should get to know each other. Alatheia Winder. Tiffany Roth."

Tiffany stopped and stared at me, and I regarded her back in silence. I wondered if she was as unsure how to proceed as I was. Her hair was blue, and the color completely worked for her, not that I would dare say as much out loud.

Another girl sat in front of Tiffany, but Phoenix didn't bother to introduce me to her.

"Hi," I finally managed, deciding I should say something.

"Hi," she replied, then sunk in her seat. "Ah, sorry. Unexpected. I didn't know Phoenix knew my name."

For his part, he fiddled with something on his computer and wasn't paying attention to us, or at least he pretended to be occupied.

I swallowed. I could be brave. I fingered the pearls, then I managed to ask, "Why wouldn't he know you?"

"Because he hasn't ever spoken to me in the ten years we've gone to school together. It's still nice to meet you, Alatheia. He mentioned you're an artist, too?"

I didn't ever confess it, not to anyone but the Lents, so heat flooded my face. "I can sketch a little bit. I think he's being kind."

He tapped his pen on his desk sharply. "I'm not."

Tiffany leaned forward. "Well, maybe at lunch we can see each other's work. Almost no one here draws, I swear. It's too. . .small for this crowd, but I love art. So, yeah, let's sketch together, if you're available. Um, sorry. This is such a Pullman thing to say, but I don't recognize your last name."

I blinked then realized what she meant. "Yeah, that's because I'm the Poor Relation. My aunt is Tricia Samuels." Tiffany made a face, so I had to decide what her expression meant. I never talked about myself or said anything about my family. In this case, I admitted, "She's such a bitch."

Tiffany gave me a huge smile. "She *really* is. Sorry you have to live with her, but I love that stream, if you were referencing what I think. How do you feel about the guy they just introduced? Do you think he's the Real Deal?"

Phoenix leaned forward, interrupting unabashedly. "He's the Real Deal. I know it."

They did love my newest character I'd added to my web novel, *Poor Relation*. He was also a Poor Relation, so each of the Lents thought it was based on some part of themselves. Personally, I knew it was just fiction, but they loved it.

A girl sat down in front of Phoenix, spinning in her seat to beam up at him. He rolled his eyes and went back to his computer.

"You." She nodded at me. "You're a new girl. Who are you?"

Tiffany sat back in her seat. "Fuck off with your attitude, Bethany. No one wants it here."

The statement earned her a glare from the new girl and my unrelenting devotion. *Do I have to answer her? Can I pretend I speak a different language? Probably not.* Finally, I blurted, "I'm Alatheia Winder."

"Oh...I heard about you. That's right. We're not Hamptons people, ourselves. Why stay in the country, right?" She pulled out a lollipop and popped it in her mouth. I wished she would just suck on it and shut the fuck up. I stole a quick glance at her shoes. *Yep, open-toed stilettos with her school uniform.* She wasn't just rich, she was snotty, and her next question proved the shoe theory when she added, "Didn't you try to seduce your uncle?"

I took a long breath. *There it is. I haven't met these people yet and they already have opinions about me.* Phoenix jolted, but he never got a chance to answer because Marco Madison, who I had met at a party at his house this summer and who played water polo with the twins, slid into the seat next to her.

"Don't you watch the news? That dude was arrested for rape. Seems like she might have just gotten lucky and got away from the creep. Support the victim or whatever." He shrugged. "Leave the girl alone. Besides, Julian hits people who say shit about her."

Bethany widened her eyes. "He does?"

"Don't talk about my family." Phoenix didn't look at her or Marco, but he answered them nonetheless.

Tiffany frowned. "I'm sorry that happened to you. What a psycho he must be."

"Dude." Apparently, Marco really liked that word and didn't just use it at parties. "I need to pass this year. I barely slid through last year. Not only is my old man suddenly up my ass about grades, but I've got to get my GPA up to stay on the water polo team."

Phoenix shrugged. "Wrong Lent brother to talk with about that."

"Yep." Marco took out his computer. "Also, you don't go to the Hamptons, Bethany, because your mother left your father for some Eurotrash. Turn around and stop being a bitch to Alatheia. She's nice."

Never, not in any of my previous schools, was anyone ever as nice to me as Marco and Tiffany were being. I blew out a breath, chalking it up to the Lents. They could add miracle workers to their list of qualifications, as far as I was concerned.

The teacher, Ms. Collins, entered then wearing very severe boots. She'd pulled her steely gray hair into a tight bun, without even a hair daring to escape, and her dress was as shapeless as a black sack.

The bell rang but no one spoke; the room had gone silent when the teacher arrived. Phoenix bent over to grab his large headphones out of his bag. *Is he going to put them on in class?*

"Good morning, ladies and gentlemen." My neck swiveled and I stared at the small speaker mounted above the whiteboard. It must be the principal, and I noticed her tone seemed upbeat. "I'm so happy to have you all back for another year at Pullman. I expect great things of all of you. Before we start the pledge, we need to wish Toni Lovelace a happy birthday. She is one of our new eighth graders. Happy Birthday, Toni."

Marco laughed. "Sucky day to have a birthday. First day of school? That blows."

"Mr. Madison, language." The teacher frowned at him.

He shook his head. "Which part bothers you, suck or blow?"

He really must have amused himself because he burst into laughter. The look she shot him said she wasn't amused. More announcements followed from the speaker, about club fairs and a fall dance. Afterward, she asked us to stand for the pledge of allegiance, which we did. Finally, we took our seats again.

The teacher stared at all of us from the front of the room, her pinched expression severe.

"I am Ms. Collins. I unfortunately know most of you, which I find disappointing. I thought some of you would be out of here by now. If you *are* here, you failed a class last year. Failure is not acceptable, and I find it atrocious that people have let you skate by without repercussions. I personally don't care who your parents are. In my day, the children of the rich had more expectations put upon them, not fewer." She walked up and down the aisles, and when she passed me, I could smell baby oil. It tickled my nose and seemed strange coming from her.

She continued, her tone droning. "I have files on all of you, but I don't trust files. I want to see your character for myself. When I call your name, you will rise at your desk then answer questions that I pose for you."

Phoenix rolled his eyes dramatically, and I was glad Ms. Collins didn't see it. She didn't seem the type to have much of a sense of humor or a forgiving nature.

One by one, she called on people. The first boy had failed math, per her file, so she made him answer sums out loud like he was in elementary school. He slumped down in his seat when it was over, muttering *it was precalculus* loud enough everyone could hear it. This wasn't her trying to judge us. She liked this. She was getting some kind of...joy out of it.

Over and over, each student followed suit in their turn.

Everyone was forced to do some menial task related to what they hadn't been able to successfully accomplish the year before. Truthfully, I had no idea what Phoenix failed, but I waited for my turn with a sigh. I'd failed nearly everything.

When she reached Phoenix, who would go right before me, he rose.

"Mr. Lent, back again. My most frequent offender, returned again."

He stared back at her, unimpressed by her censure. "Yep. I'm back."

"Not a surprise. You would never be allowed to attend this school if your parents weren't so important. Your brothers are honors students. Doesn't it bother you that you are so dumb?"

I caught my breath. I never spoke out in class, I never bothered teachers, but I couldn't tolerate her summation of him. *Dumb?* I jerked to my feet before I really thought it through.

"Are you crazy?" I shouted the question, and everyone, including Ms. Collins, stared at me. My fury wasn't done, though, so I added, "He's *not* dumb. He is probably the smartest person in this room. In any room, actually. And if you don't know that or can't see it after so many years with him, then maybe there is something wrong with *you*."

She stared daggers at me but then turned back to Phoenix. His eyes were so wide, I was afraid they might fall out of his head. He even breathed a little heavily. *Oh shit. Is he pissed at me for saying something?*

My gaze darted around the room, and I noticed Tiffany smirked while Marco flung around in his seat to watch the show.

"Is that so? Are you the smartest person in any room? Let's see, then. Mr. Lent, tell me, can you define mitochondria? Or is that too easy for you?"

He rolled his eyes. "It's the powerhouse of the cell."

She stared at him. In that moment, I realized she hadn't expected him to know.

"Next." He crossed his arms over his chest, arrogance oozing off him. "Keep going, Collins. Ask me anything you want. I'm here for it."

She pointed at him. "I don't like your attitude."

He shrugged. "I don't like your dress, but let's keep going. Come on. Ask me whatever you think I am too stupid to know."

I took a deep breath. *What is going to happen now?*

4

"Fine. Mr. Lent, what is the capital of Mozambique?" She lifted her eyebrows in challenge.

Phoenix rocked back on his feet. "I'm betting you don't know the answer unless you memorized it for this kind of thing. It is Maputo, pronounced from the Portuguese."

I blew out a breath, impressed despite myself. He made it through science and geography, but how much further would she push him? I essentially caused the whole mess. On his own, he would have probably put her off with just a nod, not caring if she thought he was stupid, but I just couldn't let it linger. *He is too. . .important.*

She placed her palms on her desk and gazed at him. "Give me a metaphor from something you've read. Make it something important."

He rubbed his eyes. "I'd love to know how you define important but okay, fine, we'll use *Romeo and Juliet*. By calling Romeo the sun, Shakespeare emphasized how important Romeo is to Juliet. It's a met-a-phor."

He spoke the last bit slowly.

She stalked closer to him. "So, perhaps you don't belong in this class? Maybe you are just lazy. Maybe you think you don't have to pass classes. Maybe you're just a bad person, or perhaps you think we're all supposed to feel sorry for you because you were kidnapped as a child. Do you think we should feel bad for you, Mr. Lent?"

A muscle ticked in his jaw. Only I stared at him, since everyone else diverted their eyes.

I took a step in front of him as if I could physically bar her from doing more damage. "That is the worst thing I've ever heard anyone say, and I've heard some really awful things," I said to her.

She ignored me. Phoenix very slowly smiled at her. "Sure. I think you should feel sorry for me. I'm a total fuck up because I was kidnapped. I'm just a problem, and I need your tender guidance. How else will I ever make it in the world?"

He sunk into his chair but not before he added, "If you ask me all those questions again, I'll get them all wrong. Every last one of them. I'm staying in this class. Sorry. You'll have me all year."

She breathed hard but rounded on me. "*You*. The new girl, Alatheia Winder."

I met Phoenix's gaze across her shoulder, but I braced myself. It would be bad, but it was my own fault and I would do it again, given the chance.

I could feel Phoenix's gaze on me. The whole class stared, actually, but only his mattered to me. "That is me."

"Do you know what your name means?"

Did she? "Truth."

"Yes. And truthfully, I don't think you belong in this school. I don't know how you got in at all, honestly. You failed every class last year."

She wasn't wrong, but in my defense, it was hard to care about grades when my aunt's boyfriend tried to rape me and then I got the shit beat out of me because he wanted me. I wasn't telling her that, though, so she could just judge.

I didn't comment. She didn't actually ask me a question. Meaning I didn't owe her a reply. I was there, so the how and why were really none of her business. Her petty, mean nature shined through as she glared at me.

"I bet you would say it's because you're dyslexic." She said the last word like it tasted bad.

That wasn't why I failed, but honestly it would be sufficient explanation if I wanted to use it as an excuse. Then again, she might know already why I actually failed. Everyone else seemed to, as I had predicted. She might even bring it up, so I steeled my spine for the hit.

"I don't believe in dyslexia," she said then shook her head. "It's a made-up excuse."

Phoenix leaned forward, crowding into her space. "I don't think it's the kind of thing you get to decide whether or not it is real. It exists. Your opinion on the subject is not interesting to any of us, since it is fact."

She ignored him, keeping her eyes trained on me. After a few moments, she strode to her desk and came back with a book. Never breaking eye contact, she handed it to me. "Read it. Aloud for the whole class."

I might as well be naked, I realized, and blew out a shaky breath. It would be less humiliating than me trying to read aloud. I didn't bother to reach for the pearls, since I could be brave for Phoenix but not for myself.

It was *The Bell Jar* by Sylvia Plath, and I loved the book. For a second, I smoothed my fingers over the familiar cover.

"Read it. Aloud," she repeated sharply. Somewhere in her file, she probably already read that it would be a huge problem for me.

I cleared my throat. "Okay, the thing is, I can read really well silently. I love to read. I've read this book, actually, but aloud is a different thing entirely for me. I think that you know that, and you're trying to make me feel bad."

She clenched her teeth. "Read it."

"Right." I opened the book. My pride shriveled up and died, since Phoenix was about to have a front row seat to how dumb I could really be. Other dyslexics read aloud with no problems, so why couldn't I?

I took a deep breath. The words moved on the page, scattering as if trying to escape my gaze like they always did. I tried to concentrate, to make them stop. With everyone's eyes on me, it was impossible.

"You've made your point." Phoenix's words barely reached me, the ringing in my ears so loud and the beating of my heart a thrum.

I have to do this. I'm never getting out of it. I began, saying, "It was a queer, sultry summer, the summer they electrocuted the Rosenbergs, and I didn't know what I was doing in New York. I'm stupid about executions."

I wished I just read it, that I could simply say the words, but I stumbled through all of them, tripping as if I'd never spoken before . Finally, she stopped me, grabbing the book from my shaking hand. "You don't belong here," she repeated and we both knew she was right.

I sank into my chair not looking at anyone. Not at Phoenix, or at anyone at all. He proved he was smart, that she was wrong about him. In my case, she proved I wasn't on his level and never would be. *A third grader could have read better than me.*

"Alatheia," Phoenix pounded a fist on his desk, imploring me to meet his gaze. Ms. Collins moved on to someone else, but he interrupted her. "What do those lines mean? Why do you think Plath wrote them like that?"

I swallowed. Why would he make it worse? Why would

he bring everyone's focus back to me when it finally began to move away?

"Um..." I wanted to throw up, but I automatically answered, trying to shift the attention away from myself. "I think that by bringing up the Rosenbergs that fast, by immediately talking about them, she's letting us know that there is death. It's cold. Public. It certainly sets up the book to the reader as not being lightweight. She lets us know, *hey there is going to be some real stuff here and we have to deal with it.* It's all almost claustrophobic, right? The heat. And she is stupid about executions. I mean, who is smart about them?"

He smiled at me, his eyes so kind, I wished I could float away in them. "You are. You are probably smart about executions. You could probably tell this whole class everything you know about them." He held up his hand to stop me. "Don't, but I wanted to remind you there's more than reading aloud."

Ms. Collins glared like she wished we would just spontaneously combust and die.

When the bell finally rang, it felt like a life raft. *Are we really going to have to do this every day?*

I rose and Tiffany grabbed my arm. She had eventually identified things on the periodic table for Ms. Collins, which didn't seem to bother her at all. I wished I had her confidence.

"Meet me at lunch. Let's look at each other's sketches."

Phoenix shook his head. "She'll be with me. Come find us in the courtyard."

Her grin seemed amused. "Okay. Sure. I'll bring Hal." She scooted away, calling over her shoulder. "He's my boyfriend. Phoenix loves him."

Next to me, the youngest Lent brother groaned. "He is a douchebag."

Bethany stopped to stare at me. "You sounded pretty

stupid when you were reading, but then it was like...you're smart? I can't make you out."

I left it, since there wasn't anything I could say that would change her feelings about me. She failed biology because when would she ever need it? She said as much, without any shame or hesitation. With a final fluff of her hair, she left the room.

Marco shrugged. "I don't want to read aloud, and I don't want to read to myself. Screw it. Why bother when there are so many other, better things to do? See you, Lent. See you, Alatheia."

Phoenix and I walked next to each other toward our next class. We couldn't touch, but it was just nice to be with him.

"Red," he said as we exited the classroom.

"Yes?"

He put his hands over his heart. "No one has ever, and I mean ever, said anything like that about me before. What's more is you believed it. You meant it. That is. . .everything. Why wouldn't you look at me? After that bitch did the reading stunt."

I shook my head. "If I talk about it now, I'm probably going to cry. I don't want to be the girl who cries on her first day of school in the hallway." Already, everyone thought I tried to seduce my uncle, and after that class, they thought I couldn't read. I didn't want to add crybaby to the list.

He nodded. "Fair enough. Show me your schedule." I pulled it out and he took a photo of it. "English, okay, but I have a different one. Why did they put us in different classes?"

I stared at him, surprised. "Probably because I failed it last year. Did you?"

"No. I made a D, actually. I'll be outside all your classes to walk you to your next one. Wait for me." He smiled. "You do know I think you're amazing and brilliant, right?"

Well, then you're wrong. At the classroom, he left me with his hands over his heart again.

After Collins, though, my other morning teachers were fine. They mostly left me alone, which was my preference. I tried to text Barrett while I waited for math to start after English, but my phone wouldn't let me send a text. I frowned and the guy next to me smiled and pointed at the phone.

"You need a VPN on it to get around the block. Download it at home." He nodded. "You're friends with the Lents, right? I saw you this summer."

I cleared my throat. "Alatheia."

"Davis." He smiled. "I know Phoenix pretty well."

The class started, which saved me having to say anything else, and I was grateful for it. Art was my last class before lunch, and true to his word, Phoenix walked me to every one. I was grateful to not get lost. The school retained its old mansion look, so it seemed filled with long, confusing hallways. I couldn't imagine trying to find my way around by myself—not to mention there was apparently a senior hallway that ate the twins, because I still had yet to see them.

I sat down with Phoenix at lunch after visiting the cafeteria. He paid for my food, because my aunt still hadn't put any money in my account. *What else is new?*

We no sooner took our seats than the door swung open to Julian and Jeremy, followed by a number of guys I didn't recognize. Except for Marco, whom I'd hated in the Hamptons. After today, he improved greatly, especially since he told Bethany to suck it.

"Hey," Jer said as he scooted in next to me. "There you are. You look really pretty in the uniform, which is nearly impossible."

"Missed you," Julian said, but he kept his voice soft. "How are you? How is it going?"

Marco scooted onto our table. "Why are we all here, anyway? This is the Junior lunch area."

"You didn't have to come." Jeremy said then shrugged. "We didn't tell the whole team to come. You followed us."

He smirked. "Oh Captain, where thou goest, we goest." He then laughed like he'd just said the best thing in the world.

"Thanks for helping." I said to Marco. "With Bethany."

"Oh." He glanced my way then shrugged. "Yeah. She was out of line, not that it is unusual for her."

"What happened?" Julian glanced between us before taking a bite of his apple. I stared at my sandwich, my stomach churning just thinking about it.

"Bethany was being a bitch about the uncle thing. She was nothing compared to what Collins did to you." He whistled. "Dude, it was bad. I thought it was monumental with Phoenix, but then he ate her alive. You? That was bad."

Julian took my hand. "Baby." I should tug my hand away because he needed to stop doing that in public, but I wasn't going to tell him not to when I needed his touch. I would miss him too much. "What did she do?" he asked.

I shrugged one shoulder as if it didn't matter. "She just showed everyone how stupid I am."

Phoenix shook his head, his lips dropping into an instant frown. "No one thought you were stupid."

"Well, I kind of did." Bethany admitted as she scooted into place at the table. Where had she come from? "Then I changed my mind because of Phoenix."

Is she sitting with us, too? Really? I met Julian's gaze after he stared at her, his mouth open in surprise. The entire water polo team seemed to be listening to every word we said. While I stared at them all, I noticed Tiffany with whom I could only presume was Hal approaching with lunch trays in hand. He was taller than her with glasses, and then Phoenix groaned again. *What is his deal with Hal?*

Tiffany sent Bethany a scathing look. "Really?"

"Sure. You're not the only one who wants to be friends with Alatheia. I mean that was quite the display today. I wrote you off and then had to write you back in, which almost never happens."

Lucky me.

"I still don't know what happened." Jeremy set down his food. "Is someone going to explain?"

Phoenix rubbed his eyes, and I noticed he'd been doing it a lot lately. *Is he not okay? Is he getting enough rest?* "We'll get into it later. Not now," he said.

Jeremy sighed. "Fine. Has anyone heard from Barrett?"

Which reminded me of my useless brick of a phone. I held it in front of me. "I can't get through to anyone. I was supposed to text him, but my phone won't send messages. Someone named Davis said I need a VPN on this too."

Phoenix held out his hand, so I passed him my phone. "I'll get that fixed for you, but don't talk to Davis."

Julian grinned, nudging his brother with his elbow. "I thought he was your friend."

"He can be my friend, not hers. He's not good enough to be her friend." He jerked his chin toward Tiffany. "They're going to be friends."

This is the strangest lunch I've ever had, but I'm loving every second of it. Before the bell rang, Tiffany and I managed to show each other some sketches. She loved to do scenes at the park, and I had some nice ones of animals in my travel sketchbook. I wasn't going to show her any I drew of the guys, deciding in that moment it was something between just us.

By the time lunch ended, Phoenix fixed my phone and it

dinged with incoming messages. I tucked it into my back pocket, walking with Tiffany to our next class.

"So, Phoenix is your boyfriend?" Tiffany asked when we were finally alone. I headed toward science next while she had social studies. The guys scattered, with the water polo players following the twins back to their senior hallway while Phoenix disappeared. Hal followed him, but I still didn't know their deal.

I shook my head, focusing on her question about Phoenix. "Just my friend."

"Well, I don't know about that. The vibes. . .you two *definitely* have something in the works, but then again, two of his brothers fawn all over you, too. You'll have to let me know when you decide which Lent to date," she joked, and I bit my lip. She would never know how loaded her statement really was.

Bethany stared at our drawings, comparing them as not intended, from over our shoulders. "That one is the best," she decided, pointing at my squirrel. "They're all cute. Barrett was the hottest, but he is gone now, out of range at university. Brown, I think."

I almost corrected her—*Columbia*—then I decided I might prefer if she didn't know how close Barrett remained.

Tiffany held out her hand, ignoring Bethany. "Give me your phone, and I'll give you my number. Then you text me from yours."

I followed her directions, then a second later, I actually had a contact in my phone who wasn't a Lent. I never honestly thought I might make a friend.

"Me too." Bethany put out her hand, demanding my phone.

I scowled at her. "You said you thought I was stupid."

"Yep." She smiled, and I picked up on the genuine warmth in her expression. "Then I told you I changed my mind. You should think I am stupid, too, since we're all in that class together. Let's be friends. I'm not so bad, once you get to know me."

Absolutely gobsmacked, I passed her my phone. *Okay, now I have two phone numbers.* One I wanted, and the other. . .I didn't know what to do with exactly. After she gave me her number, she left to go get some coffee.

"If I'm being entirely honest," Tiffany sighed as she admitted, "She's not so bad. There are worse people here, much, *much* worse. They all leave me alone, though. I'm too rich for them to fuck with, luckily."

I'm not. She knew it and I did, too. Bethany might make a great pseudo-friend, if I looked at it as strength in numbers. I could probably also add Marco because he made the Euro-trash joke. Maybe Bethany was slightly misunderstood.

"You do know Phoenix does a lot of drugs, right? I ask because Hal does, too. It isn't easy to be around all the time, but he's really a sweetheart, even if I'm the only one who gets to see it." She shrugged. "They used to be best friends, Hal and Phoenix? I don't know what happened. Hal doesn't talk about it, but I know he misses Phoenix."

I cleared my throat. "I appreciate you sharing, but like I said, we aren't dating. Phoenix and I are just friends." *Who sleep in the same bed and kiss a lot.*

Tiffany nodded, her expression saying she saw more than I admitted. "Yeah, I get it. I protect Hal, too, so let's be friends and keep our secrets."

She left and I didn't know if she really was okay with what I said. I hoped she understood I wasn't prepared to talk about Phoenix's private business, nor would I ever be.

Finally, I glanced down at my phone, and I realized one of the notifications meant Barrett had texted.

All good?

I smiled instantly, heat warming my cheeks before texting

him back. *Other than missing you? Phone didn't work for a while, but Phoenix fixed it.*

"Red," Phoenix appeared from around a corner as if I summoned him with my thoughts. "Time to get to the next round of hell."

That afternoon, I had social studies, science, and theater before I got to watch the twins play water polo. Theater would be my last period of the day.

Which then dragged on as if it would never end. Most of the teachers handed out rules and syllabuses for their class anyway, so it didn't even feel like real classes. People kept saying hello to me, and I tried not to appear shocked by the attention. Everyone knew Phoenix, though, and the general consensus seemed to be we were or would be together soon. No one asked about our dating status, they just let me know they knew Phoenix when they introduced themselves.

Probably why he's walking me to classes, I realized. *He wants everyone to know we're friends to keep me safe from the bullies.* My heart warmed at the knowledge.

When the bell rang at the end of the day, I took a deep breath. A weight seemed to lift off my shoulders, because I made it through my first day—at least that was behind me.

"Alatheia," the theatre teacher, Mr. Kaus, called me forward before I could duck out the door. In his thirties, the only defining thing I could say about him after one class was he smiled a lot. "Come here for a second?"

I went to his desk. "Yes?"

"It's a small school, so I heard what happened this morning in Collins' classroom. She has been here forever." He took his glasses off and cleaned them with the edge of his shirt. "But that doesn't make what she did okay. We will be preparing monologues to deliver this year, but I wanted to let you know I will *never* call on you to do one without giving you time to prepare. I will tell you the day before, if that sounds fair? I don't want you to worry. What she did. . .well, I am personally sorry. Not every teacher at Pullman is quite so. . .yeah."

I nodded at him, understanding the unspoken bits. "Thanks. I appreciate that."

"Let's have a great year," he said with another of his smiles.

As far as first days, overall, mine went okay. Collins might be crazy but she wasn't my first insane teacher. Barrett leaned against a locker when I turned the corner, and my smile blossomed.

"I finally get out of this place, but I have to come back because you're here, Sweetheart."

I grinned, so happy to see him. "They just let you in?"

"I'm Barrett Lent."

I nodded, not caring if it meant he could be there. "How were your classes? How was everything? Did you have a great day?"

"I hated my first class and loved the second a surprising amount. We'll see how that goes."

When I was close enough, I could smell his clean scent, so I let myself take a deep breath of him, filling my lungs and wishing I could fall into his arms. "Did you eat anything? Do you need anything?"

He shook his head. "A hug from you, but I think we're both resisting that one. How about we go watch the scrimmage then go home? You can tell me what the fuck happened in your first period that made Jeremy text me because he doesn't know about it. Something about the details he heard has him worried."

I sighed. "I may have made it worse on myself and Phoenix. We'll talk about it, but I don't know that there's much we can do for damage control. I just. . .yeah."

A piece of brown hair fell in Barrett's eyes, despite his

recent haircut. I almost brushed it away, so I literally had to catch myself and tuck my hand in my pocket. "Let's go see them play," I agreed.

He stopped, his gaze serious as he considered my expression. "Just tell me you're okay? That whatever happened this morning, you're okay."

It was so sweet, it took me a second to be able to answer past the emotion in my throat. I let myself touch the pearls before I spoke. "I'm okay. I survive things. Somehow. Today wasn't as bad as other days. I wasn't alone."

"You're never going to be alone again," he whispered in my ear. "Sorry that it took us so long to find you."

The building next door housed the gym and the pools. People wandered around while the guys from Dallas did stretches on the other side of the pool. As we took our seats, the Pullman guys came out of the locker room, already warmed up. Julian told me how they had to be there an hour before the competition to swim.

I spotted the twins in tiny Speedo bathing suits— Pullman colors in green, red and blue. I saw them shirtless all the time, but never in public, and heat flooded my cheeks as my heartbeat picked up a notch. *Wow. They are gorgeous.*

All the guys were built, and they exercised to stay in shape, but I'd never seen one of their games. I forced myself to think about something other than Julian's and Jeremy's abdominal muscles, fanning my cheeks. Barrett put away his phone, glancing over at me.

"Mom is still in treatment, " he said then frowned. "I try to check on her, but that's the only answer they give me."

I hated that for them. "You shouldn't have to deal with so much. I'm sorry."

"It helps to have you. Oh, yes, I always forget about the Speedos." He drew his attention from his brothers back to me and he grinned conspiratorially. "They hate the Speedos. In crew, we actually got to wear clothes."

"Do you miss it?"

He shook his head and then nodded. "Sometimes?"

"You could still do it, right?"

Phoenix scooted past us, his eyes vacant. *Okay, so that's where he's been.* "Did I miss anything?"

I shook my head. "No, they're just starting."

"Good." He pointed at Barrett. "You're here."

His oldest brother patted him on the back. "I am."

A whistle blew.

5

I don't know what I thought a water polo match would be like, but it wasn't what I expected. They treaded water, rushed up and down the pool, threw and caught. Marco seemed to be able to come entirely out of the water to block the ball, hanging in the air for what seemed like impossible seconds. Whistles blew, people shouted. They climbed in and out of the pool.

I didn't understand the game, and I wasn't sure how any of them didn't drown. Every muscle in my body tensed, trying to be sure they were okay. Ultimately, Julian and Jeremy scored most of the points, passing smoothly between themselves, and Jeremy in particular seemed to almost have his back to the goal as he sank the shots.

The Dallas players were great, too, though, and I couldn't help but think the teams were well- matched.

Barrett winced when Julian took a hard hit. "We're really good for this area of the country. They'll probably win States, but it's nothing compared to how schools in Dallas play, and Dallas loses almost everything to the schools in California."

I found his idea interesting. "So, you're saying it's a regional thing?"

"Development of the programs started at different times." He shrugged. "Also, weather."

"I guess that makes sense."

The quarters were short, and the guys rotated in and out of the water in intervals so no one got too exhausted. They took elbows to the face, kicks to their bodies, and I couldn't even see what was going on under the water. I never realized how brutal it was to play water polo. I knew they were tough, but they showed a whole different level of athleticism I couldn't fathom.

No wonder Jeremy passed out on the couch face down and didn't stir until woken. Maybe his shoulder really does hurt.

Julian got pulled for a foul, and the clock said he would be out for five minutes, although I missed his altercation. Everyone seemed to be doing everything at once, making it nearly impossible to track every single play.

But then the game ended, and we lost by one. They climbed out of the water, Julian shaking out his hair and Jeremy wrapping a towel around his waist.

They both turned and scanned the crowd for me, so I grinned and waved.

"Wow. That was...amazing," I said, failing to come up with a better description.

Barrett nodded. "It was. They're great. Come on, Phoenix, it's over."

He got to his feet and stretched. "I think I should avoid the pool when I feel like this."

I sighed and bit my lip. Despite wanting to chastise him, I bit back the words from the tip of my tongue. He knew he shouldn't use drugs, since I wasn't lying when I said he was the smartest person in every room. If he chose to do them anyway...

"Do you need to get out of here?" I asked then took his hand.

"Yes," he said and nodded. "Tell the wonder twins I enjoyed their game. See you later."

He turned and left, dropping my hand without further comment. I blinked. Was he mad at the twins? I glanced at Barrett. "Did I miss something?"

He shrugged, watching his brother leave with concern. "It's an old argument. We didn't used to resist giving him shit for using. Actually, we gave him an ultimatum about getting clean and even staged an intervention. It all went down last spring, but as you can see, it was unsuccessful. We weren't speaking to him much when you came along. He was pretty good this summer, so it seemed like maybe he was getting better. As if you really were the magic we know you are. But we're back to the way things were, apparently. This is Phoenix during the school year. At least he got up this morning and was relatively with it all day. Try not to worry. It does nothing."

I elbowed him. "I don't want you to miss out on the college experience because you are worrying " —I deliberately used the word— "about *us*."

He laughed. "Listen, okay, point taken. I worry, but that's not why I'm here. I've lived on my own in the city pretty much since I was fifteen years old. Yeah, I know it sounds fucked up, but that was when my parents really started to leave me alone. The twins kept their attention for about another year. Phoenix stayed with them because, by then, I think the parents didn't have a clue what to do with us. I don't need to go live in a college dorm to have independence. Besides, it's mostly people puking from drinking too much. I have had my independence for a long time. What I want is to be with you." He paused and lowered his voice. "And because we are who we are, I want to hang around with them while they hang around with you. Phoenix will pull it together eventually. For now, I want to go home and eat dinner with you."

I leaned on his arm. "If you change your mind, if you *ever* change your mind, I want you to know that I'll get it."

"I know you would." He smiled at me. "Hard not to touch you. So hard. Okay, music club on Friday night?"

I grinned. "Sounds good."

"Hey, new girl, "a woman called, and I turned to see a tall brown-haired girl my age walking toward me in a bathing suit.

I glanced around, sure she was talking to someone else. "Me?"

"Yes, you. Have you figured out your PE requirement yet?" She put her hand on her hips, considering me grimly from her considerable height.

I swallowed, feeling as if a spotlight had been trained on me. "My what?"

She laughed. "Yeah, they didn't tell you, which is a constant problem, but it usually works out for us. We're the women's water polo club here at Pullman, and we're different from these guys. They're PSAA but we're only a club. Don't get me started on the difference in funding for women's and men's sports in this school." She held up her hand like she wanted me not to speak as she rolled her eyes in obvious frustration, which was fine, since I had no intention of interrupting her. "Anyway, we practice when they're not using the pool, which works out to be three times a week. We play games against other clubs in the area, but we're down one player and we need that player to keep our status as a club."

Interesting, but why was she telling me? Then it hit me and I swallowed hard. I tried not to be too hard on myself for being so slow, but I wasn't typically invited to things. I cleared my throat. "You want me to play?"

She nodded. "Four months with us takes care of your PE requirement."

Barrett nodded. "It does."

Julian and Jeremy arrived, dressed in matching Pullman tracksuits and carrying backpacks.

"Sarah?" Julian said to the girl, who still hadn't introduced herself to me. "What's going on?"

Barrett slipped his arm around me. "Sarah was asking Alatheia to join the club for water polo."

"Really?" Jeremy sloped his brows down. "I don't know that it's really Alatheia's thing."

Sarah laughed. "I'm talking to her, Lent, and I didn't ask for your opinion. Or your big brother's, really. Or your twin's. I'm talking to *her*. By the way, you totally had that guy. You just needed to swim left, and you would've nailed the goal, maybe a second one with the five meter he was bound to do."

Jeremy visibly swallowed, considering her words as if impressed. "Thanks for the input."

She turned back to me, saying, "Yeah, so do you want to play water polo, help me out, make some friends, get some exercise, and take care of the fact that you need to do PE anyway? Otherwise, you'll end up doing something else with someone a lot less charming than me."

All their eyes were on me, even if it didn't feel like a life-or-death decision. I didn't know if I wanted to play or not, so I wasn't sure how to answer. "I just saw water polo for the first time today, and I'm not a great swimmer. I can swim, but it's more like I can survive in the water rather than any intentional grace. I for sure can't do whatever they just did in the pool."

She grinned, confidence oozing from her like a drug. "By the time I get done with you, you'll be a swimmer. Like I said, we're a club team, and a pretty bad one anyway. Come on. Try it."

I jolted. "Right now?"

"Why not? The guys are done. Let's go." She nodded toward the locker room. I swallowed, since I hadn't even agreed to join the club yet.

"Hey." Julian caught my hand, snagging my attention. "You don't have to do this if you don't want to. Or you can try it. If you hate it, just don't do it again. We'll figure out how to handle your PE requirement, I just didn't think of it yet. We handled Phoenix's. What did he do again?"

Barrett sighed. "An independent study where he was supposed to be professionally skateboarding."

I shook my head. We didn't need to make up a PE for me. "Okay, I'll try it, but I can't promise I'll be any good. I might be terrible. You may regret asking me to do this."

She snorted, dropping her hands from her hips finally. "Doubt it. Let's go."

I turned around, glancing at the guys. "I guess I'll see you later?"

They all agreed, but Jeremy frowned. Something about the situation didn't track for him, so I wished I could read his mind to find out what.

I followed Sarah into the locker room, where about a dozen other people changed. I didn't know any of them, but Sarah pointed to the left. "Grab a bathing suit from the rack in your size. Towels are over there. Leave your stuff in a locker."

"Sarah," I said again, trying to make her understand. "I really don't swim all that well."

Her smile was fast and confident. "You will soon. Can't get stronger if you don't get started."

True enough words for many things. Without other options, I made my way to the rack she indicated and grabbed a bathing suit, happy there were a few that looked like they would fit. I changed quickly and stored my stuff away, my palms slick with sweat. I'd never played a team sport, other than generic gym classes, so I didn't even know what to expect.

"She got you, too?" a girl said from the corner. I glanced at her, finding a skinny pretty girl with light brown hair and glasses.

I smiled, admitting honestly, "She sort of caught me by surprise out there. I'm still not quite sure what I'm doing here."

"My mom said I have to do something with myself if I want to go to college. Sarah's mom knows my mom, so here I am." She shrugged. "I'll be entirely awful at this, I'm sure of it. I'm Valerie."

I put out my hand and we shook. "Alatheia."

"Cool name." She walked past me, dancing a bit on her toes. "Why do our bathing suits have to go up our asses like this?"

I couldn't disagree, since they gave me a permanent wedgie. *Do they need to see our ass cheeks?* I glanced around. Other than Sarah, two other girls looked comfortable, but otherwise, the rest of us lurked pathetic and uncomfortable looking.

"Okay," Sarah said and clapped her hands. "We have a week to get ready for our first game against Greystone. They're just a club team, too, so no stress. It's not like we have to play any of those teams in Greenwich." Sarah frowned. "But they are about as good as we will be, which is to say that we are all terrible. Everyone, in the water. Let's go." She clapped again, and I wondered if someone should get her a whistle. Imagining her whistling for my attention, I frowned and realized I didn't really want that at all.

We headed back out to the water, the smell of chlorine biting at my nose. They had a smaller practice pool and the playing pool. Overall, the room seemed so much quieter than when the water polo team played, save for two people who were sitting in the stands—Julian and Jeremy.

"No," Sarah yelled at them, gesturing with her thumb at the door. "Out. I won't have you here during my practice, Lents. No way. Go deal with your own team. Your *varsity* team. Leave mine alone."

Jeremy rose to his feet. "We'll leave, but this is fucking ridiculous, Sarah. The room is open to the whole school. I could sit here all day every day if I wanted."

"Really?" She stormed over to him, facing off toe to toe. "Is that why I can't use this pool when you're using it? Is that why I have to cancel my practices if you need times I have already reserved?"

The twins hated water polo; they were only captains because it was one of the things they had to do for the family. Still, I didn't get the impression Sarah understood that about them. *Does she actually believe they are. . .forcing her out?*

"I don't make the rules." Jeremy said then shook his head. "I can promise you I have never purposefully taken the pool when you wanted it. We practice at five-thirty in the morning, and I don't make association rules about when and where we play games."

They shouted the words at each other, so Julian grabbed Jeremy by the arm and tugged him. "We're going but we're not leaving. We'll be waiting outside."

"Why?" she laughed. "I am not going to let your friend drown. Is she one of your girlfriends? Whatever. I don't care. Go, out."

Julian laughed. "You can't ban us from the hallway."

Sarah turned around, hands on hips again. "Everyone in the pool. We're swimming laps. Now."

I jumped in the pool, terrified not to obey her. I probably would do whatever Sarah wanted, especially if she kept barking orders. Cold water stole my breath, so I shrieked when I came up for air, startled. I wasn't alone. Several of the girls, Valerie included, yelped some version of the same surprised shriek.

"We won't feel it if we swim," Sarah pointed out, jumping in without any startlement whatsoever. "Let's move."

We started to swim, and I realized I wouldn't possibly be able to keep up.

৩৯৩

SOMEHOW, I didn't drown. I could barely tread water for the amount of time they wanted let alone sprint across the pool, but I managed not to die. The starters were set, with one goalie and six players. Sarah needed a requisite amount of alternates, though, to give her main players breaks. I hoped no one ever needed a break during a game, since I would be utterly happy never seeing another drop of water.

Still, I survived the practice, and pride made me feel good about it. We didn't have another practice for two days, so I would get a break—because the boys hogged the pool, in Sarah's words.

"Good work, Al."

I blinked. *Does she mean me?* Sarah patted me on the shoulder. "I thought you might just be a warm body, but you have heart. I'll make you into a helluva polo player."

In that moment, I wanted to prove her right.

"Showers, ladies," she shouted. "Then you can go home."

Al? No one calls me Al. My cheeks heated, but I liked having a nickname, even if it was a terrifically masculine one. The hot shower water felt so good against my frozen skin from the pool, easing my muscles and making me sigh. I would have to get tougher if I wanted to survive the sport, I realized.

I no sooner had I closed my eyes than the shower curtain

was ripped back, the clank of the rings on the curtain making a clatter. A girl I'd never seen before stared at me, her lips curled in disgust. Blonde, blue eyed, and dressed to the nines, her expensive black shoes matched the rest of her black outfit. Her beauty could likely make most men gasp, and I certainly did.

Then I grabbed my towel, covering myself quickly.

"Which one are you dating?" she shouted, pointing her finger at me in judgement. She wasn't on the team, so I didn't even know why she was in the showers.

I wrapped myself in the soaked towel, water still streaming around me, and tried to get around her but she shoved me back, not letting me pass. "Which one are you dating? Because Jeremy Lent is mine."

"What?" I managed to squeak. "What are you doing? What do you want from me?"

She repeated, getting in my face, "I asked you a question. Jeremy is mine. You are *not* with him."

Jeremy is hers? What the fuck? Did anyone tell him?

"Hey, Maggie," Sarah said, also totally naked but obviously not concerned by the fact as she posed with her hands on her hips as boldly as normal. "Go away. Jeremy Lent isn't yours, and he never was. Sorry if you thought so, but you don't belong in here harassing my team. If you bother my player again, I'll shove your face in the toilet."

Maggie's eyes widened, possibly startled by Sarah's nudity. Regardless, she ran, and I blew out a relieved breath. A lot of traumas had marked my life so far, but assaulted in the shower was a new one.

Sarah frowned at me as I stood there still shaking with a combo of fear and fury. "You take a lot of shit, don't you? Between the uncle thing and now the Lents...I don't know your story, Al, but no one fucks with my friends or my players. Maybe you will eventually be both since you're already one."

I'd never know what I would have said in response, because she stormed away as boldly as she did everything else.

With my heart racing, I sank to the floor, since it felt like the strength went entirely out of my legs. I only needed a few seconds to catch my breath, but I determined that Sarah would be my friend.

I almost giggled. *I certainly don't want her to be my enemy.*

৩%৯

WITH MY HAIR STILL SOAKED, I exited the locker room carrying a bag with four Pullman swimsuits.

"Hey..." Julian offered his hand, and I was too exhausted and overwhelmed to concern myself with whether or not I should take it. I entwined our fingers and he drew me against him.

"Lents," Sarah said as she approached. "Your friend just got assaulted in the shower because Maggie Benty thinks that you're hers, Jeremy. You might want to do something about that, but for now, I stopped it."

She stopped to punch my shoulder on her way past. "Good job today, Al. See you."

I didn't have time to soak up her positive attention since Jeremy whirled me around, his hands on my shoulders. "What? Are you okay?"

Julian didn't release me, even when I tried to shake off his grasp. "Are you?" He shook his head, before shooting a glare at his brother. "You should have known better than to dip your dick in crazy. Seriously, dude."

I took my hand back to cover my ears. "Don't want to hear that."

Jeremy shoved his brother. "Don't talk like that around her."

"It's the truth. Handle it. Tell us what happened." He tucked me against him protectively, and I took advantage of the position to inhale his scent. "But let's do it over dinner since you've had a very long day. You require some Chinese food and maybe a drink."

Jeremy turned his back on us for a second, his shoulders looking tense. "Tell us, please, what exactly happened, Princess."

I would take the food and pass on the drink. I didn't think I would ever feel safe enough to risk drinking after I saw what it did to others.

I explained, "She was crazy, if I'm honest. I've never seen this girl before, then she yanked open the shower curtain and screamed at me. She asked me who I was dating, then explained how Jeremy was hers. Sarah got rid of her for me. She said she would shove her head in the toilet."

Julian laughed, then caught himself, trying to keep his expression serious. "Sorry. It's not funny. What happened to you is awful, but Sarah absolutely would shove her head in the toilet. She used to shove Jeremy's head in the toilet when we were kids. She doesn't play around or make toilet threats she doesn't mean."

I let them lead me out of the school, my jaw popping with a yawn from my day. Jeremy added, "She won't get near you again, I promise you that." A muscle ticked in his jaw.

Crisp evening air made me wish for a sweater, the warmth of the day lost as the sun set. Streetlights lit up the night in a way that only existed in Manhattan. As I walked past the elegant brownstones and high-end boutiques, street noise became a familiar chorus, filling the night with honks and screeching tires. The city never slept, or so it seemed, with everyone having someplace they needed to be fast.

As we walked, I asked, "Did you wait for me because you thought something bad would happen?"

I remembered Sarah's bitterness at the start of practice, and considered their faces carefully.

Jeremy bumped his shoulder into me. "Julian just told you Sarah put my head in the toilet before. She isn't my favorite person, and she never will be. I don't love the idea of her spending time with you, but no one will mess with her. Did I think Maggie was going to go nuts on you in the shower? No."

His brother quickly added, "Maybe you should have, because you should absolutely *never*..."

Jeremy held up his hand. "Don't. Just fucking don't."

Julian laughed, his tone bitter. "If I don't say it, it doesn't make it any less true."

"He's no virgin, despite what he might have you think," Jeremy said then shook his head.

I really didn't want to have that conversation. "Can we not? I mean, I know you guys have known lots of people that way or whatever." I should use the word, but I had to blow out a breath before I could make myself do it in front of them. "Had sex, I mean. The thing is, now you want to be with me, right? So I can't be thinking about your pasts, or I'll go through every day wondering if I'm sitting next to one of your former lovers. I think it would drive me crazy."

Jeremy stopped walking, and we almost ran into him since he was slightly ahead of us. He regarded me seriously. "It hasn't been *that* many people, but I understand what you're saying."

"I don't know..." Julian said then chewed on his bottom lip.

His twin rounded on him. "You don't know what?"

"Maybe she *should* know our pasts. Wouldn't that be

better? At least she would know why she's getting assaulted in showers then, right?"

Jeremy looked almost wild, as if he genuinely feared my judgement. "She just said she didn't want to know."

Julian raised his hands in surrender, but his eyebrows said there was more to the topic. "Okay."

We walked a bit again before I had to ask, "Why did she shove your head in the toilet?"

"Jeremy took her favorite pen. He wanted it, but it was hers. Sarah comes from a long line of very wealthy New Yorkers who don't take shit, so Jer had to learn the hard way."

Jeremy took my hand, his fingers warm against mine. "That much is true."

"What happened with Phoenix and you in Collins' class?" Julian asked, his voice low as we approached home.

No, it's their home, not mine. I needed to remember that. They lived there, and I might be staying with them, but it wasn't where I lived. I couldn't even tell anyone that I was staying there, other than the doorman. *Maybe discretion is a job requirement for doormen.*

Regardless, I started at the top and gave them the whole hellish story about Collins' class. It seemed only fair to admit my own stupidity and how I made life more difficult for their brother.

They didn't respond as I expected, though. Instead, Julian pressed me against the outside of their building, his breath hard against my face, his lips close to mine. "Thank you. Seriously. That was possibly the most amazing thing anyone ever did for Phoenix. You're a gift to all of our lives, and fuck that woman for making you read. I guarantee, she knew you would struggle because she knows what dyslexia is, regardless of her bullshit. You're crazy smart."

Jeremy cleared his throat. "I hope she's not crazy, since

you just pointed out we're not supposed to dip our dicks in crazy. God knows you want to do that with her someday."

That shouldn't have been funny, but it was. It just fucking was. We laughed, all of us, as though we'd never laughed before. By the time we stopped, tears streamed down my cheeks.

Julian kissed them away with a lingering smile. "I love the sound of your laughter. I want to make you laugh and smile every day."

His twin nodded. "Agreed. And Collins will pay."

I smiled despite his dire warning. "You can't go around punishing everyone who is mean to me."

The doorman opened the door, so I followed them inside. Jeremy lifted his eyebrows, as he clarified, "Yes I can. I absolutely can."

By the time we got in the elevator, I leaned into his body like it was the only thing that could keep me upright.

I breathed him in deep, filling my lungs with his scent before I asked, "How did I end up playing water polo with the girl who shoved your head in a toilet? Today was overall really strange."

If I was honest, I would admit I wanted to be Sarah's friend.

"It was." Julian nodded. "But I think the rest of us realized today that we have to share you with everyone else. You were just ours, but now you're going to have people in your life that aren't in ours. We'll just have to get used to it."

Jeremy kissed me. "One day down. One hundred and seventy more to go."

Ugh. Why did he have to mention that part?

6

Barrett had placed Chinese food around the table before we got there, and he grinned at us when we entered. "I set it up."

"Thank you." I walked over to kiss him on the cheek, stomach growling at the scent of food.

He nodded. "Sure. The guys texted when practice was almost over. Did you hate it?"

"No, but I want to go change. They can tell you what happened afterward. Is Phoenix up in his room? I want to make sure he's okay."

Barrett sighed. "He's not here. I asked if he was joining us for dinner, and he just said no. One word. I checked the tracking app, and he's only three blocks away, I think at Jo's."

Jo, his drug dealer. I hated him. I reminded myself that Jeremy said he would punch him when he saw him next, and I couldn't work up any sympathy for him.

I changed my clothes and arrived to find Barrett had obviously already heard about the whole day from his brothers. His whole demeanor had changed, especially the way he held himself, stiff and rigid and ready for a fight. It was his first day of college, so I really didn't want to add to his levels of stress.

"I'm okay," I said as I walked over to him. "Actually, all in all, it wasn't a bad day. I don't want you to worry about me."

He shook his head, smoothing my hair away from my forehead. "Don't you worry about me, she says. Aren't you worrying about me worrying right now?"

I grinned, because he called it. "Sure."

"Then you're going to find a way to deal with me worrying about you, too. What Maggie did wasn't okay. Collins, either. Although I don't know why we didn't know she was giving Phoenix shit before now."

Jeremy motioned for me to sit, so I squished in between Barrett and Jeremy. Julian sprawled across from us, as shirtless as his brother and wearing shorts. They both held a beer.

After we all ate—including an eggroll each, because that was essential according to Julian—Jeremy spoke again. "Maybe he didn't tell you because you're not his father. Despite you taking care of all of us—and I know you have— it's not your job. I can't speak for Phoenix, but I know I don't want my life overflowing onto yours. Maybe he's just handling shit himself."

Julian laughed. "Badly."

I stretched in my pajama pants and a tank top—my preference, if I could wear anything at any time, the most comfy outfit possible. Despite my arguments to the contrary, apparently I couldn't just live in pjs full time. I glanced at Jeremy and realized I would probably feel the same as him, in that position. I wouldn't want someone else responsible for my choices either.

Barrett blinked rapidly, as if surprised. "I didn't try to raise you. At least I never thought I did. I only wanted to make sure everyone was solid." He squirmed in his seat.

"Alatheia and I are going to a jazz club Friday. Anyone else want to come?"

Jeremy groaned, but Julian nodded. "I'm in."

"Great," he said then smiled. "Celeste Demille is in town, playing at Lincoln Center, but I have it on good authority she is going to Miller's the night before. Obviously, I'm going."

I swallowed, recognizing the name. "She's been playing jazz since the sixties mostly in New Orleans, right?"

His answering smile was huge. "That's right. You are so awesome."

Julian tapped on the table to get my attention. "Are you busy now?"

I knew what he wanted, since I had promised to read the play. "I'm done eating, and I have time."

Jeremy glanced between us. "What am I missing?'

Julian shoved his shoulder. "I finished my play, and I asked Alatheia to read it."

"Oh. " He seemed genuinely curious as he scanned his brother. "That's awesome. Can I read it?"

"Yes, but after her." He nodded toward Barrett. "You can, too, if you want later."

Their oldest brother sat back in his seat, uncrossing his legs and stretching before he stood. "Sure, I'd love that. I actually have to do some reading for school, too, so I'll be in my room unless anyone needs me."

Jeremy yawned. "I am going to watch television."

I translated that to mean he would fall asleep on the couch, though I couldn't blame him. My muscles were already starting to ache, and I didn't do half of what they did in the pool. Despite that, I managed to follow Julian to his room, where he pointed at the desktop. "Can you read it there or do you want me to print it out for you?"

"Computer is fine. I am actually more comfortable with it than I would be holding a bunch of printer paper."

He clicked to open the file, glancing back at me with his devastatingly handsome grin. "Me too. It's different than holding a book, but all that doesn't matter right now. Anyway, my play is tentatively titled *Ghostlighting*."

I swallowed, not sure if I could handle it if he went full gore. "Is it a horror thing?"

"No, it's about the ghosts we carry with us—literally and figuratively. It may be really stupid, so I have to let you read it before I chicken out. Anyway a ghostlight is the light left illuminated on the stage when the theater is empty." Uncertainty tinged his voice, but I understood his hesitation well enough since I felt the same way ever since I showed them I wrote *Poor Relation*. Something about having someone else reading and judging your work made the nerves sensitive, regardless of who you were.

But an ache formed in the pit of my stomach as I worried about what I would say if it sucked. *Shit.* I couldn't lie to him, because he would know... Julian ran a hand through his brown hair, his blue eyes full of nerves and worry.

I squeezed his hand. "Is there anything you can do so you aren't actively watching me read?"

He nodded, glancing at the doorway. "I can go watch television with Jeremy."

I grinned, realizing he would probably also pass out. "I'll wake you when I come out."

"No, he falls asleep in front of the television like some old guy, but I don't. Besides, I'm going to be antsy because you're reading my work. See you in a bit."

I turned toward the computer, blowing out a breath because it wasn't like I knew a lot about plays in general. Maybe I wouldn't even be the intended audience.

But I started reading.

Immediately, the story sucked me in, and I felt as if I was Elizabeth Short, the beautiful dark-haired heroine.

"Hello," she said, then nodded to the audience per the stage direction. "I'm Elizabeth Short, but you know me by another name." Stage direction instructed her to pause, and I imagined her lips quirking with an impish grin. I could picture her as though she was real. "History has called me the Black Dahlia."

Okay, I'm hooked. Julian used the play to describe a family —a really traditional one, with a mom, dad, two kids, a teenage boy and a grown daughter—all just going about their lives. Then everything is upended by the sudden and mysterious death of a neighbor. Even more interestingly, each of the characters dragged a ghost along with them through the plot. The father walked with the shadow of his father—long dead but ever chasing his steps, trying to be the man he imagined his father to be. The mother had her mother's ghost, whispering all the things she should be doing throughout the day like a taskmaster. The older sister carried her living mother's dreams from when she was young, before she became a parent and changed her path. The brother had his fifth-grade teacher, who died in the night and didn't return to school the next day.

Dahlia herself remained in constant dialogue with her dead neighbor. Minor characters filled out the story—a police officer, the neighbor's mother, but everyone had their own ghost.

I finished it in an hour, and by the end, tears streamed down my face. I wiped them away with a sniffly sob. It was a beautiful play, so different than I imagined when I thought of his writing.

The Black Dahlia started and ended the play, but the story didn't focus on her. She haunted the play, like a figure removed from the action and yet part of it at the same time.

I sat back in my seat, wiping my nose and breathing slowly. Julian would probably get a big head, but I would be raving about the play. My fears of telling him bad news were squashed by his amazing writing skills.

I tiptoed out to the living room, hoping not to wake them if they fell asleep. Sure enough, Jeremy was out cold on the couch, snoring. Barrett played the piano, his fingers almost strolling across the keys, and I was surprised I didn't realize it was him playing.

They left the television on, but with the volume so low, I wasn't sure anyone could hear it over the music. Julian wasn't really watching it anyway, instead scrolling through his phone. He looked up when I entered and then jumped to his feet.

With his arms crossed over his chest, he approached me, one brow arched defensively. "How bad?"

I blinked at him, still slightly sniffly. "How bad? Not bad at all. Brilliant." I wiped at my eyes again. "You made me cry. Julian, you are so talented. Thank you for even letting me read it and..."

He kissed me, square on the lips, the gentlest of caresses to steal my words away. His body practically vibrated against mine, his emotions so vibrant I could feel them press against me as clearly as his lips. Finally, he pulled away, taking my hand and dragging me with him into his bedroom. With a click, he shut the door behind us.

Before I could sputter out a laugh at his eagerness, he asked, "Really?"

I nodded. "Really. I wouldn't lie about your writing, though I was afraid you might suck and make things horribly awkward for us both. No, it is actually incredible. Seriously. I know you said you wanted to be a playwright, that it was your goal, but I had no idea you were this talented. You're an artist."

Julian hugged me so tightly I had to put my head down on his shoulder. "Thank you. I...I do feel like this is what I am supposed to be doing, but I also don't want to be ridiculous.

I'm the rich kid of a rich kid. Sure, we live this impossible, hidden life, but I don't know that it means I have anything interesting to say. Sometimes it seems ridiculous to think I have something important to say that people should hear."

I pulled back. "What? But you do. You completely do."

"Well, thank you. I mean, seriously." He kissed me again, but this time, his lips weren't gentle. Instead, he claimed my mouth, his tongue hungry and asking. He stroked his fingers down my cheek, and I shuddered against him, answering his needs with some of my own. I trembled, even. It felt different, somehow. Despite all of them kissing me—as frequently as possible—this one was different, or my response was.

He led us toward his bed, which seemed like a great idea to me, especially when his weight pressed me down into the mattress. We rarely even entered his room normally, making it strangely intimate and special.

He whispered near my lips, "Nothing happens that you don't want to happen. I am just going to kiss you."

I nodded, nuzzling my nose against his. My body ached, needing more of his. "There...there is going to come a time where I want more than kissing."

He smoothed my hair, watching me with the cutest smirk. "Well, I sort of hope that will be the case, of course. But for now, I don't want you to feel pressured about anything."

I didn't but he was sweet to point it out. Then again, Julian seemed to prioritize me from the first moment we met. "I think that I should get on birth control first," I admitted.

Julian tilted his head, not disagreeing. "Good call."

I bit my lip, because the logistics would be a bit complicated. Although it likely would be easy enough to ask a doctor for a prescription, I didn't have access to my insurance information, nor did I think my aunt would be willing to provide it. Phoenix said he would look into that but didn't know the status. But in bed with Julian wasn't the time to worry about such mundane things.

I kissed him instead, drawing him down to me, and he greedily accepted my offer. He kissed my lips like he owned them, his shirtless torso hot under my hands. I traced my fingers down his back, feeling his skin and the hardness of his muscles bunch under my touch. He moaned, jerking his hips against me but continued to kiss me, nothing more.

I closed my eyes and sank into the feelings, lost in a sea of the taste of him and his touch. My control slipped away so easily with my eyes shut, the darkness the perfect place for my needs and cravings. He was hard, his need obvious and grinding up against me, and part of me thrilled to be wanted by him.

I wanted him too.

A lot. It seemed my skin caught fire under his touch.

I pushed things just a little further, and tugged on my shirt, freeing myself so I only wore my bra, and more of our skin could touch.

He stared down at me, his eyes wide. I kissed his bottom lip. "Just kissing still, but like this?"

His nod was fast and his mouth hungry when it found mine, practically gulping me down.

"You're so fucking beautiful," he whispered in my ear between kisses before he dragged his lips across my throat. "They write poetry because of you."

I could have argued, but right then, I wanted the illusion. Besides, he was absolutely perfect himself. "Have you looked in the mirror lately?" I pointed out.

He shook his head. "I don't compare."

We kissed again, over and over, until I was sure I would never need air again. I only wanted Julian to breathe life into me with his kisses. When he would grind his hips into me—

seemingly unconsciously—a thrill arced through me so I moved with him.

Finally, with a sigh, he stopped, rolling onto his back, and drawing me against his side. "Sorry," he said, sounding out of breath. "I need a minute. To stop, actually." He panted, but he kissed my temple and my cheeks. "I love you. Got to stop. Okay?"

I wasn't sure I followed, my mind practically drunk on needing him, but I couldn't complain about his warmth or listening to his heartbeat. "That was...yeah," I agreed, at a loss for words.

He grinned before he kissed my forehead. "It was. You are...yeah."

In an awkward move, I managed to pull my shirt back on, trying not to feel self-conscious that he could still see me. The piano had stopped from the other room, but I could still faintly hear the television. I reached for my back pocket, realizing I'd left my phone by his computer. "What time is it?"

He sighed, one arm thrown across his eyes as if to block out the world. "Does time have to exist?"

I couldn't think of a good reason to leave him, so I kissed his side then closed my eyes. "No, or we can pretend it doesn't until you have to get up for water polo tomorrow morning."

After a while of holding me, he moved, leaning back on his elbows. "If we stay here much longer, I'm not moving until morning, so we should get ready for bed. It's late, I think."

I nodded. "You're probably right."

"Alatheia," he said and took my cheeks in his hands and kissed my lips. Once. Then twice. "I spent the whole day thinking about you. All day. I hated you being so close, yet I couldn't see you all day. Just know that when we're apart, I'm thinking about you every second I can think."

I wrapped my arms around him, breathless with the force of my feelings. "I think I was just trying to survive. It wasn't awful, but everything is new. I thought about you all day, too, in the midst of my chaos."

"Fair enough."

When he would have gotten up, I stopped him, entwining our fingers and making sure to make good eye contact. "What you wrote is just amazing. I think I might be carrying ghosts from everything that happened, if I'm honest. My mom for sure, and maybe even my dad? My relatives? Anyway, I loved the way you talked about the ghosts, and I think it is going to resonate with a lot of people." With a smile, I gave his fingers a squeeze. "Are you carrying any ghosts of your own?"

"Fewer since I met you, if I'm honest. I thought. . .I thought maybe I would always be alone. How on earth could anyone want to be with me under these circumstances? But my heart knew your heart. So, yeah, I am carrying a whole shit ton of ghosts, but I feel like they aren't as heavy anymore. We'll work on yours, too. Alatheia. This is forever for me. You are it. I know we're too young for me to say that and you to believe it. I get it, I do, but just know...that's where I am."

I shook my head, but not because I doubted him...exactly. "It's hard for me to think about forever. I just hope they don't send me away to a boarding school in Switzerland or some-where," I confessed.

"If they can't be encouraged to change their minds, either by us or by my parents or by Granny, then we will go with you to Switzerland. If you're there, we'll be there. I'm not sure about Barrett, actually, but we can go to school wherever you go. I don't care where I graduate from. We'll figure it out, I promise you that."

I wanted to believe him, so for the moment, I allowed myself to revel in the illusion of pretty happy ever afters.

When we reentered the living room, Jeremy was still sprawled snoring on the couch.

Julian shot me a quick grin. "We should leave him. Waking him is going to be like poking a bear."

I scowled, because I couldn't leave him sitting up on the couch. "I'll get him up. He won't be a bear to me. If he is, I'll forgive him, but where's Phoenix?"

Julian sprinted back to his room, returning a second later with both of our phones. He passed me mine, his eyes glued to his own screen. "Hasn't moved, still over at Jo's, and I don't know what time he'll get back. As far as I'm concerned, if he isn't here when we go to bed, he loses out on the snuggle that night. Normally, he gets automatic rights to you because he can't sleep without you. I don't mind it, because I like him better sleeping, but he can take the floor if he isn't going to get his ass home."

I frowned as Julian left the room, because I couldn't just let it go. Instead, I sent Phoenix a text message. *Coming home?*

I waited a second as if he would answer instantly, but he didn't. I decided to check my other notifications while I waited for his response.

Tiffany sent me a gorgeous unicorn, and I guessed it was her latest art piece. I sent back a heart emoji, hoping it wasn't weird. I hoped I wouldn't overthink every single interaction, but I feared I would because I'd never tried to make friends before.

I really shouldn't overthink it, I decided, flipping to the next message. Bethany texted too, selfies in her school uniform but with her hair in three different styles. *Which one?* she demanded.

She wants my opinion on her hair? I typed back honestly, *I have no idea. All look good.*

I noticed a water polo group chat that I didn't have before, and I scrolled through the messages discussing a schedule for practices. . . I had never in my life had so many messages, not to mention on the same day.

Bethany answered my text first, saying, *I'll try all three this week, and we'll see if you're right.*

I chewed my bottom lip, deciding whether or not I should reply, then remembered Jeremy. I placed my hand on his shoulder, squeezing gently. "Jer, don't sleep here. Come on, let's go to bed."

He blinked awake, kind of moaning before his eyes cleared and focused on me. "Hey, Princess. What's going on?"

"Bedtime," I explained, enjoying his sleepy loose limbs.

He nodded and kind of wobbled his way into the bedroom after giving me a passing kiss. I stared down at the phone, not sure what to do because Phoenix still hadn't answered me. *Maybe he isn't going to.*

I ran a hand through my hair. I didn't think I would be able to sleep a wink worrying about him.

I wanted to ask the guys what to do, but I hesitated, afraid he would think I asked them to check on him if they went over.

Finally, I entered the bedroom to find it silent. They had each taken their places already, with Jeremy on the mattress on the floor, already fast asleep. Julian and Barrett left me a spot on the bed in between them, but they also seemed unconscious.

I reminded myself that his brothers would be worried if something was actually wrong, turned off the light, and climbed between them. The soft bed enveloped me, their scents so warm and safe, yet different. I sighed, realizing I was used to having Phoenix beside me every night.

The twins snored, a familiar and comfortable sound, like a white noise to me at this point. As I settled down, adjusting the covers around me, I let myself drift into the sounds in the room.

Despite my best efforts, I couldn't sleep, though. Perhaps my ghostlight glowed too bright?

Barrett laughed, a low sound, and I wasn't surprised because sometimes he talked in his sleep. He rolled over, pulling me against his chest. "Alatheia," he whispered, his eyes not really open. "There you are. Sleep."

Julian rolled over too, his forehead snug against my back. They were there, and all would be well. I tried to force myself to sleep by closing my eyes.

I must have slept, but it didn't feel like I got much rest. I woke when the twins got up for practice, startling awake as they tried to sneak away. Julian kissed my shoulder, audibly exhaling before he climbed out of the bed. I lifted my head, glancing around the dim room to verify Phoenix never showed up. I hoped he would have snuck in during the night.

Jeremy crossed the room, giving my foot a gentle squeeze as he passed. I rolled into the place where Julian had been, stealing what remained of his warmth as I stared at the ceiling. Barrett murmured and then opened his eyes. "Why so far away?" he grumbled, his voice rougher than usual.

I smiled then rolled into his open arms. "I don't know. Just...not able to sleep."

"Try to doze in my arms for a little bit. We'll have coffee in an hour."

I didn't disagree, tucking into his warmth and heartbeat.

They had lived with Phoenix's comings and goings a lot longer than me, and none of them seemed worried. If they could sleep and not worry about it obsessively, then I would have to figure it out, too. Time passed slowly, my eyes closed and breathing slow as I listened to the twins leaving the apartment. The air conditioner switched on and off, cooling us with a gentle breeze. Outside, cars honked their horns and a siren went off. Finally, Barrett's alarm jangled.

He rolled over to turn it off, so I hugged him when he

rolled back. *His arms are safety.* It sounded stupid in my own head, but it was all I could think right then.

"Good morning." He kissed my head. "Did you sleep okay? I passed out before you came to bed. I guess it was a long day."

I smiled, staring up into his brown eyes. "I slept, but Phoenix didn't come home unless he slept in another room."

He nodded. "And you're worrying about him." He didn't phrase it as a question but then it wasn't one. "He doesn't think. Unfortunately, this won't be the only time he sleeps at Jo's, unless he is willing to take some steps to stop. Jo is a factor. I don't know why he was like that yesterday. But... yeah. I'm sorry."

"You don't have to be sorry. You didn't do anything wrong," I said, trying to brush it off as I got out of bed. "I'm going to go make us coffee."

I tried to pretend I didn't think about the fact Phoenix promised to make my coffee, since he wasn't there, and I still needed to make it through my second day of school regardless.

❧   7   ❧

I dressed in my uniform then started on laundry from the day before. I never minded picking up, mostly to spare the maid from having to do it. Rosalind Lent didn't live here, and she wasn't seeing her sons very much at the moment. Still, she paid for them to be comfortable, which meant I benefited from her generosity with her children.

It didn't mean I had to make things harder for the staff. Instead, I tried to make their lives easier, hoping they would be less likely to get rid of me.

I shook my head. Jules said we were forever, but was I not capable of comprehending that time, or did I not believe him?

Barrett poured a mug of the coffee I'd brewed when I entered the kitchen. After a glance at me, he said, "I know it's the same outfit every day, but I'm never going to get enough of you in it."

I hugged him, only blushing a little at his compliment. "Okay, so today you have Intro to Con Law at eight, Philosophical Foundations of Justice at ten-thirty, and Music and the American Experience at six p.m." I made a face after I said the last one. "It's your late night."

He rocked with me, just slightly, almost dancing with me in the kitchen. "Yes, my late night. I'll be off all afternoon while you're busy then just when you get home, I leave. Still, I'll be home by ten, so if you went to bed early, I promise to crawl into the room quietly."

It wasn't the first time we had the conversation, because it came up ever since he got his schedule. "It's your bedroom. I'm not going to go to bed in your room, especially if it might keep you from being able to use it."

He kissed my nose. "Sweetheart, it's *our* room now, not my room. The others barely use their rooms, if you haven't noticed. If I need some kind of space when I get home to do something, I can use Jeremy's room. I don't care about the space anymore, just that you're nearby."

We sipped our coffee, and I glowed under his attention, so I cleared my throat. "Okay, well, I'm not sure I buy it, but we'll see."

"You're sweet to care. I will be looking forward to bed." He frowned. "So last night I couldn't get a few thoughts out of my head. I ended up playing the piano for a little while so I could think."

I took a deep breath to get a good whiff of his scent, hoping to keep it with me all day. "Yeah, I saw you."

He blinked. "You did?"

"Yep. You must have been pretty heavily concentrating to miss me watching."

He nodded, his gaze going distant. "Right. So, I cleared my head and went back to my homework, but I have thoughts about Collins."

I scrunched up my nose. "Yuck. Really?"

"Right?" Barrett laughed. "Listen, Collins should be long gone, and I don't know why she hasn't retired. People don't get to stay at the school if they're mean to the kids, normally, since we're rich and entitled. Yet she is still there and has been forever, which means someone or something must be protecting her. Due to that, please be careful, even if it might be impossible not to trigger her. I don't know our best options, and I hate not knowing, but we are protected. Nothing will happen to the Lents unless our secret comes out, but you're a different matter. You're not a scholarship kid, but your family won't protect you. If she figures that out, I don't know how we'll be able to protect you from her." He kissed my nose again. "But I'll figure this out, and then I'm going to stop her."

I tugged on his shirt. "Not your job, lawyer. Your job is to go learn something and have some fun."

He shrugged. "I have many jobs. See you tonight." He winked at me as he left.

I caught my breath, realizing it was my first time actually alone in their apartment. Usually, the space seemed filled with their energy, noise, and it seemed bizarrely empty without them.

Like right after the holidays, I thought, *when the decorations come down and everything seems just a little drabber and dull.*

With a half hour until I should leave, I headed into the living room and thought about watching the television. Soreness in my arms from swimming made me stretch, and I sighed.

The door opened and closed behind me and I turned, wondering what Barrett could've forgotten. But it wasn't him. My breath caught in my throat, shock jerking through me in an adrenaline hit. Phoenix lurked in the doorway, disheveled as all hell, red-eyed, and looking worse than I had ever seen him.

I rushed to him but stopped just short of throwing my

arms around him. Not only did he smell like smoke, his body language spoke volumes—*leave me alone.*

I read the message, and I controlled myself.

We stared at each other, not speaking, because I worried so much about him, even if he didn't want me to touch him. Finally, I couldn't stand the silence anymore. "Are you okay?"

"Why wouldn't I be okay?" He lifted an eyebrow, the derision in his expression hitting like acid.

A question instead of an answer. Deflection. I might not know what was wrong, but I knew he wasn't just tired.

"Is something wrong? Did I do something?" I asked. *The big change is me, so I must be the problem.*

He ran a hand through his dark hair, his dark eyes wounded as he seemed to realize my fears. "No, you didn't do anything. I hung out with friends last night, no biggie. I'm allowed. It's not like I have a bedtime. Do I have to, what, check in with you and get permission before I go somewhere?"

Ouch. I stepped back, his point hitting me squarely in the ego. None of them needed to answer to me, and he wasn't wrong. As soon as I was out of his way, he stormed to the back of the house. My heart beat so fast I could hear it thrum in my ears. He usually wasn't so cruel, not even when we didn't know one another and he stole my wallet.

The shower came on from his room, and I jerked at the noise.

Snagging my backpack, I decided I didn't want to stick around for him to tell me off again. I would just go to school early, sit outside, and wait to get into the building. *Better than waiting here with Phoenix, anyway.*

I kept my head down and my heart sat firmly in my stomach as I tried to think of what I did to deserve his attitude. Did he just hate going to school with me? Was I annoying or something?

I kept my head down the entire walk, only paying attention to the red and green indicators before crossing roads. The guys hardly paid attention to them, instead seeming to instinctively know it was time to go or stop, but I wasn't that well versed in traffic.

When I made it to school, others milled around talking to one another. The sound of wheels behind me on the sidewalk made me turn around quickly, so I wouldn't be run over.

Abruptly, the skateboard stopped in front of me, and I looked up at Phoenix. His wet hair and half tied tie made me think he rushed.

"What the fuck, Alatheia. You couldn't wait for me?"

Are you serious? For a second, I considered not answering him, gaping like a startled fish. Then my fury caught up to my mouth.

"Why would I wait for you after you said those things to me?" I shook my head. "Why would I stand there and wait to take more?"

He threw his hands in the air. "What? I didn't say anything that awful. I think maybe you're being—"

I put out my hand to stop him and he actually instantly went silent. "You were mean. Cruel. You treated me like a Poor Relation, and you know you did, because you did it on purpose. Whatever you intended to say, you can stop right there. Don't belittle us both or bother trying to gaslight me. You owe me nothing, which you made clear today. I don't even deserve a text back when I'm worried about you."

Phoenix's façade seemed to crumble right then, outside of Pullman, where we stood on the street. I swallowed, not allowing myself to feel bad for him, despite his raw and bare expression. *He was an asshole*, I reminded myself.

"You hurt me," I finished.

Then I turned my back on him and headed toward the stairs.

"Alatheia," his voice caught me, so I turned around. "I'm sorry, Red. I don't know...why I did that."

"I don't know why you did, either." I popped the earbuds Barrett gave me in my ears to end the conversation. I would listen to music for a while, tune him out.

He grabbed my arm. "Can we talk about this?"

I shook my head. "I need some time. I don't really want to talk to you right now, not after I spent the whole night afraid. I suppose I'll reach a point where I'll just be able to keep on keeping on the way that your brothers do when you spend the night at Jo's or whatever. Until then, I won't bother you with my expectations. I'll leave you alone."

I spun and left him outside, pretending I had somewhere to go. Looking busy was a great way to avoid facing being alone, a lesson I learned a long time ago.

🐉

I MANAGED to find my classroom, take my seat, and keep my head down. The musician we planned to see Friday night wailed in my ears, and I hoped to keep her there until I absolutely had to remove the headphones.

As I pulled out my laptop, Phoenix knocked on my desk, grabbing my attention.

I stared up at him, shocked he would proceed with our argument in class.

He leaned close to say, "Please don't leave me alone." His gaze implored me. "*Please* don't. You are not and will never be the Poor Relation to me. Not ever. I spent the night at Joe's because I can't face all of this. I can't do another year of this. I don't know if I can make it."

The rest of the class settled into their seats, and Tiffany grabbed my arm. "More to show you. You sure you don't think it sucks?"

I mumbled something like *of course not* but I kept my gaze on Phoenix. To him, I said, "Going to Joe's doesn't fix that. We had Chinese food. Julian finished his play. Barrett played the piano. Jer fell asleep in front of the television. Maybe being with us would have helped."

"Well?" Bethany said as she spun in a circle in front of my desk. "Do you like my hair?"

She had picked the up-do out of the three styles she had sent me. Marco threw his bag down and stared at Bethany. "Did you do something new to your hair?"

She threw her pen at him, and he laughed.

Phoenix took my hand for a second and linked them between the desks. "I'm sorry."

I already forgave him, if I was honest, as I squeezed his fingertips. I just wasn't sure what to do about it after such a long night.

The announcements rattled through the speakers, wishing another person a happy birthday, followed by the pledge and some school news. The minutes passed, then Ms. Collins stood and moved to the center of the class.

"Today, we are going to speak about intentions and setting goals. All of you can be successful...if only you would try a little harder."

I listened to her ramble on happily enough, since I didn't have to read aloud.

By the end of class, I was happy that Phoenix managed not to snore. His eyes drooped until they closed and he was out cold at his desk. Fortunately, he remained quiet, and Collins only seemed to notice when someone made noise or was disruptive while she explained how we were all failures.

The bell's chime couldn't come fast enough for me. I put my hand on his arm to wake him the second it was over.

"Phoenix, time to get up."

He lifted his head, blinking blearily at me. "Shit. Did I fall asleep?"

I smiled at him. "Yep. Maybe you need a bedtime."

After giving him a parting smile, I popped the earbud back in, hoping to make it through the rest of the day unscathed.

By lunchtime, I found my normal school rhythm, keeping my head down and my personality unobtrusive. Unlike other years, though, everyone seemed to want to stop and talk to me.

Because of the Lents. I might not understand the fascination, but I was sure it would pass.

I stepped into the courtyard and got yanked into an alcove where they stored extra chairs. Phoenix tugged me into a hug.

His body shook against mine—probably from exhaustion and whatever he took that day. He muttered into my hair, "I am so fucking sorry. Please."

I closed my eyes, inhaling him into my lungs and enjoying his warmth wrapped around me. "I forgive you, okay? I just feel a little bit wounded. I'm still learning how to do this, and I won't bother you again about coming home or anything."

"Yeah, well, I'm going to come home. Every night." He whispered the promise in my ear, then kissed my neck. "I do have a bedtime—whenever you want to go to sleep. I don't know why I sometimes fuck things up for myself, I just do it."

I would be happy to stand there all day and let him hold me. "You matter, okay? A lot."

He kissed my neck on a space where my skin was exposed. "Forgive me?"

"I have."

Phoenix nodded and pulled back. "Sorry, I just needed to hold you for a second."

We joined the table already rapidly filling up with all the

same people from the day before. The female water polo team joined us at the next table, and Bethany seemed to have brought two new people, too. They looked me up and down but then actually smiled.

Two empty seats remained near Jeremy, one across from him and one next to him. I took the one to his left while Phoenix slumped himself into the one across. He then dropped his head onto his arms, muttering something about needing a nap.

Julian slid into a seat at the table, but not before whacking Phoenix on the head. "Get some sleep at home then you can make it through the day."

Their youngest brother lifted his head but didn't otherwise respond. Laughing people surrounded us, and Jer put his arm around me. "How is today going?"

I sighed, feeling part of a group, a strangely satisfying sensation. "Fine. Nothing today of note, not even Collins."

He nodded once. "Glad to hear it. We have practice after school."

I knew because I memorized their schedules like it was my job. I hated the idea of not knowing where all four of them were, proving that maybe I was more than a little bit needy.

With that thought, I pulled out my phone and texted Barrett. *How's today?*

Groan, he texted back and I smiled. *He sums things up so well.*

"Hey, Al." Sarah walked over to me. "Good job yesterday. How's your soreness?"

I wasn't focused on it, but since she mentioned it, I noticed my discomfort. "My arms hurt the most."

"Yep. They will. That'll stop."

A girl marched out into the courtyard, and I gasped when

I recognized Maggie, the shower screamer. I tensed and Jeremy squeezed my shoulder. "Don't be scared."

"Alatheia," she said then pursed her lips. "I'm sorry for my behavior yesterday. I'm on some medication, and it has strange effects on me."

I blinked, startled. *What is happening here?*

She put her hands behind her back. "Can you forgive me? Maybe we can even be friends."

Jer shook his head. "She isn't going to be your friend. Not ever."

Maggie visibly swallowed. "Can you forgive me?"

Julian cleared his throat, and Phoenix shifted in his seat, glancing between us. "What did I miss?"

"A lot of stuff." Julian shook his head. "Later."

The courtyard had fallen silent, everyone apparently curious if I would forgive her. Maggie stared at me, her pretty blue eyes rimmed red and puffy. *What happened to her since we last met?*

I shrugged. "Sure, let's just let it go."

She nodded and then stared at Jeremy. "Won't happen again."

"I'm sure it won't." He squeezed my shoulder.

After she exited the courtyard, it exploded in volume, everyone talking at once. Bethany grabbed my arm. "How did you get Maggie to fucking apologize to you and what did she do?"

"I...I did nothing." I would ignore that second part, since I didn't want to discuss the shower incident.

Sarah crossed her arms over her chest. "That you, Lent?"

"I don't know what you're talking about." Jeremy went back to his lunch.

For their part, Phoenix and Julian whispered together and Phoenix widened his eyes. "She did what?"

Jeremy explained, "Yeah, I know, really bad. Normally, you would handle it, but if you're going to go non-communicative at Joe's place, then you're going to miss things. It got taken care of."

Phoenix grinned at Jeremy. "I forgot how brutal you can be."

"Not me." He shook his head, but I didn't believe him. *Not even a little bit.* Once the buzz moved on to other topics, like a pep rally and an upcoming homecoming dance, I nudged Jeremy.

"Tell me the truth," I whispered.

He chewed on his bottom lip then answered me in the same low voice. "I can't tell you how much I want to kiss you right now. I don't think I ever appreciated the amount of restraint in my family."

He was being deliberately obtuse, so I scowled at him before admitting, "Same, I promise." After kissing Julian last night, I planned to be more honest about it. He widened his eyes, and I kicked him under the table. "But you know that wasn't what I meant."

He sighed. "Daniel filters a lot of money to people trying to start high end businesses. Her father opens men's fashion houses, high end stuff. I texted Daniel that I needed him to intervene on something, because Maggie went way out of line and needed her rope tugged. He tugged her dad. Then her dad tugged hers."

I closed my eyes. "She is going to hate me even more now. She might have publicly apologized, but she won't forget it. Trust me."

"No, maybe that's how it was in other places. But we learned how to defend ourselves with a good offense. We always have to be the biggest predator in the room. Julian might pretend he doesn't know it sometimes, but Phoenix and I never forget it. And Barrett? With him, it depends on the day."

I closed my eyes, knowing it would blow up in my face regardless of his assurances. I might not know when or how, but it would. "She was pretty convinced you were hers," I pointed out.

He snorted. "Well, like she said earlier, she is on a lot of medications."

Lunch ended, and I didn't manage to eat a bite. Everyone got up, and Julian leaned over to whisper in my ear, "Baby, don't worry about the Maggie thing. You're with us now. You're all good."

He was wrong, but I would figure out how to handle it when it happened, just another ghost I would drag around until it exploded. I shook my head, realizing Julian's play was going to resonate with me for a while.

Sarah nudged my shoulder. "It's sweet they did that. I'm not surprised, since you seem to be good friends with the Lents, but someday I want the story. You'll have to tell me how you managed to befriend the most unfriendly group of people ever."

I shook my head. "Don't talk about their family like that."

She lifted her eyebrows, beaming at me. "I like that. You're loyal, too. No problem. I'll be loyal to you, you be loyal to me, and I won't speak about the Lents like that again." She shook her head, glancing around as if afraid to add, "You know girls like Maggie don't go away forever. They're like the plague. They flare up every so often."

Phoenix watched us but gave us some space.

"How do you avoid it?" I asked her. "How did you manage to be you and not get swept up in this world?"

She shook her head. "My family is a *plow our way in, ask questions later* setup. You'll find your way, too. In the meantime, you've somehow managed to make friends with Bethany and Tiffany, who absolutely don't run in the same crowds. Not to mention us. Not bad for your first day."

I laughed. "You know I don't ever have friends. Not usually."

"Well, you'll have to let me know which way you prefer it."

One day in and my life is already hardly recognizable.

◌⚎◌

SCHOOL ENDED and I made my way outside, since the twins had practice. Barrett wouldn't be home until very late—he might have even gone home and come back already. I could probably check on the app, but regardless, he wasn't near me. I didn't know where Phoenix was or if he would be coming home. I certainly wasn't doing the dance again in my own mind.

As if I conjured him, he appeared next to me, skateboard in hand. I wondered if he kept it in his locker, or where he kept it all day, since I hadn't seen it since morning.

"Going home?" He looked so hopeful, so I almost laughed.

I lifted my brows. "We're not supposed to say things like that here."

"Red, we're skirting breaking all the rules with you. Jeremy's arm was around you all through lunch. I guarantee it garnered some questions, especially after the Maggie apology, but most people already think you're dating me. So, yeah, you're right, but I'm wondering how long we can do this without utterly screwing it up anyway." He cleared his throat. "Are you, though? Going to the place That Shall Not Be Named?"

I thought about it, because although it was my plan, we didn't have to head right home. "Are you exhausted?"

He probably should be, but he shook his head. "I took something an hour ago, so I'll be wide awake for a while."

I hated that. So much. I didn't even know where to put all the hate, so I swept it away by blowing out an annoyed breath. I couldn't fix the situation on the sidewalk—hell, I might never be able to fix it at all. "Okay, you have the board with you. Why don't we go somewhere where you can skate and I can watch? Doable?"

I didn't feel like doing my homework. I wanted to watch Phoenix skate, and I didn't want to overthink it.

"Really?" He shook his head. "For real?"

I laughed, because he sounded as if he truly couldn't believe it. "Yes, so where can we go?"

"There's a place below the Manhattan Bridge. We can take the subway, then we'll have to walk. You up for that?"

I nodded. "Are you?"

He dropped the skateboard, putting one foot on it and offering me a hand. "Jump on, Alatheia. I can't wait to show you."

I stepped onto his board like the day when we chased the PI through the streets together. I held on to him and let him lead us away from Pullman. Phoenix didn't think he could make it through another year of school, but I wasn't sure either. Maybe we just all needed to make it a different kind of a year?

When we reached the skate park, I realized he wasn't lying about the location. The park was nestled beneath the Manhattan Bridge, literally. There were skaters all over, varying from the too young to be doing that to the practically too old to be doing it too. And everyone in between. The graffiti-covered walls were artistic in places and dirty and mean in others. The sounds of the constant wheels on concrete, plus cheers and grunting bounced around me. I stared at all of it, taking it in.

Phoenix seemed to know everyone, though he outright ignored the little kids on the periphery. By the time dusk tinged the sky pink, only his friends remained.

He introduced me to most of them, but as I sat on the ground watching him, I didn't think I remembered anyone's name. *Too many new people in my life*. Everyone seemed transient and no one stayed very long.

Remembering the past couple of years, tears threatened to spill, because I realized even if they didn't think so, the Lents could vanish overnight, too. They said they would come with me if I went away to boarding school, but it wasn't realistic. *Their lives are here.* Phoenix seemed like he might live three different kinds of lives all by himself, between school, drugs, and skating.

I like two of the three.

Not to mention their secret family life and their whole existence in the Hamptons.

I thought about Barrett, probably in some college classroom, and the twins at water polo, but they would be in college next year, too. They wouldn't be flying off to sit with me in whatever boarding school Aunt Tricia shoved me in.

As I watched, Phoenix pushed off with one foot, ready to go again. The people in the skatepark looked at him with respect, but not because of his name or his money. No one cut him a wide berth or rolled their eyes at him. He was one of them, and crazy talented.

Sometimes he even managed to go vertical, or vert, as they called it. The air seemed to capture him, holding him upright until he maneuvered himself back to the ground with practiced ease. Doing it one more time, he turned to grin at me.

"Do you want to try it?"

I blinked in surprise. *On his board, no pads, with everyone else around quasi-professional skaters? Do I want to fall on my ass in front of them?* It sounded terrifying, if I was honest.

"I'm good," I said and got to my feet. It was getting late, and the twins would be getting home soon. "How about if we get going? I want to stop at the grocery store near the house and grab some things. I want to make dinner." A thought dawned on me, because I didn't want to force Phoenix to go home. I wanted him to enjoy his afternoon. "You can stay here, if you want. I remember how we got here. I'll just reverse engineer."

He shook his head. "Don't be crazy. Of course I'm coming with you. Cooking? This is a new thing?"

"A trying it thing." I smiled at him. "You were so good. I mean, you're really incredible. How did you learn how to do all of that? " I gestured back at the skatepark as if encompassing all of it.

He set down his board and offered me his hand as he did every time. "Hal and I tried it together. We used to be best friends. We did everything together."

Hal? I searched my memory for a face in a sea of new names then I remembered—Tiffany's boyfriend, the one who did drugs, too. She mentioned Hal missed Phoenix, but I didn't really know the dynamic.

I jumped on the back of his board and held onto him, leaning my forehead against his back and wrapping my arms around him. I trusted him implicitly, so I simply held on tightly because he felt good in my arms.

We reached the subway, though Barrett would probably have preferred it if we'd gotten a car service. At the bottom of the stairs, Phoenix caught my hand, squeezing our fingers together before he brought them to his mouth to kiss them.

I put my head on his shoulder while we waited, comfortable with him. "Can I ask a question?"

"Always. I know I was a dick this morning, and I'm sorry. Don't be...intimidated around me. I'm still me."

I stared up at his hard profile, biting my lip and considering my words carefully despite his claim. "Why did you stop being friends with Hal? All Tiffany would say is he uses too, and he misses you."

He looked down at his feet. "When his parents cued into what he was doing, they blamed me for it. Truthfully, Hal is who got me into the stuff, but he blamed me, which was whatever. He got my parents involved, or at least Kit and

Mom. Eric is actually my dad, as you know, not that it mattered. They all stared at me with such disappointment. It's not like we have an awesome parent-child relationship to begin with, if I'm honest. They know who I am. Daniel actually said *I never thought you'd do this to someone else.* It was horrible." He looked away. "Rather than take responsibility for the fact that he got caught, he screwed me. Now, he doesn't even get it, because he doesn't know."

I nodded. "About your family dynamic?"

"Right, but it's not even that. Things are tenuous for me with them. If my brothers didn't love me so much, and cover for me, I wouldn't still be here. They would've sent me away to who knows where a long time ago then thrown away the directions of how to find me again."

I caught my breath, because although I didn't think his parents would abandon him, I didn't know for sure. Rosalind had been half out of her mind the whole time I knew them. His fathers seemed like they were always running in circles—sometimes figuratively, sometimes otherwise—to keep things together.

But at the end of the day, it wasn't what mattered. "I'm sorry that happened. Hal is obviously not to be trusted."

He shrugged. "Maybe he's changed but I doubt it. He's arguably more of a junkie than me but probably not much more."

"Hey," I said and squeezed against him tighter. "Don't talk about yourself that way. I don't like it. Do you want to stop doing what you're doing?"

The train chose that second to arrive with a screech. People started darting around and he pulled me onto it with him. I was on one side and the board was in his other hand, which meant he had to wrap his arm around the pole for support while he held his board at the same time.

I wasn't going to get an answer to my question right then. My timing couldn't have been worse. Then again, it was totally possible Phoenix would outright not answer me.

Instead, he kissed me, hard on the lips, stealing my breath and my thoughts. "Yes, but you're going to have to let me do it in my time. I've got some things to work out first, okay?"

"Whatever you want, however you want it. I won't press."

He nodded once as we jerked forward. "I know, because you're you. But I don't want my brothers to *keep on keeping on* as you said earlier. I've got to think about some things. I don't want to be the weak link you all eventually have to release."

I hated how little he thought of himself. "You're a genius, Phoenix. Anyone who doesn't see or get it is an idiot. You're essential. Besides, you might all be replacing me when I have to leave for boarding school."

"We're not circling around that topic. You know I'll follow you."

The subway clattered, a familiar noise and part of the city soundtrack in my mind. Conversations would vanish into silence, with the sound of the train dominating all. I couldn't understand a word said over the speakers.

We arrived at our stop and rushed off to make our way back to street level.

It was still hot outside, even sticky, so I fanned my shirt away from my body, trying to stir some air. "When does it start to feel like autumn? Last night teased it."

"Fall comes in about a month or so. I bet if you wanted, Barrett would take you on a drive to Vermont and Maine to look at the leaves changing colors. It sounds like the kind of thing he would enjoy."

I groaned. "You know you would want to come with us. Besides, it wouldn't be any fun without your running commentary. Plus, we'd have to go get his car right? Drive to the Hamptons, retrieve the car, and then leave for Vermont?

He probably wants to stay on campus and have fun or something, not drive with me to Vermont."

I was talking a lot, rambling, so I shut my mouth.

He grinned despite my nerves. "Hop on," he said and offered his hand.

I held on tight while he rode us home.

To his home. Not mine. I needed to remember that, since the rug could be ripped out from under me at any moment. I had to keep reminding myself.

"Hey," he said and stopped abruptly. I almost fell off, but he kept us both upright then pointed. "Isn't that the fucking PI?"

I looked around, scanning faces to see if I could spot him. "What?"

Then I saw him. He stared straight at us, about a block from the apartment. My lips thinned as I recognized him.

Phoenix lifted his hand to give the man the finger. I laughed, unable to stop myself. *So, we are back to this.* My family hired him before to follow me, not that it made any sense. I didn't go anywhere besides school.

Let him take photos.

Quickly, we ducked into a nearby grocery store to grab the few things I needed to cook a simple meal. I hoped I could cook, anyway. Aunt Amelia cooked for 'call me Ted' sometimes, and I watched her. Maybe I hoped she would be like a mother, despite me so completely failing in San Francisco. Maybe I just wanted her to like me? Regardless, I recognized really quickly people like her would show me favor if I gave them a ton of attention.

We made it all the way to his home and inside the building without getting into it with the PI, which had to be a win of some kind.

Stepping into the apartment, we came up short when we saw Kit and Daniel. *That's right. Dina said they were coming back.*

"Kit. Daniel." Phoenix stepped around them. "To what do we owe the pleasure?"

Kit ran a hand through his hair. "I thought you would all be home. Alatheia, good to see you."

Is it? I could never make out exactly how the elders in their family felt about me. Maybe they liked me? Maybe they thought I should go away. Maybe both. *Sometimes it seems my life is full of maybes.*

"Hi," Daniel said and smiled at both of us. "Good to see you're both well."

Kit leaned against the wall. "You didn't answer when we asked about the others. Where are they?"

"The twins should be almost home. They had practice tonight," I said as I carried the bags to the kitchen and set them on the counter. "Barrett has class until eight-forty-five ."

Their oldest father—not a genetic father to any of them—nodded. "Okay. Alatheia, I'll talk to you for a minute then we can wait for the twins. You can all relay our conversation to Barrett."

Daniel sat down on the couch, so I considered Barrett's father. They could practically be twins except Barrett had slightly lighter hair than his father.

"Hold on, Kit. How was school? You're two days in now, right? How is it going?" He looked between us.

Phoenix hadn't said a word. Was he going to answer or would I be monologuing with his family?

He sighed. "Fine. I mean, it's the second day. I'm not failing yet, if that's what you're asking."

"I wasn't." Dan smiled as though Phoenix didn't just snap at him. "I'm glad it's going fine." He paused. "How about for you, Alatheia?"

I stared at him for a second, considering my response carefully. "Also fine."

"Good. Did it help? The phone call I made? Did it help with the girl?"

I cleared my throat, since I meant to broach that topic with them. "Yes, but I don't want you to feel like you need to do things like that for me. I don't want to be trouble."

He waved away my protest. "Don't worry about it. Sometimes it's the only way to handle bullies—you have to bully them more. It's not nice but that's life."

Kit clapped his hands together. "Okay, listen, I have been looking into you and..."

The door opened and then closed, so he paused as the twins joined us. Julian nearly choked on a sports drink when he saw them.

"Hey," Jeremy said and set his bag down on a chair by the table. "What's going on?"

Daniel grinned at them, but even I could see his strain. "We wanted to see you."

"And talk to Alatheia," Kit finished.

Julian pulled me to him, sitting us both down on the big lounge chair next to the couch. In a second, he tangled our legs. "About what?"

The air conditioner chose that second to turn on, which added to the chill in the room. Daniel was trying, but Kit wasn't. My guys, without Barrett as a buffer, were making no effort whatsoever.

Jeremy sat down next to Daniel, Phoenix actually rose to take the other side, which left Kit standing. Maybe he realized it because he looked around quickly then took a seat in a smaller chair.

I cleared my throat. "You were saying? You looked into my family?"

"Right, so there is no record of you being born in Colorado."

I blinked, a chill icing my bloodstream. *Is it the AC or just the feeling like everything is about to explode?* "What?"

"You weren't born in Colorado, hard stop. Actually, I haven't been able to find your birth record anywhere." He held out his hand. "I don't think it's surprising you were worried about your family, since even a simple search proves something is wrong. We have two options. We can hire a guy I know, more of an ex-spy than an investigator. Although I'm sure he'll find answers, he is a bit like using a shotgun in a knife fight."

Jeremy shook his head. "So you don't want to pay for him?"

He shook his head. "I'll pay for him. When have I ever turned away something because of money? No, I think we have a faster, easier option, a far simpler way to find answers."

I looked between them all, not sure what he meant. "What is that? My mother told me I was born in Colorado. It isn't just some lie my aunts and uncles made up, because I know that was what my mom said."

The volume of my voice increased with every word, panic threading through my tone despite my best efforts. I couldn't even seem to stop it.

Julian squeezed me. "I'm sure she had a good reason. She loved you. You know that.

Daniel nodded quickly. "If your mom lied, it was for a reason."

Kit sighed. "Listen, there is no way to get through this other than to go through it. I'm not sure why your mom lied to you, Alatheia. I don't have enough information to reach any kind of conclusion, but if you want your birth certificate, you may have to go get it."

Go get it? "How?" My heart raced and I might have actually stopped breathing. *My mom lied to me. Is there anyone in my family who didn't lie to me?* She always told me I was born there, where we had been living when my father died. It didn't make sense for it to have been anywhere else.

"My suggestion is you walk in and take it when she's not there." Kit rose. "Get me your birth certificate, and we'll go from there. I don't want to take any steps forward without that, just in case."

Phoenix shook his head. "Just in case of what?"

"Just in case other steps have to be taken. This is bad, you guys get that, right?" He aimed the question at his sons, but my stomach churned in response.

I closed my eyes. His wife called me a charity case. As the days passed, increasingly, we proved that was what I was. I wanted a family. The Lents—at least the ones I knew— wanted me to be part of their family. *But how can I be anything when I don't even know who I am?*

"Excuse me. Give me a minute, please." I squirmed until Julian let me out of his embrace then I rushed into the bedroom where I slept. Barrett's room, stolen from him for our shared use, despite him saying he didn't mind. It was probably true, since Barrett didn't worry about having a place to belong, about having something that was his. He knew his place in the world even when things got slippery.

I sank to the floor, rootless and practically nameless. I only owned clothes Dina had bought me, making them basically charity. Otherwise? Old, ratty sneakers tucked in the closet, my computer, the things I used to create the *Poor Relation*, Dina's notebooks, and some toiletries. That was it. There were my school uniforms, but the guys paid for them.

I didn't have anything, not even a birthplace to call my own.

No way would my guys leave me alone for very long, so I sniffled and rubbed at my nose. Jeremy was probably already pacing. I went into the bathroom and locked the door, since they respected my privacy there. None of us bothered anyone in the bathroom.

I turned on the water to cover the noise then I sank to the floor to cry into my knees. Big, gasping, senseless sobs racked my body despite me knowing tears fixed nothing. Not when everything was broken.

Why did it hit me so hard? So I wasn't from Colorado, big deal. I was from *somewhere*, we only had to figure out where. Despite the logic, my sense of self felt shattered.

To their credit, it was a good long time before I heard the gentle tap at the door. I wasn't surprised it was Jeremy knocking.

"Princess," he said then knocked again. "Let me in, okay?"

I wiped my eyes. Since I'd cried so hard, I probably needed water. Wasn't it just being self-indulgent? I needed to pull myself together, and my legs were wobbly, but I managed to get up to open the door.

Jeremy took one look at me then tugged me into a tight hug. "We're going to get answers. Tonight."

Tonight? I sniffled on a choked sob slash laugh. "What are we going to do? I promise you, we can't just walk in and demand my birth certificate. They'll refuse. Even Dina won't be able to get it."

"There is an event tonight. Granny confirmed your aunt plans to attend. I don't know about your uncle, but Daniel doesn't think they actually live together. Rumor has it he sleeps at his office."

Did he? I never realized it, but it made sense.

"Are you saying we should go *steal* it?"

Phoenix leaned against the doorway, his smile whiplash fast. "It's not stealing. It's your birth certificate, but yeah, we are getting it. Afterward, I can open a bank account for you, too. If we have it, they can't get you a passport to ship you out of the country, either. Sure, they could order another copy, but we'll have one, too. We'll put a tracker on your name, so I can see if they've done anything we don't want."

I loved it when Phoenix concentrated on a problem. Right then, he looked like he did on his skateboard—focused and ready.

"I took your wallet. I'll find your birth certificate and anything else they might be hiding about you."

Julian called to us from the living room, "Come on. Let's figure out dinner."

I stepped out of Jeremy's arms back into the living room to find the fathers gone, the apartment just ours again. "Why would she lie to me? Never mind. I'll go make dinner. I bought groceries to cook, so let me do it."

"You're cooking?" Julian asked then tilted his head.

"I'm trying, at least. I have homework, too. You guys, I don't know if we should break into her apartment like that. There is a PI trailing me. We saw him today." I shook my head. "I'm rambling. I'm sorry."

"More like train of thought." Jeremy clapped his hands together, just like Kit. I never noticed him having the trait before, as if it were inherited, something he got from the man who was technically his uncle. "That's okay. What are we cooking?"

We? "You want to cook with me?"

"Yes."

I took the chicken out of the bag, hoping it wasn't too warmed. "It's been on the counter since I got home."

"Is that okay?" Jeremy asked Julian who shrugged. "Should we look online?"

"Let's go out to eat. You can cook tomorrow." Phoenix said as he took the chicken from me and threw it out. *That is so incredibly wasteful.* I bit my lip, hating the waste. "We need to go eat and get this done before Barrett gets home. If he gets home, then we won't do it. You know it and I do, too. No way will Barrett go along with it, even if it was Kit's idea."

I couldn't argue his point, but it made it all seem way riskier. "Then we shouldn't go?"

"No, we should." Julian said as he followed Phoenix toward the door. "It's a good idea. Come on. Afterward, you can do your homework. We'll go to eat, get this done, then get home. Easy peasy, no problem. Don't forget your apartment key. We'll go now."

They all waited for me, and I gnawed my lip for a moment, weighing my options. Should I do it? *Yes.*

I wasn't born in Colorado. I needed to know where I came from, and the information was strangely essential.

"Get a car to pick us up at the backdoor. The PI doesn't need to see anything we don't want him to see. He won't even know you left the building."

I hoped it would be that easy. *Is anything?*

৩✖৩

WITH MY STOMACH stuffed with salad, I stood outside of the building with trepidation.

"Hi," Julian smiled at the doorman. "She's grabbing some stuff and then we're going to see my granny."

The doorman smiled at him, chatting about the Yankees. Julian bantered back with him while my stomach churned. Hopefully, he wouldn't even notice our silence past Julian's charm. The doormen of our building—their building—were tougher. Less easy to distract with conversation. For the moment, the fact was helpful but Dina lived there. I didn't like the thought of her at risk.

The wind blew against me, and I shuddered, a chill icing my spine. I still wore my school uniform, as did Phoenix. If we got arrested, we would be on the news in our Pullman gear. I could picture the news reports—the school would be horrified. *Collins can tell everyone how we're failures and didn't belong there.*

I stepped inside then headed for the elevator as Julian laughed again.

"Leave him." Jeremy said and took my elbow. "He can stay here, giving us a distraction."

I followed behind him because I didn't know what else to do.

❧ 9 ❧

Jeremy, Phoenix, and I got in the elevator. Familiar pine scent assaulted me, somehow more comforting near Dina's apartment and the ground floors, like the woman herself, and less as we rose up the building. I practically gagged before we reached the proper floor, like Pavlov's Dog. *Woof Woof.*

"Remember, we're on camera. They can't hear us, but they can see us. Make sure you look bored." Jeremy stared at his phone, and likely to outsiders appeared to be doom scrolling.

I pulled out my own device, copying him and leaning against the wall. "I hate that we're doing this without telling Barrett."

"Well." Phoenix stared at the floor. "If he knew we were here, he would panic. If something goes wrong, he won't get in trouble and can say he didn't even know what we were doing."

I sighed. "You two won't get in trouble, either. Just me. You know your family will get you out of any trouble, and besides, you're not getting in shit because of me."

Kit already threatened to send Phoenix away if he got in

trouble again. I blinked, anxiety heightening even further at the thought. "You shouldn't come with us, Phoenix."

"I'm the only one who can get this done. Don't obsess, Red. It's no biggie. Your wallet was more challenging, and we're not even breaking into the apartment. You have a key and are here to regain your own documents."

I hoped he was right, but when nothing went right, I started to assume it would go wrong. "She might have it in a safe, in which case this is a waste of our time."

The elevator doors dinged open, and Jeremy nodded. "Yep, in that case, we leave. No harm. No foul."

I added, "There are also cameras in the apartment. I didn't get the impression she particularly monitors them, but she could."

I turned the key in the door, using every ounce of bravery I could muster.

"Even if she checks the cameras, we came to get your birth certificate because you need it. It is your property. We aren't talking about stealing her fucking diamonds. If we're on camera, they'll just see what you didn't take." Jeremy looked around then pointed left. "This way, right?"

He was correct so I followed him. I pointed out, "She could alter the videos to make it look like we stole something."

"Okay, now we're getting into some super-duper spy shit," Phoenix said with a laugh. "I don't think it's going to be a big deal. How often does she look at your birth certificate? She probably won't even notice it is gone, so let's just get this done. I doubt it's going to be in your uncle's home office. My mom doesn't keep anything in the dads' offices, instead storing her documents in her bedroom."

He was remarkably well versed in stealing things, so I considered him suspiciously. "Have you done this before?"

"Specifically? No. But I took things from my parents."

Phoenix led us into my aunt's bedroom. It helped that all the apartments were designed with the same floorplans, identical to his grandmother's place.

Jeremy whirled around. "Really? What did you take?"

"The police reports about my kidnapping years ago. Back when I was twelve. It's not important right now."

I had never actually entered my aunt's bedroom, not in all the time I lived with her, so I glanced around in curiosity. Tan walls, very boring compared to Dina's preference for bright red. Perfume bottles sparkled from the armoire next to a photo of my aunt and uncle dressed up together. I didn't have time to study any of it right then, but I memorized as much as possible. I'd seen this from the doorway before but never like this.

Phoenix opened up her closet without ceremony, revealing more clothes than I could have imagined. Despite the smallness of New York City apartments, her closet was huge.

"Is your granny's this big?" I stared at it open mouthed.

Phoenix didn't answer, but Jeremy got on his hands and knees to look under the bed. "I can't say that I've ever been in my granny's closet. Have you, Phoenix?"

"Found the filing cabinet I was looking for," he replied, ignoring the question. "Red, come over here. There are two. You grab one, and I'll grab the other. If you find your birth certificate, see if they have anything else about you, okay? Anything they already have is something we don't have to order."

My knees hit the plush carpet, and at first I mostly found a lot of folders pertaining to my cousin. Papers for her husband...then finally, I stumbled on one that said Alatheia.

I caught my breath, excitement making my hand shake slightly. "Found something."

"What?" Jeremy came up behind me, his head leaning on my shoulder.

The front door opened and closed, the noise as loud as gunfire in the otherwise silent apartment. I caught my breath, somehow managing not to scream.

The guys heard it, too, both going still. "Move." Phoenix whispered, pushing us all into the closet and closing us inside. Jeremy pushed me back against the wall of the closet, so that we were somewhat hidden against the plastic covering dry cleaned dresses and gowns.

He tucked me behind him, while Phoenix remained somewhere on the other side of the closet.

My aunt came into her bedroom, her voice resounding as she chatted on the phone. "I have to change shoes, Amelia. I won't make it all night in these. I don't even know why I bought them. I should just wear Rossis all the time. I am getting too old to put up with the other brands cutting my feet." She paused. "What? Are you serious? If I'm having surgery, it's to fix my nose finally, not bothering with my feet."

I realized she likely talked to my other aunt in Chicago— the one who didn't believe her boyfriend, Ted, tried to rape me. He currently faced charges from other people, but she was still a bitch. Just months ago, she tried to ruin my life in the Hamptons.

Jeremy squeezed my leg, obviously feeling me going stiff. His meaning was clear. He didn't want me to make a noise, but I didn't want to get my aunt's attention. Truthfully, I didn't even want to breathe. I closed my eyes, imagining her finding us.

She won't get to beat me. Jeremy and Phoenix won't allow it. I breathed just a little bit easier knowing they offered me a modicum of safety.

Please don't let this be the biggest mistake I've ever made.

I put my head on his back and tried to hold on.

"Once I change shoes, I'm going. It's going to be boring. It's always boring. Oh, did I tell you I saw one of those Lent brats in the lobby when I came in?" She paused again. "No, I don't know which one, but how can anyone tell them apart? I don't know if she's sleeping with him, either, before you ask. I don't know which one the little bitch is fucking."

Julian. She must have seen him talking with the doorman. I winced at her word choice, since I hated her speculating anything about us. I also hated that she used that word in a way that made anything about our relationships sound so awful.

She opened the closet and walked over to her shoes, grabbing a black pair of Rossi's without otherwise looking up.

"No, I don't know anything about what she is doing, but I can say we need to hire a better PI. Surely, we can afford better than this." There was silence. "She's a *teenager.* I hate that it's come to this, since it should've gone away all those years ago. It was supposed to go away."

What is she talking about? I couldn't ask her for answers and the closet door closed, making her voice fade into the distance as she exited the room.

Jeremy held his hand up, gesturing for us to stay still. I didn't have any intention of moving, struggling to even think past the thousands of questions flooding my mind. Somewhere in the distance, I heard a ding. *The elevator. Okay. All right. She's gone.* Phoenix jumped up at the noise. "Dude, what were the chances?" He burst into laughter.

With me? Unfortunately very high. My luck wasn't nearly as good as that of the Lent brothers. I moved from behind Jeremy, wanting to get out of there before she decided to swap purses. I grabbed the folder with my name on it and rushed toward the door.

Jeremy was right on my heels. Quietly, I closed everything up so that she wouldn't know we were ever there. It was only luck that she hadn't gotten naked. That would have been awful, and even though I hated her, a violation of her privacy. *Changing her shoes is one thing, her clothes another.*

I wanted out of the apartment, and I hoped I would never have to see it again. If life was kind, maybe I wouldn't have to.

In silence, we boarded the elevator and Phoenix met my gaze. "You okay?"

"No." I gripped the folder against my chest with no idea what was inside it. I wasn't going to look until we got to their granny's.

Jeremy squeezed my shoulder. He grinned, as if the adrenaline was still rushing through his system from almost getting caught. "Can you believe it? I mean, shit. What were the chances?"

Darkly, I said, "High."

Julian's face was pale when the elevator doors opened and we joined him in the lobby.

"I just don't think they have a pitcher this year," the doorman said, clearly continuing an ongoing conversation with Julian.

Are they still talking baseball? Jeremy whipped out his key and the two of us followed him quickly into Dina's apartment. A second later, Julian followed.

My heart was in my throat. I could hear it in my ears. *Is this a panic attack? A heart attack?*

I put my hands on my knees, breathing fast and hard, almost dropping the precious folder. That was when I noticed Daniel stood there in the living room.

"Did you get it?"

Daniel held out his hand expectantly when I looked up, so without thought, I handed it to him.

I forced myself to breathe, admitting, "I have no idea what's in there."

He tapped it against his hand. "It is going to find its way to Kit's desk. We won't tell him how it got there."

Julian looked between us. "She went upstairs, and I couldn't reach you. What the fuck did I miss?"

"Language." Daniel squeezed Jeremy's shoulder as he exited the apartment quickly.

Dina's sigh drew my attention her way. "Kit is going to get himself disbarred. Telling teenagers to go steal paper-work..what was he thinking? He should have asked me to do it. I'm a dotty old woman, and I could claim I was senile."

Everyone laughed, especially since Dina likely would be the least senile elder I could name.

Julian raised his voice to get their attention. "I'll ask again. What happened?"

Relief at not getting caught finally hit me, taking the starch out of my legs, so I sank onto the floor. Jeremy sat next to me, tugging me onto his lap easily.

"The whole time, I kept thinking it was fine if she found me." He cleared his throat, emotion clogging his voice. "But she couldn't find you."

"Same," Phoenix agreed, and I noticed him stuff his shaking hands in his pockets. For Phoenix, it was a long stretch of not going down the k-hole, so I hoped he was okay.

It did beg a question, though. "What would you have said you were doing in her closet if you got caught? I mean...do you have a thing for expensive shoes?"

I meant to be funny, but they laughed like it was the best joke ever. Even Dina threw her head back, drawing a couple of startled snickers from me, too.

Then I breathed in deeply a couple of times before resting my head against my knee. *The important part is we didn't get caught.* "I would never tell on Kit. If they asked, I would say it was my idea. I wouldn't narc him out."

"I know, dear." Dina put her hand on my head. "I know

you wouldn't, but don't be so fast to take the blame, either. Save it for things you've actually done. Then make sure you go through life doing enough interesting things that, when asked, you can proudly take the blame for them."

Phoenix shook his head. "I would take the blame, so it doesn't matter anyway. Everyone always thinks the worst of me, so it's not like it would be a stretch."

Julian sat down on the couch. "I kept the doorman busy... *the whole time*. She couldn't talk to him because I kept him so busy, in fact."

"Yeah, she noticed you." Jeremy nodded then told everyone what she said to my aunt.

His twin grinned. "Brat? Been awhile since I heard that one. Okay. I'm a brat. But we have the folder, so Kit can get things done."

I wished I'd had a chance to see more than my name on the outside of a folder, but that was on me. *Why did I just hand it off?* I closed my eyes. *Panic. I acted out of panic.*

"Will he tell me what was in there?" I asked, hating that my voice broke a little.

Dina touched my hair again, so I opened my eyes. "I'll see to it that he does."

An hour later, we were back in their apartment, so I sat down to work on my homework. Phoenix wandered into his room, and I worked hard to not wonder what he did in there. *Hopefully not drugs.* The twins pulled out their computers, also working on homework.

I glanced around, sighing at the normalcy of it all. As though we weren't just playing at being thieves, breaking into a house and stealing documents.

We're just doing our homework, no biggie.

Barrett got home about an hour later, just as I was closing my laptop. I retained nothing of my work, going through the motions but not concentrating. Hopefully it wouldn't bite me in the ass at test time.

"Hey," he said as he tossed his bag on the kitchen counter. "Well, this is going to get old. Twice a week with all day classes feels like a lot, but at least I was interested and..." His voice trailed off. "You all look a little strung out. What did I miss?"

Phoenix leaned against the door frame of his room, his glazed eyes proving my suspicions about how he'd spent his hour.

"Let's just get to it. We knew you wouldn't like it, so we did it before you got home." He explained our exploits before Barrett even managed to sit down. By the time he finished, he had sunk into one of the chairs next to me.

Silence permeated the room, a gaping hole filled with our confessions. Maybe none of us really processed all of it, or maybe it was just me, but somehow telling Barrett about it made everything seem more stupid.

He rubbed his eyes. "I don't know what bothers me more, the fact that you got stuck in a closet and almost got caught or that you did it when you knew I couldn't even try to talk you out of it." He shook his head. "Actually, what bothers me more is that Kit told you to do it. Let me tell you something, had I been here, you wouldn't have gone, which he knew."

Barrett headed to the kitchen then came back with a beer, which he drained in one long pull from the bottle. Then he added, "Not to mention I could have helped you. If I was there, we would've known she wasn't coming back, because I would have confirmed her arrival at the event. I could help you, too. I'm not just some stick in the mud."

He practically shouted the words, his temper clearly getting the best of him. Guilt hit me, as he likely intended, but I rose and put my arms around him. "I guess maybe we knew that your good sense would prevail. Despite that, we wanted to go get the folder."

He hugged me back. "Don't leave me out of your plans in the future." He kissed my hair. "What did the birth certificate say, anyway? I'm honestly curious where you were born."

I shook my head. "I handed the file to Daniel without looking at it in some kind of blind panic. It would have taken two seconds to look, so I'm feeling pretty stupid right now."

"You got a file with your name on it then, right? We'll at least know soon what was in it, but if we need to break in to get your birth certificate again because it's not in that file, I'm going, too." He released me, and gave me a final warning stare. "Got it?"

Jeremy nodded, but he also grinned. "I still can't believe we hid in a closet."

It really was the strangest day.

❧

THE GUYS all slept around me, Jeremy on one side, Phoenix on the other. Barrett sprawled over his mattress, one hand off to the side while Julian lay on his back, eyes closed, mouth open. Phoenix snored with the twins, the way he did when he was exhausted. *Probably from staying at Joe's last night.*

The Lents could sleep through stress, but I couldn't. I didn't mind, since I would probably only find nightmares if I managed sleep in my current mood.

As quietly as I could, I snuck out of the bedroom, closing the door behind me. I could read Dina's journals to pass the hours until dawn. I knew myself well enough to know that if I started working on the *Poor Relation,* I would never get to sleep.

Instead, I opened her journal, excited to venture back into the past with her again. When last I read, she had visited

Louisiana and was convinced something was amiss with the other side of the lake. Or the second lake? Why did they refer to two lakes as one? It was confusing to me.

୧୨୨

DECEMBER 6TH 1966

Hello to myself,

I am sure only I will ever read this, so I'm talking to myself again. Maybe someday, I'll be senile and not remember all of this, so it will be good that I recorded the events. Or maybe I just need something to do while they all go fishing, since I really don't want to spend any more time talking to their mother today.

It isn't that she's overtly hostile or anything, but I know she doesn't like me. I think she thinks I'm the reason they're planning to head back to Manhattan. They don't see it, but that's fine. I do.

The guys are different here. In some ways, they're more relaxed. In other ways, I miss New York. Nathaniel doesn't laugh as much here, I've noticed. Victor is always kicking the dirt in front of him, as if the soil itself offends him.

Ed is always quiet, but he is so much quieter here. Only Robert seems the same.

So...I asked Robert to take me back to the other side of the lake.

He ran his hand through my hair when I asked. "Why? Why do you even want to go?"

I took his hands in mine. "Because I can tell you all don't want me to go, which means I need to see it. You didn't just leave here because you wanted to open a store, and I know it. You left here because there is something you don't like, which makes me nervous. I'm ready to commit to our relationship, ready to say let's give it a try, but I can't do it if you're hiding things from me. That's unfair to me."

He nodded, agreeing easily to my logic. Sweet Robert. "You're right."

We got into the car together and drove to the other side, and he stopped and parked. It was foggy, so I needed a sweater, but that was actually kind of nice after the heat of the day. We talked as we strolled, the night still around us, cricket song leading us as easily as the fireflies. Eventually, we stopped in front of a boarded-up house, and his hand tightened around mine.

"We used to live there."

I was shocked, reconsidering the structure I considered ramshackle at best. I thought they spent their whole lives in their beautiful white house, and had no clue they came from humbler roots. "When?"

"Back when I was born." Robert stood right next to me, but his gaze never seemed so distant before. "You've noticed there are two sides of this place—the wealthy and the not wealthy. We lived on this wrong side of the lake. Eventually, my fathers made a lot of money, becoming the wealthiest family here. We moved across the lake when I was ten, but we weren't so wonderfully accepted despite having the money to be among them. Sure, everyone plays nice now, but we were too much of a reminder that things over here aren't always so nice."

I took his hand again, his fingers icy in mine. "What kinds of things?"

"Women. . .aren't always treated with the kind of respect they deserve, for starters. When we left, we thought we could leave two things behind. Firstly, the way we're never quite good enough. Secondly, the memory of how bad things can be."

I didn't ask him for more details. I might've lived an incredibly sheltered life, but even I knew what he meant.

"It'll never be like that with us, Dina. Never. I promise you. Not ever."

I believe him.

He kissed me in the shadow of that other house. He is so steady, always the one to remind everyone else about how they should or shouldn't behave.

Oh, their mother is calling me. She wants something.

My question really is. . .can we pull this off in New York? I guess we're going to find out!

For now,

D

※

I PUT down her journal and stared at the wall for a few moments, processing her life. He wanted her to see how the women on the other side of the lake weren't living such genteel, pretty lives compared to hers. Rosalind used that phrase on me—she said I wasn't *in the Life*. *Is this what she worried about? That I would get involved with her sons without understanding the situation?*

Dina didn't even know I would like her grandsons when she gave me her journals, but she'd trusted me anyway. I leaned against the couch, wondering what my guys knew about the lake, especially on the other side. Why did their fathers think Phoenix's kidnapping had something to do with the lake at all?

I rubbed my eyes. I didn't have any answers, not even the location of my own birth.

The door swung open from the bedroom, so I glanced over quickly.

Barrett stared at me in the low light, his eyes still bleary. "Can't sleep?"

I shut the diaries and set them aside. So far, none of them had asked me about the contents, nor had they peeked or even asked for a peek at her writing.

"No." I rose, stretching. "Thank you for being you, Barrett. I'm sorry if we made you feel you weren't perfect just the way you are. I admire how you know what to do in any situation. I love that you are always so sure of what is right and what is wrong, with no gray area."

He shook his head. "I only know you're right. Everything that isn't you with us was wrong."

❧ 10 ❧

The genuine sweetness of his confession touched me, not going to lie. I opened my arms and he walked into them, reaching behind me on the couch to lay us both down, so I pressed against him. We might not have been in bed, but I absolutely needed to be held by Barrett right then.

He yawned. "Tell me why you can't sleep."

I shook my head, instead distracting him with a kiss. I wanted his mouth, not words. His sweet gentleness, easy since he never pushed for anything else. I closed my eyes and let the night move over me, safe in Barrett's arms with his mouth against mine.

"I love you," he whispered to me in between kisses. "I love you so much."

I loved him, too, but he didn't give me the breath to try to say it. It was nuts that I couldn't make myself, but part of me still thought it would jinx things. The second I said it aloud, it would all fall apart. Instead, I hugged him tighter, rocking against him.

He was mine until the universe took him from me, at

least. I could hold on as long as I wanted, to remember every moment.

I must have eventually fallen asleep in his arms, because I woke up back in the bed in the morning. I snuggled between Jeremy and Phoenix with no memory of getting there, but I smiled, since I couldn't complain in the least. Barrett loved to carry me back to bed, which made our whole interlude almost seem like a dream.

Jeremy brushed a kiss on my cheek before he rolled out of bed. I closed my eyes, and dreams swept me back into darkness.

The smell of coffee woke me again, more permanently, as Phoenix whispered in my ear, "I know I missed my coffee turn yesterday, but today I didn't forget."

I smiled at him. He looked so hot in the sunshine, and had zero clue, which made him somehow hotter. Feeling heat flush my cheeks, I managed to say, "Thanks."

"Yep," he said and kissed my temple. I felt his lips curve into a grin against my skin. "We hid in a fucking closet yesterday."

Yes, we really did.

OUR ROUTINE BECAME COMFORTABLE, or as much of a routine as three days could create. *School. Water polo. Homework. Sleep. Hanging with the guys. Rinse, Repeat.* I loved it.

I glanced at my phone, always filled with texts—though no one else seemed to realize how epic that accomplishment alone was for me. Bethany wanted to know about her clothes, for instance. Had anyone ever asked me for fashion advice before, and why would they? I never considered myself particularly on trend and she only saw me in uniforms. Still, I gave her my opinion when she wanted it, even though I didn't feel as if I knew her well enough to judge. I became very familiar with her shoes and her hairdos. For the life of me, I still wasn't sure why she went from being mean to wanting to be my friend.

Tiffany talked to me about paintings, which I loved so darn hard. I mean, a *lot*. I could text about art with her all day every day, and it would've been my idea of the perfect life. Still, the Hal factor banged around in my head. *Why would Phoenix introduce me to Tiffany when he knew she dated a guy he wanted to avoid? Unless he doesn't. Is it his way back into the friendship, like a backdoor? Am I just overthinking it? Are both things possible? Probably not.*

My water polo buddies mostly bitched about our bathing suits in their texts. I hated them, too. Eventually, I even added a response or two to that group chat. *I can be funny... sometimes.*

Neither Kit nor Daniel answered my questions about the folder, which honestly—that was a crock. They told Barrett when he asked why they would keep the information from me—when he sent them a rather scathing text the next morning—how they were working on it and would know more soon.

Which officially told us nothing.

Phoenix offered to go break into his parents' apartment upstairs to find out for us, but we'd all told him no. *Enough of that. We suck as thieves, so why bother pretending to have the skill?*

Then it was Friday, which meant I made it through my first whole week. We were all going to the Jazz Club that night with Barrett, so there was that to look forward to later.

I just had to make it through my first water polo match. *Easier said than done.* Despite two additional practices, in our first game, I just tried not to drown. I chased the girl I was supposed to be guarding up and down the pool, but not with any skill or usefulness. I mostly wondered how long I could keep my arms moving and my legs kicking before I sank to the bottom of the nine-foot pool and never came up.

When I managed to actually get close to her, she scratched me under the water, and I was pretty sure she left marks. Somehow, I kept going. Once, when the ball came my direction, I managed to toss it to someone else before Sarah whistled then gestured me out of the water.

I panted on the side of the pool, pretty sure I would die any moment. I also hoped I didn't look too pathetic and was self-aware enough to hate myself for not being able to walk it off. What would the *Poor Relation* say right then? I needed to know, so I focused on that rather than my burning chest. In my most pithy non-Alatheia inner voice, she smirked her familiar half grin at the audience. She would brag about how hard the game was, how incredible. Maybe if I wasn't fighting past cramps and exhaustion from being out of shape, I would find other sports fun, too, like her. Gretchen the *Poor Relation* loved the game, and other sports, honestly. I smiled, causing severely chlorinated water to go in my mouth, and I wiped it away. Trying not to spit. *Maybe I will be cool like her, too. Eventually.*

Luckily, Valerie didn't seem to be in much better shape than me. In fact, we all sucked other than Sarah and two other seniors—Carrie and Jamie. We did end up winning the game, so I breathed a sigh of relief past my pains. I pulled myself out of the water at the end of the game.

I grabbed a towel, remembering the swimsuit for surprisingly the first time all game and hating it still. Someone named Violet's mother had them made for us, even embroidering on our names. I couldn't fathom having a mother like that. Mine wouldn't have the time, past working hard to support us and struggling to get by, if my memory served.

And taking drugs. I reminded myself of the rumor and wondered why she would've sewn up holes in my clothes if she had money for drugs. Sometimes, in odd, usually inappropriate moments, my dark sense of humor thought about her dying of a drug overdose, and I wasn't always kind. I just couldn't get why she wouldn't have cared enough about herself—or about me—to stay away from drugs.

In my dream, she accused me of forgetting her, but I could no sooner stop breathing than forget my mother. I just didn't know any more if I ever really knew her at all.

"Hey," Julian pulled me into a hug and I *oomph*ed my way into his arms.

"I am going to make you soaking wet," I complained.

He shrugged. "Don't care."

His arms felt good, so I gave myself a few moments despite my logical-self knowing we were in public view, so therefore unable to show affection openly. When I released him, I didn't want to let go, so I held his gaze a second too long. "Thanks for watching me. I mean, I should be embarrassed. I can hardly swim compared to how you play, but—"

"You were great, especially for your first ever game. And with almost no practice? No, seriously, you were great." He grinned at me. "I'm very proud of you."

Jeremy nudged his way through the crowd and stole me from his brother. "I am, too. Don't let him fool you. We were all terrified watching, and we learned there's a big difference between seeing you do it versus us doing it. When that girl got an elbow on you, I almost dove into the water to take her out."

Julian shook his head, his smile crooked. "He's not kidding. He almost did. I probably would've gone, too, if I didn't have to watch him."

"Hey," Barrett said and tugged me against his side to give me a squeeze. "Well done. I mean, I really wish I got you set up with rowing, which is arguably much safer. Despite that, fantastic job. Go get changed, though. Phoenix is already outside, and we'll wait for you out there."

Do I want to know why they sent him outside? I decided not to ask and instead nodded. "Give me a minute."

Valerie ran up to offer a one arm squeeze while we walked into the locker room. Sarah laughed about something and suddenly my life felt so normal. No one judged me or acted like I did anything terribly wrong, which was both bizarre and refreshing all at once. I got tugged into several hugs when I finally reached Sarah.

"Good work, Al," she said. "We're going to make a water polo player out of you yet. First game, and you didn't drown plus you helped the team a lot. I knew you belonged with us."

I grinned at her, the sense of belonging wildly unfamiliar and addictive.

I showered—no Maggie interruptions, thankfully—and changed back into my school uniform. By the time I met the guys outside with my damp hair braided, I hummed to myself.

"You're happy," Phoenix said as he tugged me into a hug. "I can't stand being in there, though, sorry. The chlorine makes my eyes water."

I thought the redness was from drugs, but he actually seemed to still be with it at the moment, meaning his eyes were irritated. "You didn't have to come. I would've understood."

He shot me a baffled expression. "What? No, I'll be there. I'll get some drops or something, because I wouldn't miss it. Besides, I have to keep the twins under control. They want to go kick ass every time someone gets near you."

"Not a lie." Jeremy laughed then his expression turned dark, his tone ominous as if we planned to drag him into a meth lab. "We need to get home and changed to make it to the jazz club, if we're still going."

Barrett shook his head, putting his arm around me to guide me forward. "So go do something else. We're not dragging you to see one of the great voices of our time."

"Not of our time. From a time long ago, a relic borrowed from another time," Jeremy said then laughed. "I'm not letting the three of you take her out on a date without me. That's ridiculous. If we're group dating this week, I'm part of the group."

Group dating. I rolled the word around in my mind, trying it on for size, since I never thought about it that way. *We play house and we are going on a group date.* A thrill shot through me, since if I was honest, I loved our situation. I loved them, even if I couldn't say the word. *Saying the word will make everything implode.*

"Okay." Jeremy walked backward, his gaze trained on our faces.

I reached for his shirt, tugging at the fabric. "Don't do that. You're going to get hit by a car."

"No, I won't. I have mad walking skills, Princess." His smile was infectious, so I grinned back. "If we're group dating, then we're also going to solo date. We agreed to the routine for sleeping—Phoenix won that one too easily—and now we need to date her one-on-one. Otherwise, Phoenix just wins at solo time, since you actually get to see her in class, too."

Their youngest brother shook his head. "While I am not going to disagree with me winning, being kidnapped as a child probably means I'm the opposite of lucky."

Julian slung an arm around Phoenix. "Absolutely true, but admit it...Having that as the ultimate backup excuse has really turned your negative into a kind of winning."

To my shock, Phoenix threw his head back and laughed. Something about the moment sparkled, imprinting itself indelibly on my mind, the image of what life meant when it could be good.

I pulled out my little black dress once we got back to the apartment, a sleeveless number that stopped right above my knees. I didn't have to ask about appropriate wardrobe, which gave me a sense of pride as I got dressed. All summer, I'd stuck to shorts, pants, or skirts when we went out to eat, so I delighted a bit at taking the extra steps to primp myself and make sure I looked good. When Dina had picked the dress, I loved it from the moment I saw it, so I thrilled at getting to wear it finally.

My pink pearls from Jeremy in the Hamptons finished off the look, so I let my hair fall down in reckless curls. Hopefully, I wouldn't regret the decision because I became frizz lady later. Sliding my feet into black heels, I couldn't even find a thing to hate about my reflection in the glass.

When I emerged from Barrett's bedroom where I prepped, everyone looked up from their phones to stare at me, and honestly. . .they took my breath away.

They pulled out all the stops for that evening. Dressed in uniform black, the matching color seemed striking on each of them. All managed to give their outfits personal touches. Phoenix wore a blazer over an open collared shirt and black pants. His skater vibe seemed hotter in this nighttime version. Barrett adjusted his tie under a black blazer, his suit neatly tucked and buttoned up. His slicked back hair reminded me of something out of the past, but then again, he always struck me as comfortable in his formality.

The twins didn't bother with jackets, but both wore collared black shirts and dark jeans. Something about them each stuck out, perhaps in the collar, because Julian's scooped down in a way unlike Jeremy's.

"You guys look incredible." I confessed honestly.

"I think you've rendered us speechless." Jeremy offered

his hand, so I took it. "You look gorgeous." He spun me in a circle, so I giggled and almost tripped, so unprepared for actual giggling. I'm not a big giggler, if I'm honest, but they could make anyone flustered and flattered.

They called a car, so soon we sped toward the club. Jeremy ran his fingertip over the pearls, occasionally touching my neck and meeting my eyes. Each time he stroked my flesh, a shiver rushed through me. He gazed down at his phone, and I wondered if he even knew he affected me so much.

"What you said before about it being a bygone era? About her voice?" Barrett said from the backseat. "You couldn't be more wrong. Some things are eternal."

Phoenix glanced back from his seat next to the driver. "Are you two going to do this all night?"

"Probably." Jer didn't look up.

Actually, I knew they wouldn't. If they followed suit with former trips, they would sit at the table Barrett reserved for us, and no one would check our IDs. As expected, I followed them to my seat and ordered a drink.

I leaned over to Barrett while I sipped my ginger ale. "You must have really helped them out of a financial jam for this to be so easy all the time."

"I did." He kissed my cheek. "And I liked it so much, it's all I want to do now. I would just open and help music clubs and teach, if I could, but that's not likely."

The music started up and a beautiful woman in her seventies took the stage. Despite her obvious advanced years, she stood with the ease and confidence of a woman half her age. What was more, she owned the crowd, but then Celeste Demille was famous. My uncle loved her. Although I had few good memories from San Francisco, I didn't regret learning to love jazz.

She gripped the microphone and winked at the crowd,

earning immediate applause. I joined, prepared for my hands to hurt by the time the night ended.

"Well, New York, I am bringing you some love from New Orleans tonight." The applause roared through the room again. "Tomorrow night, you can find me at Lincoln Center, but you? Y'all are my people."

The music started and I sailed away on the sound of her voice wailing between soulful notes. I meant to turn to share a grin with Barrett, but I couldn't take my eyes off of her. She owned the audience with her talent alone, and I sighed, the weight of being in the same room as greatness settling around my shoulders like a mantle. I once heard a late night comedian in Chicago talking about an actress' entrance, and I dismissed his description as exaggeration. Back then, I never experienced the likes of Celeste Demille.

Unlike some, I recognized my privilege came from the Lents, so I glanced at the brothers in gratitude. Soon we surged to our feet with the rest of the audience, everyone moving as a unit. She varied between old classics and new songs I'd never heard before. Occasionally, she let us know she was trying out a new song on us, so if we didn't like it? Well, she would play it again and again until we did. I just loved her, grinning at her flair and sass.

All too soon, the show ended. She lasted honestly longer than I probably would've, and she would appear again the next night at Lincoln Center. Twice, the crowd applauded her off the stage before she took her final bow and exited the stage.

I sank back into my chair as if someone removed the solidity from my very bones. "Wow."

"You loved that." Barrett plucked me up out of the chair and into his arms. He squeezed me so tightly, I could feel him vibrate against me. "I meant to say you loved that as much as me. Sweetheart, where have you been my whole life? How have I lived without you? Because I never thought—I mean, I didn't dream it could be so much better just because you loved it, too."

I laughed. "She was...everything."

"She was amazing. A dream. But you're everything." He kissed me then. Despite being in public, right then, we didn't care at all.

I kissed him back like he was air.

Finally, Jeremy tugged on us, breaking our kiss. "Let's go. I actually loved the show, too, both because of your enjoyment and also because that woman. Just...wow."

Barrett pointed at him. "If she can win you over, she can win over anyone."

The autumn night had chilled during the show, so I wished I'd brought a sweater for our walk home. I rubbed my arms and two seconds later, Phoenix's jacket covered my arms. I grinned up at him, my mind literally swimming with happiness. *What a day this was. Maybe my best ever.*

Is it tomorrow now? I checked my phone to see the time hit just after midnight. My lips curved into a smile at the idea of having not one, but *two* great days in a row. It was more than I dared dream of even a few months ago.

"Despite the fact that it's late," Phoenix began, "I would like to point out it is actually also early. Some people are just going out, and I got invited to a party that is starting up now. Would anyone want to drop by with me?"

Julian cleared his throat, shooting me a glance. "I'm game if Alatheia wants to go. If she prefers bed, I'm up for that, too. Basically, I want to go with my girlfriend." He met my gaze. "I also want to kiss you in public like Barrett did sometime, to tell people you're my girlfriend. I just want to say it out loud to someone."

Barrett knocked his shoulder into Julian's. "I lost my head," he confessed.

"You did, but I don't have a problem with it." He smiled at me, even as he spoke to Barrett. "What do you want to do?"

I didn't want to drag any of them anywhere if they were tired. "You two? Any thoughts?" I asked Barrett and Jeremy before making my call.

Jeremy lifted his arms over his head. "Let's take our girl-friend to a party for an hour before bed. Unless it's weird for Barrett to go to a high school party."

"It was weird for me to go to a high school party when I was in high school, so I don't think much changed because of graduation. I'm not leaving Alatheia. Who is throwing the party?"

I was glad he thought to ask, since I never remembered to care.

Phoenix smirked. "Not Joe, so chill your asshole. I kept it together pretty well tonight, I think, and you should be proud of me." He lifted his chin. "Murial Monk's house, the brownstone on Seventy-Eighth without a doorman. Easy peasy."

Murial Monk. The name didn't ring a bell for me. "Should I know her?"

"No," the twins answered together. Julian added, "But her parties are legendary in our circle. If Phoenix got an invite, we should go."

Julian held up his phone. "I got one, too."

Jeremy pulled his phone out of his back pocket and frowned at the device. "Oh, what the fuck? I didn't get one."

His twin grinned at him. "Looks like I'm winning the popularity contest this year. How did you piss her off?"

"The fuck if I know. We're going, so I can just ask her." Jeremy pushed buttons on his phone, texting quickly to someone. It sounded like they decided without me.

Barrett put his chin on my shoulder, his breath hot against my ear. "Murial's mother is a fashion icon. She used to be a super model who married a billionaire. Rumor has it, Murial hasn't seen her in a decade, which makes our parents' neglect look like active parenting. With the rich, sometimes it gets out of hand. Let's go for an hour. If they want to stay longer, that's fine, but I want to sleep and I think you do, too." He paused. "Unless you want to stay? Or go home now?"

I didn't know yet, but it seemed likely he would be right, if I was honest. Marco's party during the summer wasn't my scene, so I doubted I would fit in better at Murial's. Everyone else at least wanted to stop there, though, so I could tag along for a bit.

"Jer's already called us a car. It would be a shame to screw up his rating on the app by canceling it." I grinned. "So instead, let's go find out why he didn't get an invitation to Murial's. Don't stress. If it gets to be too much for me, you said you'll leave with me."

Phoenix took my hand, squeezing my fingers gently. "I will, too." Then he smirked. "I am happy to have a curfew and a bedtime if the privileges include sleeping with you."

Jules poked him in the shoulder. "Not our fault if you miss out then, so own it."

We climbed into the large SUV in our requisite places, as if we assigned a seating order for car rides. I sat sandwiched between the twins in the middle, Barrett chose the back, and Phoenix sat up front with our driver. I smiled, enjoying the routineness of it all. *Same can feel safe.*

I wondered if they kept the seating order from the times before I joined them, so I asked Barrett, "Where do you sit when I'm not here?"

"In the car?" He shook his head. "I don't go that many places with them, if I'm honest. We were all starting to sort of live separate lives until Julian found you."

The blue-eyed twin took my hand. "I did and I will gladly take credit for it. Still, if you want to be technical, Granny found her. I just had the good sense to wake up and pay attention when I met her."

I blushed, flattered at the sentiment, but it was hard for me to picture them apart. They functioned so much better, and seemed more at ease, as a unit. It begged the question, though—*would Barrett be happier just going to college? Without all the added family drama, surely his freshman year would've been full of adventures he would miss out on if he stayed at home. Would Phoenix have felt less pressure if he didn't have to cover up his relationship with me? Are the twins missing out on something, too?*

I chewed on my lip, the familiar guilt making me worry. I worried over whether I should feel guilty over taking all of their attention just for myself. Surely it was at the very least greedy? Insecurity was a constant presence for me, regardless of the topic, though, and I knew it as a weakness I needed to find a way to conquer. Maybe someday I would have the kind of security of Celeste Demille and Dina.

I'm not anywhere near there yet.

🦋 11 🦋

T
he brownstone towered above us, eating up what appeared to be most of a city block, nearly the size of Pullman. I blinked up at the elaborate facade with awe and reverence, thinking when their family died off, maybe some other private school would buy the estate.

Wealth didn't intimidate me anymore, at least. Not since I created the *Poor Relation* to berate the people who hurt me for being poor. Somewhere in creating dialogue for her, it stopped being the end game for me. *Love is what matters. Self-determination.* The Lents showed me both were possible. I smiled a secretive smile as we headed up the steps, thinking about my secret life with their family, who maintained constant secrecy about something so pivotal to who they were as people. *Money isn't as scary when you know secrets*, I decided.

Teenagers pushed in and out of the front door, nudging past each other as they passed. Someone wearing a Pullman uniform slid down the banister, hit the ground then laughed to get up and repeat the ride. The level of noise before

142

entering meant they didn't give a shit about authorities getting called, which usually said a lot about a party.

Truly the purview of the very, very wealthy.

"This is huge," I muttered to myself, as if I had to at least confess it aloud.

Julian chuckled and said, "They make us seem like we're the Poor Relation."

"Really?" I couldn't imagine anyone making him feel small.

He laughed outright. "Hell yes. My uncle Stephen always tells us how we should remember there's richer, hotter, more successful people than us. We should always remember that although we eat those who would harm us, there are people who can just as easily eat us, too."

I didn't want to attend that kind of party, if I was honest. I wasn't interested in swimming with sharks, and I certainly didn't want to swim in waters where sharks feared to swim. Still, I followed them inside with my mask in place, hoping we weren't stumbling into some kind of trap.

I hoped my expression would come across as distant and unapproachable, yet not overall interesting in the first place. It worked in Chicago, at least until Ted destroyed things for me.

As soon as we passed the threshold of the doorway, someone called, "Barrett!"

The oldest Lent genuinely smiled as he got swallowed by a group of what appeared to be his actual friends.

"I heard you're not sleeping there. I'm so jealous," I overheard one of them say. "My parents made me do dorm life."

I left him to it, following Phoenix, who stopped to greet a bunch of people I at least recognized from school. I didn't know their names, but they were familiar enough faces, especially compared to the seniors, who were totally new to me.

Normally, they stayed in their own hallway, so I never saw them.

Phoenix said, "Hey, I need to meet up with someone. I'll come find you shortly, or send someone after me if you want to leave early."

"Have fun," I said, resisting the urge to kiss him goodbye by only about a heartbeat.

His gaze said he saw my hesitation and recognized it before I covered it, so he squeezed my fingers quickly.

"Thank you. You mean everything."

As he vanished into the crowd, I spotted the twins surrounded by their teammates. I didn't see my own team, so I thought about joining them for about a second.

A hand grabbed me, and I spun to face Bethany. "Alatheia!" she practically screamed. "I am *so* happy you're here."

If her breath didn't give it away, I saw a beer in her hand as she wobbled into me. *Okay, she's drunk.* Then again, that seemed the consensus rather than the unusual for the crowd. "Bethany," I smiled, glad of the familiar face. I added, "Are you okay?"

She pointed at me. "I am *so* good. So. Good." Her smile got bigger. "I knew we had to be friends after I understood. Because I get *it*."

It? At least one of us knew what she meant. "It?"

"I get *it*," she repeated loudly as Tiffany arrived, slinging an arm around my shoulder.

Instead of greeting me, she considered Bethany. "I can't figure you out, Bethy. I really can't."

"Don't try." Bethany flung her hair over her shoulder and vanished into the crowd again, as mysterious as a ghost. I still didn't know what she meant, but perhaps it was for the better.

Tiffany slurred, but less than Bethany. "So, how are you?"

Before I could answer, her eyes lit up. "Come with me. I want to show you something."

She tugged my hand and led me from the room. I spotted Hal in a part in the crowd—standing in a corner watching us — but he vanished as quickly as he appeared, in the same crowd as Phoenix but not speaking. I bit my lip, unhappy since I knew why.

I found myself in an elegant parlor, and barely took in the vastness of it when she pointed upward. "Look."

My mouth fell open, startlement taking my breath for a second. "Is that a Warhol?"

"It sure is." She grinned then stared up at it. "No one ever cares or seems impressed when I show them, but I knew you'd get it." She sipped her beer.

I still gaped, trying to take in my proximity to arguably one of the Great Works. "Is it real?"

"Oh, it's real. I hear they have a second one upstairs, but I've never been invited up there. You have to get summoned upstairs to see Murial."

Like some kind of queen. Their world struck me as so bizarre. "Do you fit in here?" I asked her, honestly curious. "I mean, are you on the outskirts of this world or do you fit? I just feel like the Poor Relation."

Her smile was huge and she nudged her shoulder into mine. "I love when you call yourself that. Speaking of which, maybe they'll eventually do an episode on that. Me, though? I fit, but I'm no Murial. I'm not even as important as your friends the Lents. If it was a level system, I'm just under them, but I fit with them. Doesn't change the fact that I hate most of them, though. Then again, I think we all kind of hate each other. Doesn't everyone kind of hate their friends, or is that just a high school thing?"

That sounds...awful. "I don't want to hate you."

She shook her head, laughing. "You won't, and I won't

hate you, because you're different. I might fit into this world, but my plans don't really involve it, if that makes sense. I want something else, so I think we're safe to be friends who don't secretly hate each other."

A spark of sadness marred my mood. "I think most people—or at least people who don't live like this—don't hate their friends."

"I hope you're right." She said then stared at me. "How do you know the Lents? No one knows. I heard all kinds of things, and I didn't think I cared until this very moment."

I ran a hand through my hair, a thousand possible answers rolling through my head before I said, "I am their granny's companion."

"What does that mean?" She said then shook her head. "Do you run errands for her or..."

Abruptly, she stopped speaking, turning her head to face the girl standing next to us who I didn't even hear come into the room. It took me a second to place her, but then I remembered I saw her over the summer. She approached Julian on the street, having hooked up with Jer, but she couldn't even tell them apart.

I never got her name, but I remembered her shoes. She wore the same kind of strappy sandals, her pinky toes pinched white from pressure. I instantly remembered her hair, with its constant beach wave and perfect brown color.

"Alatheia, right?" Her smile read as phony. "Murial wants to see you upstairs."

Tiffany's eyes widened, shock evident on her face. "Why?"

"Because she does." She flipped her hair over her shoulder. "Run along." With a wiggle of her fingers, she dismissed Tiffany, who practically scampered away.

This place is so damn strange. "What if I don't want to go upstairs? I'm good here."

"It's not really...optional?" She snapped her gum. "Follow me."

I focused on her black, strappy shoes, vaguely different from the pink ones she wore when we first met, and followed her. I couldn't help but think she must be in constant pain. *Shoes say so much about a person*, I reminded myself.

"What's your name, anyway?" I asked her as she headed upstairs. I reminded myself as I followed her that Murial's family could eat the Lents, meaning the repercussions of whatever happened upstairs wouldn't be something where they could save me. I was on my own, so to speak, yet again.

She tossed a smile over her shoulder, as if surprised I asked. "I'm Greer."

Eyes seemed to pin me as I followed her up the stairs, and I glanced down to realize quite a few in the crowd stared with curiosity. I didn't spot any Lents, so I pulled out my phone to text our group chat. *Got summoned upstairs to Murial.*

I didn't even know who she was or what to expect. Greer pulled out a keycard and used it on the door before pulling an elevator open. I froze, staring at the box as if it were a bear trap.

"I'm not getting in that. I don't know where you're taking me."

I might be dumb, but I'm not stupid.

Her hand squeezed my arm gently, nudging me into motion. "I get it. Intimidating, right? Like I said, I get it. I understand your position, and I remember you. You're the Lent grandmother's companion, right?" Something in her smile oozed poison. "It's so kind how they're being nice to you for her. My family does things like that, too. We paid for our housekeeper's daughter to go to college."

I almost lied and claimed my family was rich, but I stopped myself, figuring she would know better anyway. I didn't even know how I was related to my own family or

REBECCA ROYCE

where I was born. Instead, I gritted my teeth and stared her down, refusing to get into the elevator and saying, "That was very nice of you."

Her smile brightened, becoming somewhat genuine. "I know, right? So, Murial wants to meet you. You'll go meet her, then you can go downstairs and leave, if you want. It's like nothing even happened. If you don't go, things go badly for you and the Lents, so you satisfy her curiosity or you face her wrath. You decide, elevator or not?

She spoke the last two words slowly, like I was a bug getting squashed beneath her spiky black shoe. I resisted snarling back at her, because she couldn't even tell which twin she fucked.

Jeremy really was a man-whore for a long time, so dating him meant I would constantly end up facing off with his former hookups. Did I honestly want to fight every single one of them?

Besides, Murial wasn't something the Lents could get me out of, so why not just face it? I said simply, "Sure."

I couldn't think of a way out of the meeting, other than faking my own spontaneous combustion. I followed her into the posh elevator. I remembered the cameras in most buildings, and figured Murial might be watching me even as we rode the elevator. The Lents would find a way to get me out of it, though. They always did, their success track record perfect so far.

I swallowed hard, the movement making my stomach flip. We only traveled up one floor, which seemed a waste for an elevator. "Couldn't we just have taken the stairs?"

"They're closed for the party. No one comes up or down without invitation." She side-eyed me, glancing at her feet. "Besides, these shoes don't really scream stairs."

I bit my lip, because I guessed her feet had to be killing her. *Nailed it.*

A small crowd filled the space of what I could best describe as an upstairs historic parlor, the gilt and style likely from when they first built the house however many ages ago.

About a dozen teenagers in various states of intoxication milled around the room, seeming wildly out of place in the elegant space. I spotted at least three more outside on the balcony, where sound flowed in from the city through the opened doors.

Scanning the walls, I noticed a painting and froze. *I know that man.* Downstairs, they had a Warhol, but upstairs hid a Rembrandt. For a second, I forgot how to breathe, drifting toward the canvas.

"It's beautiful, right?" a girl said who I'd never met before. I glanced around to realize Greer had vanished while I stared enrapt at the art.

I blinked at the stranger, still a little jarred by the art. My brain still cycled through a symphony of *holy shits*.

"Are you Murial?" I asked in response, saying the first thing that came to mind.

She nodded. "Yup, nice to meet you, Alatheia Winder. I know everyone at the upper school at Pullman, so I did my homework when you enrolled. Companion to the Lents' granny, you live with your aunt Tricia in the same building. As you know, I'm Murial, so this is my house, and Pullman is my school. This is *my* city." She folded her hands together, glancing around the room as if considering her kingdom. "Since we've finished with introductions, would you rather discuss the art?"

I swallowed hard, because she was *so* far out of my league on *so* many levels. Beautiful, she managed to be one of those people who didn't even seem to be real. Jet black hair, sleeked back into a single ponytail without a single bump, more proof of her unreality since not even a strand dared stray out of order. At five foot nothing she wore a men's button-up white shirt with the sleeves rolled to her elbows and the top three buttons undone. She paired it with a pair of nondescript black pants. I stared at her manicured toenails, surprised at her bare feet and not sure what it said about her.

I couldn't tell if she bothered with cosmetics, either, if I was honest. Although her face framed perfect high cheekbones, it all struck me as naturally flawless.

I might have spent every day since I turned eleven with the wealthy and elite, but I never met anyone like her. As I gazed at her, I believed her—it was her school, her house, and her city, not mine.

I turned my gaze back at the painting—a far safer subject than class. "It's beautiful, so beautiful. I've never seen one outside of a museum before."

She nodded. "You recognize it. I think we're the only ones in the room who even know it's here." She motioned toward the room, and I couldn't debate her guess despite knowing a few of the people. Davis—from one of my classes, and someone Phoenix warned me to steer away from if I could— and Greer as well as, unfortunately, Maggie.

The shower bitch.

"I'm glad to show it to you. Would you believe it was less expensive than the Warhol? Then again, everyone recognizes the Warhol. This went for so much less at auction; it was comical." She shook her head, gaze reminiscent. "Things tend to come around, if you just wait. Trends. People. By this time next year, Rembrandt could be the thing again."

I shook my head and blurted, "I think..." Then abruptly I shut my mouth. I could guess she didn't care about my thoughts on the matter.

Murial placed her hand on my arm, her fingertips cool and surprising. "No, please. Tell me what you think, Alatheia?"

"Well, honestly, I think Rembrandts are always and forever. Few things are, but you know them when you see them. They're priceless. That's why we usually only find them in museums. And—" I caught my breath, my bravery running out.

She lifted an eyebrow. "Go on."

I bunched my fists and closed my eyes. "I think you know that, too, which is why you keep it upstairs but have the Warhol downstairs where everyone can see it. You don't want anything to happen to the Warhol, sure, but you trust the cameras and your security system. This one is upstairs, because you care about this one specifically. Due to that, you keep it where you and your parents can keep an eye on it."

Murial didn't say anything for a few long moments, then her lips spread in a slow Cheshire grin. "Oh, you *are* smart. I assumed you would be asleep, like everyone else. You're not. You're smarter. Well, it makes this part easier. I do care about that painting more, and actually I love it. I treasure it, because my daddy bought it for me on my thirteenth birthday. It's the best thing he ever gave me." She took a step away, her gaze distant again. "Except my cheekbones. Those are better." She waved her hand carelessly. "Come along, Alatheia."

I followed her quickly because I didn't think I had options. When we faced off with Maggie, my stomach tightened. I knew things would go badly, but maybe I expected more time.

"Maggie did a very gross thing." She folded her arms and sternly considered Maggie. "You did, and you know it. We don't rip open the shower curtain on people. It's classless and ridiculous." Maggie stared at the floor, her expression properly chastised. "She's been in love with Jeremy Lent for years. Last year, he showed her a little bit of interest. He showed some to Greer, too, but she said he confused her." She leaned over to whisper conspiratorially, although she spoke at a volume anyone could hear. "It's easy to confuse Greer, if we're honest, but Maggie actually thinks she's in love." Murial shook her head sadly. "Jeremy was never in love with her, but in any case, she owes you an apology. A sincere one this time. Maggie?"

The other girl swallowed. "I'm sorry."

"There. She's sorry. Do you forgive her?"

All eyes in the room swiveled to focus on me. Luckily, I knew my line. "Yes."

"Good." Murial sighed. "I can't have the Lents feuding with our people. It's too messy, because I like the Lents. They know how to have a good time *and* how to behave, which honestly is a rare combination in our generation. Not to mention, they're handsome and funny and rich. One of us, if you get my meaning. We can't have things falling apart during my senior year. I'm going to be honest, Alatheia... Your name means truth, right?" She didn't wait for me to answer, barreling onward without pause. "I don't know quite what to do with you. Are you dating one of them? If yes, which one?"

If I outright lied to her, I felt like she would know it. Instead, I went for a half truth. "I'm not dating any one of them."

Since it wasn't a lie, she nodded, her gaze almost sensing my honesty. I almost let out the breath I was holding in relief. "Okay, well Maggie apologized, and I got to have a look at you. We'll look at art together again sometime soon. I heard about your art friend. Tiffany's talented, but I can show you treasures the likes of which no one else can show you. I am so glad I didn't have to threaten you to stay away from my people, since it makes things so much more pleasant. You surprised me, which is a rarity." Her teeth flashed in what I supposed was a smile, though it felt like a baring of teeth in aggression. "Before I let you leave, did you have any questions?"

Davis joined her, sipping a drink as she considered me. "Hi, Alatheia."

"Hi," I responded but I didn't bother to look at him. "Since I ran into you, why did Julian get invited instead of Jeremy?"

Murial's giggle somehow hit me as acidic and musical at once. "The best way to get Jeremy to a party is *not* to invite him. Besides, I wasn't sure if I wanted him here tonight. Maggie needs time to get over the love, so seeing him knocks her back in the Lent hole. You can tell him I said that. Davis? Take her back downstairs. Alatheia, before you leave, next to the Rembrandt is Michiel Sweerts. Bit of a deep cut, but I think it's a really interesting work. Take a look, then when next we meet, you can tell me something you've learned about him."

I blinked at her, not used to getting social homework but sure I would obey nonetheless.

Davis extended his hand, so I walked ahead of him to the elevator, my eyes on the Sweerts. The piece was lovely, but I could look it up to learn more later. *Every last detail,* I promised myself in social terror.

We stepped into the elevator, and Davis grinned at me, slipping his keycard back into his back pocket. "You can breathe again." His smile struck me as genuine, so I sagged against the wall and did take a couple of relieved breaths. "She is my cousin, and a lot, but she liked you. That's a good thing, I promise. You'll see what I mean."

I nodded, not wanting to discuss it. I only wanted to leave.

"I bet Phoenix told you not to talk to me." I shot him a glance, but couldn't deny it. "I like Phoenix, but he doesn't like me, which is okay. I'll win him over, eventually. I'll win you over, too, because I can already tell I like you. At least I like the look of you, and the way you handled Murial and the

Rembrandt impressed me. You're smart, even if you're in the class with Collins. I can't quite make you out, if I'm honest." The elevator door started to open, and I felt as if my muscles all went taut, ready to move. He continued, saying, "I'm sober. So are you. Every person up there was sober, but it's better to keep your head when vultures are near enough to pick your bones. Even if the biggest vulture flies with you." He extended his hand again, gesturing toward the room grandly.

I searched the crowd, expecting to see the Lents waiting for me. I couldn't spot them in the crowd, but I told myself not to panic.

Davis touched my shoulder as if he could read my mind. "Don't worry. They haven't left you. The twins are probably drunk in the basement with the water polo team because they heard they have to go to California this week. Phoenix is probably with the addicts in the kitchen, while Barrett is likely out back with the graduates, but likely also pretty wasted. Want me to find any of them for you?"

I didn't, I realized, but then I didn't want him to do anything for me. *I want to leave. As fast as I can.* My chest tightened, panic threatening as I gazed around the room at how many people managed to pack into the space. *How would that interview have gone if I didn't know art?* I wondered.

"I'm good," I said as I carefully moved away from his flawlessly unscuffed and unused boat shoes.

"Okay, I'll see you in class." He stepped back into the elevator and the doors closed silently behind him.

My heart raced in my throat. I wanted to puke, but I didn't want Murial to catch it on her security cameras. She wanted to look at art, but I knew she was dangerous. Maybe she would just forget me? I rushed out the front door, pulling out my phone.

A million mean things flooded my mind, all shitty texts I

could send to the group chat as a follow up to my *help* comment no one bothered to read. Barrett said we would stay an hour, yet he was nowhere to be found. Phoenix promised to escort me home, yet I didn't know where he went. Ditto for the twins...who knew, right then?

I would remember I couldn't count on them at parties in the future.

Leaving, I texted then called a car.

She didn't threaten me. In fact, it was just the opposite, so why did I feel like I had dodged a bullet? Could I keep dodging it?

I didn't know.

I got in the car, relieved as it pulled away from the house. We sped across the city, loud music playing while the driver spoke in a language I didn't understand to someone on the phone. I stared out the window, seeing nothing and yet finding everything too much at the same time.

After a nod to the doorman, I ran up the stairs to the apartment and shut the door behind me. Inside, I locked and unlocked the door twice.

My aunt wished it all got handled years ago. *Handled? What does she want handled?* It was Murial's city, so apparently I came when ordered. Davis looked at me like he wanted to eat me for lunch, and liked the look of me. I shuddered, with way too much to process.

I didn't have a single response from the Lents yet. *Why would they bother to reply to me? They are with their friends, living their normal lives. They should enjoy it.*

I sent another text, since they promised me I could have privacy when I wanted it.

Going to bed. Leave me alone tonight, please.

My words seemed clear enough. I wouldn't close Phoenix out of his own room, since he might need something. We'd already set Barrett's room up for a group, making Jeremy's the furthest away if I didn't use Phoenix's.

I closed the door, hesitated, then locked it. If they wanted apologies, it would be a problem for later. I stripped out of my beautiful black dress then dropped it wilted on the floor. Every time I wore something I really loved, I had a terrible night. *Was the jazz club just hours ago?*

Ah, there's the catch. You used the word. I loved my clothes, so it blew up in my face. Tears leaked down my cheeks as I hugged a pillow against my face, because I remembered I could never say it to them. *I need to remember that.*

❧ 12 ❧

I heard them come back to the apartment, my eyes popping open and adrenaline flooding my system when I heard them. About forty-five minutes had passed since my last text. I only knew because Jer's clock glowed on the wall. I turned off my phone after I sent the text and put it on the charger. I didn't want to know if they bothered to answer and I didn't want to obsess if they didn't. *Did they just get drunk and forget me? Didn't look at their phones even once? Was Phoenix off in k-la-la-land?*

The room smelled like Jer, which made more tears flood from my eyes. Julian's room struck me as organized, while Jer's absolutely wasn't despite the maids. Papers overflowed his desk, tumbling in excess to the floor. *It is Friday—no, now it is Saturday morning.* He wouldn't study until later, but if he pounded on the door and told me to get out, I would.

I could hear them having a discussion, but I couldn't make out their words. *Great sound proofing.* I waited for someone to pound on the door and shout *get out.* When it didn't happen, I dug my head into the pillow, realizing they weren't even going to bother. Phoenix wouldn't sleep without me, so I thought it might be a problem for them that I shut myself away.

But I needed time alone.

I closed my eyes, and dreams came fast.

I walked with my mom, but an older version of her than I'd ever seen in reality. She and my aunt Tricia were identical twins, and I remembered they looked so similar. My mom was graying and wore yoga pants and a long tunic to keep out the chill. It seemed so normal, it made my breath catch in sadness and longing.

I glanced down at my arm, to see myself at my current age instead of the child she left behind. Then I stared at her. Somewhere along the line, we got to be the same height, so I could look her straight in the eye.

She stared back at me before shaking her head sadly. The sky was tornado green. "You need to be careful. I ran away from that life for a reason. I took you away from wealth and privilege, and now, there is a tornado coming, Alatheia."

I followed where she indicated, and noted she pointed toward where the sky looked green. "Should we run?" I asked her, terror icing my veins as I watched the storm roil toward us.

"It never works," she replied with a shrug.

I woke up in a sweat. Sunlight streamed through the windows, not a single cloud not to mention green sky in sight. I rubbed at my eyes, wishing I could rub rest into them.

I pulled my knees to my chest, remembering all of the events from the night before, then put my head down on top of them. Nothing technically happened to me, not really. Why did I behave like that? The guys probably were mad at me.

I wouldn't be surprised if they asked me to leave. I would ask me to leave, if my roommate pulled crap like locking themselves away from me.

I wished I could ask myself to leave, since I didn't want to be myself that day.

I got out of bed anyway. I still wore my underwear from the night before, but I didn't want to put back on the dress. Instead, I grabbed one of Jer's long black shirts, which fell past my knees anyway. I would wash it for him before I returned it. I checked the clock, surprised to see it was only seven in the morning. They wouldn't be awake yet, meaning I had the apartment to myself.

Which was good. I wouldn't wake them. Instead, I snuck into Jer's bathroom then splashed water on my face. I couldn't get into Barrett's room to grab my school stuff, but I had my phone and charger, at least.

I grabbed the discarded dress and my phone before powering on the device. With a sigh, I sank to the bed, waiting for my phone to turn on. They probably yelled at me.

I would yell at me.

Rethinking it from their perspective, they probably thought I stormed away from the party with nothing wrong then threw a dramatic fit. It didn't surprise me that I didn't manage to keep friends before, not to mention have anyone love me.

Message notifications hit my phone like a cascade.

The first one was actually from Tiffany, but I ignored it to check the group chat with the Lents. Everything else could wait. I touched the pearls around my neck, since I slept in them for comfort. They deserved better than the way I treated them, but I didn't even know if they would let me keep them if they kicked me out. What was the rule for gifts when it came to ex-girlfriends?

My last message—*leave me alone*—was at the top. About half an hour later, a stream of other messages flooded the chat.

REBECCA ROYCE

Jeremy: *What? You went up there? When? WTF. How did I miss this? Are you okay? I'm coming home.*

Barrett: *Jer, did you leave? Alatheia, are you okay? What happened? I'll be there fast. What did they do to you? What happened?*

Julian: *Are you up, Baby? If you're up, please come out and talk to us. I'm sorry we missed all your messages and left you alone.*

Phoenix: *Alatheia, are you okay? What is happening?*

They gave up after they got home, but I didn't know if that was good or bad. As quietly as I could manage, I opened Jeremy's door and crept into the living room. Abruptly, I stopped short, shocked at the room. They were all passed out on the couches and the floor, sprawled across the room as if discarded by a storm. The twins snored, out cold on the carpet, while Barrett took up the entire big chair and Phoenix lay on the couch.

Why wouldn't they use the beds? Only Jer should have been inconvenienced, and there was a mattress on the floor in Barrett's room he could've used.

In any case, they freed me up to sneak past them into Barrett's bathroom where I brushed my teeth, which was pivotal. I needed a shower and my own regular clothes, too. I didn't feel like bothering to pretend to be one of them.

On silent feet, I crept to my dresser. I'd only slept about three hours, so they likely got less. I closed Barrett's door, anyway, to ensure my noise didn't bother them, then quickly showered. Once I was finally clean, dressed in my slightly ripped jeans and the t-shirt I practically lived in day in and day out in Chicago, I started on my laundry.

A hand touching my back made me jump. I whirled around to see Jeremy before he pulled me into a tight hug.

"I'm so sorry," he mumbled into my hair.

He's sorry? It didn't make sense to me. "For what? I am sorry. I..."

"No, we left you alone. I don't know what happened, but you got scared, and not one of us checked our phones. I was totally preoccupied. It doesn't matter. I'm sorry." He kissed my neck, free of pearls since I finally stored them properly. "I love you and I'm sorry. Tell me what happened, and it'll be handled."

Jeremy couldn't handle this situation, and I knew it, so I shook my head. "I don't know if I should even talk about it. I don't know what I would say, anyway. I can't..."

"You're exhausted," he whispered in my ear, so I closed my eyes and leaned into him. "And you hardly slept, because I know what time you got home. I liked thinking about how, if you weren't going to be with me, then you were in my bed, surrounded by my scent. I knew it would keep you safe. It may sound ridiculous, but that's how I felt." He squeezed me again, making me sigh. "Come on, let's go lay down in Barrett's bed. We can watch some television. If you don't want to talk yet, you don't have to talk."

I swallowed, because he didn't get it. "I made a big deal out of something stupid, then I made you leave your party. I'm sorry."

"You didn't make me leave the party. It wasn't my party in the first place. At Murial's party, you got summoned upstairs —which is insane—and you needed me but I wasn't there. You can make a big deal about me letting you down. You are allowed to take up space in my life. Do you understand? *Take up space.* Take up my time. I need you, too."

I shook my head, because he still didn't get it. "I need to be able to handle things myself, anyway. I can't be so reliant on all of you. What good is it if I fall apart when you're not with me? I've pushed through worse than last night on my own before, and I didn't feel like this afterward. I can't expect you to be there for me every second of the day."

"Yes, actually, you can," he whispered near my ear. "We

just found out we have to go to California for two days. I was dealing with some emotions, and lost track of life for an hour. I also got drunk, which didn't help."

I nodded. "I heard. Davis told me."

He pulled away, searching my expression. "Davis told you?"

I wiped at my eyes, pleased when I realized they were still dry. I didn't know how I managed it, but I felt as if I would burst into tears at any second. "Yeah, Davis told me. He told me how you had to go to get beaten in California, so you and Julian got drunk in the basement. He also told me Phoenix was in the kitchen with the other addicts, and that Barrett was out back drunk, but he was sober, like me. It wasn't safe to be drunk with so many vultures around. He told me that, among other things."

Jeremy's face turned to stone. "That fucker."

"What about it bothers you? Nothing he said bothered me, so much as the way he looked at me." I shivered a bit, remembering.

Jeremy jumped up on the washing machine and pulled me up to sit next to him. "So, how did he look at you?"

"Like...I don't really know how to explain it? But something about the way he looked at me felt like he could have me if he decided he wanted me whether I wanted it or not."

He nodded. "That's what made me so mad, now that I think of it. I knew he knew things he shouldn't, but where we all were, that description. It was like he was trying to own us to you?" He grimaced. "Was it Davis who made you so upset?"

I took a deep breath. "No. I mean, he even offered to bring me to you."

A muscle ticked in Jeremy's jaw. "Go on." I slipped my hand into his, realizing how much he didn't like the news. "Murial was..."

I didn't even know how to finish the statement, which he

seemed to recognize, because he said, "A lot. She's a lot. Take your time."

"Oh, I almost forgot! There is something I should tell you. She said *the best way to get Jeremy Lent to a party is not to invite him.*"

He winced. "She said that? She's probably fucking right."

"She made Maggie apologize to me again. I think...I think she meant to treat me very differently, but somehow I changed her mind because I got distracted with her Rembrandt. She has a Rembrandt; her daddy bought it for her. Did you see her Warhol downstairs? She owns Pullman and New York, too, including all of you because you fit together. She didn't want problems with the Lents, and she knows a little about me. Well, compared to most people, she knows a lot of stuff about me. And..."

He hugged me close, stopping my frantic recitation of events. "I get it. It was a lot, but fuck her. She doesn't own us, not to mention this city. Still, she *is* scary to a lot of people. We never should have brought you to a party at her place. I just thought that...well, I got pissed because she didn't invite me. Damn. I guess I'm easy to read."

I took his cheeks in my hands, making him focus on my face. "Maggie is in love with you."

He blinked as if confused. "I love you. So much. I didn't ask for Maggie's love and I don't honestly want it. I can feel that you love me, too. When you're ready, you'll say it. I'll know then it is because you feel safe. I promise not to leave you alone again anywhere like that again. In the future, you stay glued to me if you don't know the crowd, okay?"

I burst into tears then crumpled into his arms. After a few seconds of me incoherently sobbing into his shirt, he jumped off the washer, taking me with him. He nudged the door open, taking me to Barrett's bedroom. I could hear the snores from the living room despite the closed door.

Then he laid me on the bed before crawling in with me. "I don't know what would happen to me if I ever ended up in the world you came from before you moved here. How would I fit into the countryside of North Dakota, not to mention a typical public school? I know I don't know any of the rules or the behaviors or inside jokes. What if I had to move *three times* before I got there? Meanwhile, not only is my family shitting on me, they're keeping secrets, too. I don't know what I would do in your shoes, and I can't begin to guess how you've made it through so much. I only know that I love you. I will *always* love you."

Jeremy turned on the television, the volume low as I sniffled off the last of my sobs. He added, "Let's just lie here and watch nothing important."

I wiped my nose and blinked at him, but he really did seem to get it. "I never went to public high school either, I wasn't old enough, but you would've probably played ice hockey instead of water polo. Or basketball. Maybe both? Maybe we could've done 4-H club together or something. Usually, they held dances on the weekend, especially after big games. Music was a big thing."

Jer snuggled into the blankets with a grunt of agreement before he sought my lips. After the first kiss, he said, "You fit much better in my world than I would have fit into yours. By the way, I think it's totally disgusting if she's stashing a Rembrandt in her upstairs, where no one can appreciate it. Tacky. She wanted to scare you, and she did. Maybe she backed off from a full-frontal assault, but it still was a warning and attack, and you have to see it as that, so we can keep you safe."

He kissed me again then, and I got a little drunk on the taste of him. I let him lead me into deeper kisses, our mouths melding until we shared breath and time. I lost myself in Jeremy, and he didn't mind at all. He didn't seem to be in any rush, peppering kisses across my skin as if sampling a buffet. My head spun, lightheaded and happy to be that way. I could hear the drone of some sitcom in the background, but my real focus remained locked on his sighs, his gasps, his tiny moans.

Finally, he pulled away, stilling my hands in his own above my head. I closed my eyes, breathing in his scent, his easy weight on my body making all the adrenaline flow away. My lids closed, and I fell asleep as he rolled me on top of him without another word.

"She okay?" I heard, and tried to wake up. I recognized Barrett's whisper, but Jer shooshed him before he answered. "Don't wake her. Physically? She's fine. Emotionally, she went through a lot last night."

The bed dipped as Barrett eased in behind me, tugging my body against his with a sigh. I smiled, somewhere between waking and dreamland, but content to be in his arms.

"She's snoring," he rumbled as he snuggled me closer to his side. *Am I?* I tried to wake up again, but he adjusted me neatly into a warm spot, so I sighed and relaxed. "She never snores," Barrett said as he touched the back of my head.

Jer kissed my forehead, his lips warm and safe. "Go back to sleep, Princess. She's so exhausted. We can go over the whole night later. It was fucked up, in short. The rest? Later."

Silence filled the room, and darkness pulled me away from them.

The weight of the sun felt heavier, although I couldn't explain my sensations upon waking better than that. Then again, the later the hour, the heavier the sun, or so it felt to me.

I lifted my head, stretching and taking in the rest of the room. All four of the Lents lounged in the room, watching the television. I remained tucked neatly into Barrett's embrace, while the other two sat nearby. They kept the volume so low, they must be reading the captions if they even followed the show.

"Hey," I said as I tried to sit up. In seconds, Jeremy and Barrett wrapped me back up in their arms, making rising much less appealing.

"Hey," Julian said as he got to his feet. "Full disclosure? We all texted about what happened to you last night and everyone thinks it was fucked up. I mean really fucked up. I am so sorry we dropped the ball."

Phoenix lifted his head, and I saw his eyes were red rimmed. I didn't think it was from drugs—whether prescription ADHD meds or Ketamine—that he usually used in the evening. Genuine sentiment roughened his voice when he asked, "Why didn't you come get me? I told you to come get me if I took too long."

"I couldn't bear to walk through that crowd after I met with Murial, if I'm honest. All those eyes on me? It felt like every single person in that room stared at me. I just... couldn't."

He nodded, despite my confession not even fully making sense to me. He said, "I'm sorry. She should never have been able to get you alone. Who did she send to find you, anyway?"

"Greer," Jeremy said then winced.

Phoenix sighed. "You do have a lot of lady friends in that crew."

"She thinks she hooked up with Julian," I admitted.

His twin arched a brow. "She didn't."

"Well, that's that then," Phoenix said and stood, brushing his hands off on his legs. "She can't be allowed to intimidate my girlfriend. I don't want Alatheia worried about Murial on top of everything else. I mean, Maggie is cray-cray but this wasn't her. It stinks of Murial."

I sat up, reaching for him. "Phoenix, be honest. She's

more powerful than you. I might not know much, but I recognize powerful. Even Dina can't control Murial. There isn't anything you can do, and besides, she says we're going to hang out. She promised to show me art like I won't believe, and she wants me to learn about a painter. I think she wants us to be friends?"

"She doesn't have *friends*," Phoenix said, with emphasis on the word before he rubbed his eyes like they hurt which, due to redness, appeared to actually hurt. "No, I'm gonna call that one. You're not hanging out with her. If you want to look at paintings, you can go with Tiffany."

Jer imitated Julian from earlier. "I like paintings, too."

Barrett arched an eyebrow. "This isn't about us, it's about her having female companionship."

Phoenix frowned. "Fine, but if she is hanging out with Murial, one of us should tag along. Just show up wherever you're going, even. It would be stupid not to make sure you were safe, and she has to respect that. If you look at art with Queen Murial, you have one of us as an escort. You guys can't even disagree, because she could take it too far, or Davis could show up. I hate him more today than I did yesterday."

My head pounded, so I rubbed at my temples in frustration. "Why does everything have to be so complicated all the time?"

"It doesn't," Julian said and squeezed my foot. Barrett didn't say anything, seeming lost in thought.

He finally stood, clapping his hands as if he'd made a decision. "We need brunch. Food for everyone, that's what we need. Get dressed. We're going to brunch."

I rolled my legs off the bed quickly, happy at the idea of food, since my stomach growled at the thought. "The jazz club was really fantastic, by the way. I feel like it got lost in everything that happened after, but I wanted to thank you."

Barrett's smile made it worth remembering to take the

time to thank him. "I wish we'd gone home then, because it would've been easier."

I shrugged, since Murial would've found me at some point. *At least it is over.*

"She was barefoot," I told Julian, as if it mattered. Then again, he would understand because I'd told him about my shoe theory.

He lifted his eyebrow. "You might need a new category."

Somehow, I didn't think Murial fit into anyone's categories.

They showered, which gave me a few minutes to myself. Instead of worrying about how I looked, I opened Dina's journal, because I missed her. Life got busy, so we didn't have as much time to stop and see her lately. I intended to check on her later that day, and made a mental note before I started reading.

৩৯৩

AUGUST 16TH 1966

I'm married. I can hardly believe I am writing that. I am married. There, I said it again. How many times do I have to say it before it feels real? It's Tuesday now, but we got married four days ago in Louisiana. We couldn't get married here in New York City, because I'm eighteen, which is illegal here without my uncle's permission. I wouldn't bother to try to get that, but in Louisiana, they feel eighteen is an adult. Due to that, we got married on our way out of town.

My mother-in-law—officially family now—handed me her pearls as we left the house. They're lovely, but I didn't understand her choice of gift. Was it a wedding gift? She lifted an eyebrow at me, then pointed at the necklace. "So no one will ever make you feel small again."

For a second, she squeezed my hand, so I almost forgot her strange coldness all week leading up to the elopement.

Regardless, now I am Mrs. Nathaniel Lent. He's the oldest, so in their family, I guess that's how it works. Despite the words on the marriage certificate, I'm married to all of them now, which is magical. We took vows quietly, privately —all of us together, making promises only we would understand. Afterward, we went to the judge who gladly signed the papers to legally make me wed to Nathaniel. We dressed up formally, standing together as if in ceremony despite our lack of audience.

Then Ed drove us to New Orleans. It took seven hours, but we laughed the whole journey. Victor blushed at some of the bawdier jokes, but when our eyes met, I knew it wasn't just me. They could feel how intense everything became for us.

The sun had long set, and the hour was late when we arrived, but we checked into the Roosevelt Hotel. I stared at the beautiful marble floors, shined to an almost unbelievable gloss, while Nathanial took care of things, then followed them and the bags up the elegant stairwell. Colors seemed brighter, the sheen on things glossier, the vibrancy increased by my knowledge of my new grooms following me down the hallway. They booked us three rooms, so as to not raise eyebrows, but we all entered the same room with two beds without hesitation.

It shouldn't work. But it does. It really does.

The next morning, we flew from Moisant to JFK. Eastern Airlines. We dressed in Sunday best variety clothing, and the propeller plane lifted us off the ground with a lurch that tumbled my stomach as we rose into the clouds. I am a married woman. People wouldn't ever understand our arrangement. Not ever, even if I bothered to try. Regardless of the world's thoughts, I am now Mrs. Dina Lent. Mrs. Dina Newport Lent, and that won't ever change.

I don't know what will happen to us, but I am in this with them.

This is my happiness,

D

⚜

"RED," Phoenix said as he flopped down next to me. "I was fucked up last night, and I'm sorry I messed up." He turned his head away for a second, then focused on my eyes with deadly seriousness in his gaze. "I get that you couldn't get to me. I understand, and I don't want you to feel like I'm blaming you for not getting me. I wouldn't have expected you to face that kind of social pressure, if I'd realized." His lips trembled, as if emotion made it hard for him to continue. "But Barrett is never that drunk, so I figured he had things under control. The next time—if there is ever a next time—you find him. Do you understand? Do not leave without one of us. You don't have to face things alone."

I touched the side of his face, sighing because he made it sound so easy. Still, easier to agree than argue, so I said, "Okay."

❧ 13 ❧

I thought they had brought me to the restaurant on the Upper West Side before, since it seemed mildly familiar as I drank coffee and ate my eggs. I didn't have to say much, exhaustion coloring my mood, otherwise I just listened to them argue about a remake of a movie that just came out.

Barrett texted on his phone, but I couldn't even drum up the interest to ask him who it was. Noticing my own disassociation, I tried to force myself to pay attention to the moment. After all, every moment with them together seemed precious to me still.

Barrett finally set down his phone, glancing at his brothers in turn. "Two things—we have somewhere to go after this. It's a surprise, so no, don't bother asking me where. Secondly, Stephen is back in town."

Julian set down his soda with a plunk and rattle of ice. "How is Mom?"

"He said when he left that she looked much better. Eric will be back with her soon." He shook his head. "This is news to me. I can't remember them ever being apart for more than a day or two, or a night here and there."

I opened my mouth to tell them what I knew about Dina, but then snapped my lips closed quickly. It wasn't my place to share her secrets, but what would it be like at the lake if we went today? Did the world of Dina's youth continue today?

"I'm sure they would rather be together now," I said, offering them a comforting smile. "But we're living real life, right? They have to go back to their jobs."

Phoenix nodded. "Yeah, well that just makes me wonder what is happening to Eric's practice. He pretty much ignored it for a few extra weeks this summer."

Jeremy set down his fork. "He's good. People wait for him. He'll be fine, if he needs a little bit of time. He is devoted to his work normally. Mom first, then his practice."

A gust of damp September wind hit me, lifting my hair and sliding a chill down my spine. It should be hot in the city, yet autumn seemed to encroach on the warmth with unusual speed.

"Phoenix," I said as a thought dawned on me. "Did I leave your jacket in the car last night? The one you gave me outside the club. I think I left it in the car."

He shrugged. "I have it in other colors. I can just order it again."

"I'm still sorry."

He leaned over and kissed me. "Don't worry about it. Please, don't."

I widened my eyes, because I didn't live in a world where we didn't worry about losing designer jackets, so I wasn't sure if it really would be okay. Not to mention he just kissed me in public...

Jeremy grinned at my reaction before fist bumping his brother, clearly impressed. "There's nobody here I recognize. I think he got away with that."

"Maybe I check first, because I'm not a fuck up." Phoenix

winked at Jeremy, his sass telling me he took something in the car.

I leaned back, sighing. "I don't suppose anyone heard anything new about my birth certificate?"

"No," Barrett said and winced. "I doubt Stephen would know anyway. If he can't invest in it, he tends not to know much."

Julian grinned. "Sometimes he knows random things, and he'll name an old movie no one has ever heard of or rattle off every baseball stat ever recorded. The guy also knows anything and everything Greek."

Jeremy pointed at him, adding. "Every restaurant in the city, not to mention possible restaurants in cities he hasn't visited yet."

I grinned, because they didn't usually share a lot about their family. "What about Daniel? What is he like?"

"He's funny." Barrett said then nodded. "But in a gallows humor kind of a way? He's quick to say nice things and slower to criticize, but when he does—wow, it hurts."

Phoenix winced. "He's not wrong."

"He runs in, like, 5Ks and half-marathons. Marathons. Drinks protein drinks at five in the morning." His grin grew, sentimentality easing some of his worries. "What's even funnier is how he reacts when he can't get the joke. He genuinely cannot stand it, and it happens a lot."

Phoenix was finally smiling, too. "He hates it. It's hilarious."

"And Eric?" I looked between them.

"He's the quiet and sensitive one, who cares how people feel. He wants us all to have happiness and good luck, and the man genuinely thinks our mother walks on water. Oh, he also blames himself for *everything*."

It mirrored Phoenix in their generation, not that I would

be the one to point it out. He wasn't quiet, but the rest of it fit well enough.

"He makes a great hamburger but a terrible spaghetti sauce. Remember when Chef took a one-week vacation last summer? They took turns trying to cook." Phoenix twirled his spoon on his fingers like a baton, and the waiter brought the check, shooting him a side eye as Julian paid for it with his credit card.

I swallowed, curious if they would give me more. "And Kit?"

"He pushes and battles everyone. He does manage to get us what we need or want, but he worries. He is the face of our lives, and it never seemed to bother him we're not genetically his." Jeremy took my hand. "But sometimes he's mean. Judgy. Overly cautious. Unimpressed."

I wanted to ask them about Rosalind, but Barrett caught my hand, tugging me to my feet. He prepared a surprise, but we needed to move—fast. Minutes later, after jumping on a subway, we arrived at Lincoln Center. He spun by the fountain, tossing me a grin. "Wait here one second."

What are we doing? "I've never been here before."

"Wait one second." A door opened and two people came outside, and although I didn't know her escort, I immediately recognized Celeste Demille.

"Oh my god." I said aloud before I realized I spoke aloud.

Barrett held out his hand. "Come with me for a second, Sweetheart. You guys mind giving us a minute?"

Jules shook his head. "You are incredible. Go ahead, this is really perfect."

I followed him, my fingers trembling as we approached her in real life. She smiled at us as we approached, and my heart flipped in my chest.

"Celeste, this is Barrett. I mentioned him to you because he helped save the club. When he was just *sixteen,* if you will believe that part. And this is his..." His voice trailed off as he waited for Barrett to handle the introduction.

Barrett grinned. "My girlfriend, Alatheia. Pleasure to meet you. We saw you sing last night. You were incredible and I thought I would surprise her by making introductions. As you can see, it worked. She's shocked."

Celeste shook his hand warmly then managed to shake mine, despite my fangirl wide eyed silence. She and Barrett made small talk for a second, while I couldn't do more than stare at her.

She faced me, saying, "You're very pretty, but I see circles under your eyes. You're puffy, like you've been crying, too. Did this boy make you cry?"

The crispness of her consonants when she spoke coupled with her southern accent was very effective in getting my attention. "No, ma'am. I mean, I was crying but not because of him."

She jerked her chin toward the other guys. "Them?"

"No, other people entirely." I couldn't believe she even cared.

Celeste nodded and put her hands on her hips. "Well, otherwise I would've had words with them, because you look fragile as a bird today. I saw you last night. You were lit up in there, and I loved how you seemed to sail away on the music. Whatever happened?" She leaned forward, as if sharing a secret. "Fuck them. And you," she pointed at Barrett. "I'm glad it wasn't you."

"I hope I go my whole life without making her cry."

Celeste laughed, the sound as musical as her singing. She touched his arm gently, smiling when she said, "That's unlikely. You'll make her cry. She'll make you angry. That's the good stuff, but not like this. Whatever made her sad...it makes me feel like it deserves a jazz song."

I thought about my complicated life and almost laughed. I probably could write a song about it.

⚜

I MISSED DINA, so we stopped to see her, but we caught her on her way out. She always seemed busy, her fingers dipped into more things than most ever guessed.

"How are my journals?" she asked me as she fastened a pin on her blouse.

Julian shook his head. "Your what?"

"You still haven't told them? You really are good at secrets." She laughed, telling him, "I have her typing up the journals I kept for years. Don't worry, I'll be gifting them to all of you on my birthday." She spun, asking me. "How's this?"

In that second, I could see her as she must have looked on her wedding day. Joyful and dressed up, so young and fresh and full of hope. "Perfect. You're perfect."

"Doubtful but thank you." She grabbed her purse. "Don't tell them what they say. See? We're still keeping secrets. Are you all staying or leaving?"

Phoenix laughed. "We're leaving, same as you. Who are you off to save today?"

"Mermaids," she said then swatted him with her purse. "Don't sass me. I invented it. Goodnight, children. I love you." Instead of leaving, though, she tapped her purse on her hand. "No, wait. I *do* love you. In fact, I love you all so much, I'll skip the charity event in the East River tonight." She threw down her bag. "Do you remember when you were children, and you came over for your spoil-a-thons? We all would sit here and play board games and eat spaghetti until we thought we might pop?"

Phoenix shook his head. "I don't remember them. I'm

sorry. A lot of my childhood memories vanished, because they're tangled up with other things."

Her face fell, but she stroked her hand through his hair. "I'm so sorry to hear that."

"I remember, Granny," Barrett said as he took her other hand. "Back when it used to feel like it was us versus the world. Our parents would go out, but we would stay here with you. We all camped on the floor in sleeping bags, even you."

She smiled. "Okay, we'll do a spoil-a-thon tonight. No sleeping bags, and you can all go home to sleep because you don't have a bedtime anymore. This should be fun."

I blinked, backing up a step. "I can go home and let you all..."

Dina waved her hand in fast dismissal, cutting my words off. "Why would you leave? Aren't you part of them now? Unless you had something more exciting planned besides hanging out with your grandmother on a Saturday night."

Julian put his arms around her, giving her a fast hug before he said, "We have nothing better to do, but dibs on the car. Nobody else said it yet, so I called it."

I tugged Phoenix's tee-shirt to tell him, "You can remember this one."

"I'm going to make it a point to never forget it." He kissed my head.

She clapped her hands again, almost out of habit. "I'll go change then make some spaghetti. Oh, wait." She snapped her fingers. "I honestly am not sure there's even groceries here. Jeremy, could you order something? I want groceries, not finished food. I want to cook."

"Sure, Granny, on it." He side-eyed me. "So, those are her journals I catch you reading. The ones you won't talk about— is she spilling family secrets?"

I grinned at him. "Maybe, but the tea was served in 1966. I wouldn't worry. You don't even exist yet."

Julian kissed my cheek, confessing, "This was a good idea."

"Hey, I just wanted to say hi. This is all Dina's plan," I said, since I couldn't take the credit. *Even if I'm really happy we're doing it.*

It turned out that Dina Lent was a fantastic cook, which was funny since they said her son Daniel was a terrible chef. The guys each ate two plates full of pasta while Dina and I dawdled over our first, dipping crusty garlic bread in the zesty sauce.

Phoenix closed his eyes, leaned back, and rubbed his stomach. "I remember this taste. I do. Thank you so much, Granny."

"I'm glad, my sweet boy." She stroked his arm gently. "How was your first week of school?"

They all told her pretty much the same thing—everything was fine, so far as they admitted to their grandmother. Then Julian pulled out a familiar real estate board game, and they all started setting it up. I bit my lip and confessed, "I've never played." I'd heard of it, of course. Everyone had heard of it.

Jeremy nudged me with his shoulder. "Good, it will make it easier to cheat you."

I laughed at both his joke and his speedy delivery. His eyes twinkled, meeting my own and a spark of something heated my blood. Suddenly, I remembered him holding me in the darkness with the television in the background. How he said I wasn't crazy, and recognized the situation traumatized me.

And I admitted to myself, it felt like a trauma.

Julian squeezed my knee, catching my attention and shifting it toward him. I tried to shake off the ghosts of the past as he said, "I'll teach you. We'll play as a team for the first game."

"You just want to cuddle her the whole time." Barrett

shook his head, scowling at his brother. "I wish I'd thought of it."

The game was easy enough to pick up on, once they explained the rules. After a few rolls of the dice, I understood yet let Julian make the decisions for fun. I liked watching them interact, sometimes, their brotherly love and competitiveness coming out in equal measures.

Dina glanced up from the board and caught my gaze. "I'm going to break my own rule to ask you where you are in the journal. I can't stand the suspense of not knowing."

I smiled at her, actually relieved to talk about it. "You just got married, actually, so it is such a happy part of the story. In the last entry, you went to the Roosevelt then took a plane back to New York."

For a second, she blinked fast, as if fighting back tears. "Quite a night. If I remember correctly, the journal entry didn't do it justice. Some days are too full to even put down in words."

I leaned forward, my own curiosity making me ask, "Can I ask you a question?"

The guys suddenly seemed to go still, and I wondered if she didn't usually talk about their grandfathers in front of them.

She nodded easily, relaxing back into the sofa. "Of course. I figured you would have more than a few." Her voice went soft, and her gaze distant. "You've been so accepting about all of it, unlike a lot of people I told about my life. If something strikes you as weird, feel free—ask away."

I stared at my fists, the knuckles bunched white, before looking back at her, since I couldn't force myself to glance at her grandsons. "I guess I just wanted to know about the lake. The other side of the lake, specifically. Kit said that it might have something to do with Phoenix's kidnapping, but you never even knew any of them or said much about the lake at all. Robert took you to look at the old house once, but no one lived in it then. I mean, did you leave something out, or what did I miss?"

Phoenix's voice intoned solemnly when he said, "We keep so many secrets. We don't even know what was in your folder, Alatheia. Can anyone give us at least one answer? About me? About her? About *any* of us?"

She frowned at him. "Don't be theatrical. Kit didn't tell me anything about any folder yet, so I'll ask and get back to you. If there are secrets, it's because your fathers want to protect you. It's love, basically, and I don't know that you should get in their way when they're proving how much they care. I once tried to protect them. . . Anyway, no, based on where you are in the journals? I haven't left anything out, except bedroom shenanigans you wouldn't have been comfortable reading anyway. In regard to the past, all I will say is this. . ."

Her phone beeped, and she groaned as she glanced at it. Dina hated texting, squinting at the phone as she tapped with a single finger. "Stephen is on his way here, but he doesn't know you're here. He's popping by just to say hello."

She scanned their faces before asking, "What do you boys know about the history of the Lent money?"

"Department stores," Julian said in an empty tone, not even bothering to look up from the table in front of him. "Frankly, it seemed like you guys did this." He pointed to the board. "Charging rents and utilities while living off trust funds and if they're bored, maybe they also have jobs. I know they expect us to go into a trade of some kind."

She rose to fill her wine glass, not rushing to answer him. I noticed that despite the fact I regularly saw most of them drinking, they didn't even try in front of her. *Out of respect?* I wondered. Her glass sparkled with popping bubbles in pink drink, a cherry floating cheerfully in the glass as an accent.

Once she sipped and crossed her legs elegantly, she answered, "They allowed you to believe what is basically a misunderstanding. No trust funds for them, or guaranteed futures. We came to New York with money, but not like the people in the city. We earned your futures with a lot of hard work. Your fathers might have been born rich kids, but they weren't trust fund kids, either. After their fathers died, they inherited a lot of money. Some of it now fills your trust funds. They took the seeds from their fathers, and they made them blossom and became even more wealthy."

"Really?" Julian leaned forward, his elbows propped on his knees. "I never knew they worked for it. I figured they were like a lot of the others in their generation, and they just inherited it all."

"No, but you specifically asked about the lake, Alatheia. Let's start there, for now. Your great-grandfathers started out on the other side of the lake, poor but classy. They loved their wife, though, and they liked to spoil her. Few others ventured outside the community, fearing getting caught, but they took risks."

She rolled her dice then moved her little car forward five spaces. "Risks, as you know, often mean more money. Theirs started with logging, back when the wealthiest family in town was the Trosclairs."

"That's Mom's last name." Phoenix's mouth hung open for a few seconds as he just stared at his grandmother. "Well, it *was* her last name, back before she became Rosalind Lent."

She smiled. "Would you imagine that? While they took risks and gained wealth, the Trosclairs lost theirs just as fast. Her grandfathers drank a good amount down the drain, preferring the very best and by the cask. Your grandfathers had nothing to do with the downfall of the Trosclair family, but it didn't stop them from getting blamed for Trosclair troubles. The Trosclairs lost everything, ending in squalor.

Your great-grandfathers grew their wealth to surpass anything they ever had. Eventually, they died, though. They left a great deal of money to your grandfathers and your great-grandmother, so she lived the rest of her life as a wealthy widow, but the Trosclairs claimed she was snobby to them. Hilarious, really, since she came from the wrong side herself."

Dina sighed, glancing around at them before clapping her hands on her knees. "I haven't spoken about the lake in *so* long."

"Please, tell us more." Jeremy squeezed her hand. "No one else ever wants to talk about anything important, and some only want to tell us what *not* to talk about."

I bit my lip, resisting telling them that at least there were people who listened to them at all. I lived for years like a ghost, completely invisible as anything other than a walking dollar sign. I could sort of understand their situation, though, which arguably could be worse.

"I can't imagine someone telling you what you shouldn't say. Your great-grandmother on your father's side was not a nice woman, at least not to me, so I tend to think the worst of her. Your grandfathers wanted out. They spent enough time working for their fathers, and they didn't care about the game playing and gossip of the lake. In fact, they planned to leave the lifestyle altogether before they met me."

I had read as much, but she brought the experiences to life on the page.

"When they married me, an outsider, it didn't go over well within their community. For the most part, though, they just hated us silently. I thought I hid it from them, that they didn't know, but it took me too long to realize they knew all along. We visited once a year and that was it. We checked on their mama, then we went back home and back to our lives. I remember it as a happy time. We started to make money, lots of it. We worked and worked, but we liked to play, too. It was wonderful to see our work pay off—and a great distraction, since I wasn't getting pregnant."

The door opened and closed behind her, then Stephen entered the room. His face lit up when he spotted his sons. "Boys! I didn't know you were here. I planned to come see you tomorrow."

Four different versions of hello sounded, but only Dina hugged Stephen. "Having a board game night?" he asked Dina.

"It started with that, but now I'm telling them who they are and where they came from. Frankly, I was about to tell them their mother's story."

Stephen's smile vanished, stark pain entering his gaze as if it hid there all along. "Mom, really? Don't. Let their mother tell them, if she wants. She gets to tell her own story. It's hers to tell."

"No," Phoenix said and stood up so fast, the board game went flying. "It's my story, right? Your secrets almost killed me and it did kill the others. I may not remember what happened, but they died, and I didn't, and I have a right to know why."

Stephen grabbed him, tugging him into a hug. "You're right, but it goes deeper than just you and your brothers. I'm only really learning what happened that night myself. For years, I honestly didn't care about the details. They took our baby. You're not wrong, when you say it is your story, but you were *our* baby. When you went missing, I couldn't see straight past my fears. Only Granny knew and at the time, I thought she'd lost it."

Dina patted her son on the arm. "I do so love being discounted."

He laughed, shaking his head. "I know. Phoenix, your mother is coming home soon. Can you wait for her? I personally will ensure she talks about it, finally. Can you wait?"

If he expected Phoenix to agree, he grossly misunderstood his son.

He shoved out of Stephen's hold, anger distorting his features. "You all threatened to send me away if I screw up again. You take as little interest in all of us as you can yet still pretend to give a shit. My own mother hasn't looked me in the eyes for years. If you think I will just sit around and wait for you because I trust you, then you're being ridiculous." He looked away, adding, "I'm not even sure you would tell me the truth."

Stephen visibly paled, as if his son had hit him. "I will always tell you the truth."

"You haven't so far," Julian said as he rose. "He wants answers, and we have a right to ask for them. Enough already." He pounded on his chest. "I think I already know what happened, and I have for years, based on things I heard."

I wondered if he faked it, but something about his expression said he might know more than the rest of us, and I could tell Stephen saw it.

Jeremy gasped. "Really?"

Should I leave? I didn't belong here if they intended to discuss a personal family matter. Still, Dina had opened her journals to me, and the guys had said they loved me. My heart beat in my throat, and I clenched my fists, but I stayed like I had a right to be there. Even if I probably should've run while I could.

Julian continued. "They want the money, right? Mom's family. I figured it had something to do with them. Did they take the kids to try to force the issue?"

Stephen sank into a seat, his gaze distant, as if he peered into the past. "I wish it was about money. We would've paid them any amount they asked. No, I think it was payback for a slight. If Kit's instincts are right, that's what it was. But I don't even know what the slight is and I didn't see any of it, at the time."

Dina leaned against the wall, her arms crossed. "Some of it was about money, Stephen. Don't fool yourself. If you were poor and unimportant, they wouldn't have bothered."

My chin jerked in surprise, but then again, Dina usually cut to the chase.

Phoenix focused on the important part, asking, "What resentment? *Who* took me?"

Jeremy hugged Phoenix and Barrett rose, saying, "Get to it."

Stephen shrugged helplessly. "I don't know. Truly. If I did, they would be dead. We only know your mother ran for her life, and she arrived at our door. We didn't give her back, we married her. We took her away. They saw it as one more way we tried to get over them, to pretend they didn't matter. They don't like it, and they didn't at the time. To this day, some men down there think we should give her back to them, as if she were property."

Her safety immediately pressed itself to the forefront of my concern, so I asked, "Then why would you take her back there for treatment or whatever?"

It was the first time I said anything, and I panicked and looked at my fists. Jeremy laughed, adding, "What she said."

"Not everyone down there is evil, and we can't just paint them all with one broad brush. We have very close friends there, ones who also live the Life. Some are very good doctors, and one of them is working with your mom. You have friends there, too, boys. We took you there when you were young. You know this. We avoid your mom's family and their people ever since you were kidnapped, Phoenix. We might not have proof, but we knew. It took us longer than Granny to figure it out, but we caught up eventually."

Barrett shook his head. "I think we've all had enough fun. *I don't know* is not the answer any of us wanted."

"It's the only one I can give you." Stephen sank deeper into his chair, rubbing his face. "I know we're shitty parents. We had good ones, so I can tell the difference. I'm sorry about that, since it feels too late to fix it now."

Silence descended on the room, and I glanced around at each of the brothers. None of them seemed to know what to say, either.

He wasn't finished, though. "And I am sorry, Alatheia, for the role I played in you getting sent away from the Hamptons. It was my fault, and I'm sorry."

I cleared my throat. "It's okay."

"No, it's not." Jeremy shook his head. "It really wasn't."

Finally, Dina cleared her throat. "I would be happy to continue my story, if you like. Doesn't anyone want to hear how I couldn't have a baby until I turned thirty-eight?"

"No," Every male voice in the room said at once.

I smirked, sharing a secret grin with Dina. *At least they all agree on that.*

"We are too young to be this constantly strung out," Jeremy called over his shoulder as he headed into his bedroom to take a shower. None of us got much sleep the night before, and I wasn't sure whether to blame myself or Murial.

I drooped onto the couch and Phoenix sank down on the floor in front of me, crossing his legs. His hands shook, and it made me instantly sympathetic.

Acting on instinct, I rubbed his shoulders gently and he sighed, relaxing back into my touch. Julian got up and said, "I'm going to Barrett's room and if I'm honest, I might just pass out for the night. I won't even fight you for the bed tonight."

Barrett shook his head. "I'm turning in, too. You guys okay?"

"Yes," I said, focusing my thumbs on a knotted bit of muscle near his spine.

"You can't know how good that feels," he said, but he still twitched slightly. I decided to ignore it. Usually in the summer, he took something before he went to bed, and whatever it was would help with the shaking.

I whispered in his ear, "This was an awful night for you."

He snorted. "At least I got an official *I don't know.* Also a *it was your mom's family's fault,* which is more than I've ever gotten before. I wish I could remember. It's just a blank, and the more I concentrate on the blank, the less I can remember other things. It's like the blank eats my memories."

I wasn't a doctor, but I asked, "Maybe it's trauma?"

"Well, it definitely is. Still, I would love to know what traumatized me. You know, other than the obvious kidnapping and murder of the other children thing."

I rubbed a bit harder, digging into my work. "Take your shirt off? I want to touch your skin."

He didn't hesitate, despite his shaky hands. He quickly pulled off his shirt and discarded it onto the floor then lay flat on the couch so I could straddle him. "Is this too heavy?"

"Are you too heavy for me? No, Alatheia, you weigh almost nothing. I like the pressure. We could just stay like this, if you want."

I ignored him, since the massage bit seemed sort of instinctual. I started with his neck and his shoulders, working my way down until each muscle relaxed. Phoenix's body remained tense everywhere, but when I found a particularly rough spot, he would actually wince.

His body under my hands seemed all corded, lean muscle with no excess flesh, especially across his back. I remembered his tricks on his skateboard. His core strength was impressive, but I was surprised to find his back equally as defined.

"Love you," he whispered, while I ran my hands over his mid-back.

I kissed his shoulder blade in response. "We should probably hire a professional. I'm probably not doing a very good job."

"I don't want anyone else touching me like this but you. Not ever." He visibly winced when my fingertips grazed his side. *Poor guy.* I found another tough spot.

We fell into a comfortable silence, me rubbing until his breathing changed and I eventually realized he'd fallen asleep. I grinned, since it wasn't my intention, exactly, but I loved bringing him peace after a hard day.

I got up and grabbed him a blanket. When I covered him, fearing he would catch a chill while he slept, he didn't even move.

I got on my knees and kissed his cheek. "Goodnight, Phoenix."

Both twins snored nearby on the floor. Barrett sat awake, scrolling on his phone when I glanced his way. He patted the seat next to him, so I curled into his side.

He shut off his phone then plugged both of ours into chargers. "He okay?" he asked.

"Out cold." I whispered. "Should I wake him and bring him to a bed? I figured he could just sleep, but I don't want him to wake up alone."

Barrett scooted over, making room on the bed for me. "I'll get him. You stay here."

He returned a moment later with a semi-conscious Phoenix. He rolled to hold me, his eyes already closed, his breathing immediately returning to steadiness.

"Barrett," I whispered as he crawled into the bed. "Thank you."

"I'm just happy he's getting some rest tonight." He yawned.

I touched Phoenix's hair, and he snuggled into my touch. "I. . .I have come to need this so much. I don't know why I said you should stay away last night. I can't imagine you shutting me out."

He rolled to look at me, his gaze steady in the dim room.

"You were validly pissed at us because you felt abandoned. We didn't answer our texts in time, which made you mad and hurt. Not to mention you were scared, because of Murial, and who knows what coping mechanisms got you through that one." He kissed my hand then hugged it to his chest. "We need you, lovely Alatheia. You could just as easily decide you don't want us or that this arrangement is too complicated for you. We're all walking on eggshells, afraid you'll leave us."

I snorted, "Meanwhile, my family is having me followed by a PI. We really have to figure out what my aunt meant when she said something should've been dealt with years ago."

Barrett kissed my nose. "I know."

I closed my eyes. Thankfully, I didn't dream, exhaustion taking me into darkness.

THE TWINS LEFT Monday for California but they returned on Wednesday. The apartment felt colder without them, and they returned annoyed with each other and their coach.

"Why fly us out there just to get us torn up like that?" Julian iced his shoulder. "I think he's sick in the head."

Despite the travel, our lives became very wash, rinse, repeat. I loved the routine sameness of it.

I didn't see Murial at school, and I couldn't complain about her absence. I spotted Davis a few times, and his hungry eyes seemed to practically swallow me whole every time he saw me. Most of the time, I tried to avoid eye contact. I also managed to put out another episode of the *Poor Relation*.

Phoenix saw the view count then texted his fathers. He needed my birth certificate so that we could open a bank account in my name to monetize the *Poor Relation*.

They still hadn't answered. At practice, Sarah made us swim laps for an hour—a painful experience, but hard to get mad at her when she did it alongside us. Well, except the fact that she seemed to love it. I absolutely did not.

Still, the conditioning probably would help me not to drown during a water polo game, so I didn't complain.

We didn't have any big plans for the weekend, despite it being a Friday. Bethany chatted with me before Collins' class started, Tiffany drew, and Phoenix listened to his headphones while staring at the whiteboard.

As with every other day, before she lectured us for being losers, Collins headed to the front of the class to wait for announcements.

"Hello, Pullman community!" the voice over the speaker said, and I practically rolled my eyes. I'd never met our principal, but she sounded too chipper every day. I wondered if she faked it. "It is a beautiful day here in New York City, and a day for great learning here inside our walls." Some days, she read off inspirational quotes. She skipped them today, instead going right into birthdays. "We have some birthdays today—Jana Monroe from the lower school, Keith Handover, and Alatheia Winder. Happy Birthday to each of you and I hope you make it a wonderful day."

I blinked, startled at the sound of my own name. I had completely forgotten my own birthday, which should be weird, except that no one remembered my birthday. No one even actually said Happy Birthday in the past six years. Maybe I forgot on purpose, back when I was thirteen, as a way to rebel from being ignored. *It is easier to forget it than to mourn it.*

Phoenix grabbed my arm, and I glanced at his concerned expression in surprise.

"Alatheia," he said, abruptly deadly serious. "It is your birthday?"

I nodded. "Yeah. I forgot"

Tiffany smiled, turning in her seat to say, "Happy Birthday. I'll buy coffee on Saturday."

I nodded, a little thrill sparking in my system at the idea of meeting with a friend to do something. I still adjusted to the idea of friends, finding even the simple bits exciting.

Bethany swung around and smiled at me, too. "Happy Birthday."

I blinked at her, not even saying thanks because it was more *happy birthdays* than I could remember hearing for a very long time.

Phoenix squeezed my arm, grabbing my attention. "Why didn't you tell me it was your birthday?"

"Because I forgot." I repeated then shrugged. "I don't really do birthdays, so it's fine."

"It. Is. Not. *Fine.*" He released my arm abruptly then started texting on his phone.

I said, "Phoenix, really, we don't have to…"

I didn't get to finish, since Collins started class. In my defense, I tried to pay attention. Her class had to offer value, otherwise why keep such a monster on the payroll?

I noticed she used the word *intentional* about thirty times in two sentences, when she abruptly stopped and turned to me.

"It's your birthday," she said, but it didn't sound like a question.

I nodded. "Yes."

"Well, happy birthday. I hope you have a better year this year than last year. Avoid trouble this time, and it should be much easier. For instance, try not to seduce your uncle."

My mouth fell open in shock, her words hitting me with the force of a physical slap. My ears rang, my pulse a clanging noise in my head. I thought I had left the past behind me, and it wouldn't follow me here, somehow. Marco stopped

Bethany from saying it, and since then, no one had dared bring it up. The guilt, after all, seemed proved because Ted was under indictment, not to mention he wasn't actually my uncle.

"Hey," Phoenix practically shouted. "What did you just say?"

I shook my head, reaching for him. "Don't get in trouble."

I didn't want him to get sent away, and he seemed to understand my fears. He breathed heavily, but he gave me a quick nod.

Aloud, I said, "I didn't try to seduce my uncle. I nearly got assaulted by a serial rapist who is currently being charged with the same crime with another underage girl." My voice sounded strong, despite my tears. I could control my words, but not their flow down my cheeks or the heat they practically sizzled across as my face flamed. "It was hell, or as close as I've ever experienced. Then again, back then I didn't know about this classroom since it is actually hell, and you are the devil. Phoenix, *don't*."

I grabbed my bag and moved to leave, hoping he wouldn't follow me. Fueled by temper, I stormed out of the room, the repercussions hitting me with each footfall. Did I really just yell at a teacher? *And I stormed out of my classroom...*Panic made my hands shake, and I wondered what got into me. I didn't do things like talk back, normally. I usually took the abuse and moved on.

Instead, I boldly kept going. Straight down the hall, out the front door—*I am cutting school.* I never skipped so much as a class before, not even while everything spiraled out of control in Chicago. I breathed hard, the air blowing out of my nose hot and angry. *I turned seventeen today, making it a day for new things.*

Where am I going? I didn't know, but my legs kept going until I got to the park. I found an empty bench, then sat on it and looked around. Kids played, the sun shined, a normal day. Nothing to signify it as otherwise unusual at all, other than me skipping school.

Oh boy. I put my head in my hands, panic making me a bit lightheaded. *What did I just do? Shit.* I would be in sooooo much trouble. I stomped my foot. *Damn it.*

"Alatheia," a voice called out and I jolted, startled into holding my breath until my pulse pounded in my ears. *Is that... Bethany?* She grinned as she jogged to my bench then sat down next to me. "Haven't you heard me? I've been calling your name for *blocks*."

I leaned back, still shocked she left school. "No. I guess I was kind of out of it."

"Right? I figured." She looked around, crossing her legs and relaxing into the seat. "This is a good spot to look at the lake."

What is happening here? "What are you doing here?"

"I needed to see if you were okay. Don't worry, I told Phoenix I would check on you. He's probably trying to text you. Collins tried to take his phone while I stormed out, but anyway. I had to see you, *obviously*."

I couldn't think of anything obvious in the situation. "Sorry, I don't understand."

"I told you the other night, I get it." She blinked at me, and suddenly her eyes seemed way older. "Wasn't I clear enough? I almost got raped once. My old nanny's boyfriend, who stayed with us two summers ago in Europe. She brought him to our house. I haven't had a nanny in years, but she came to visit, and she brought him. I had a near miss. I didn't realize that happened to you, too, until Marco told me. Afterward, I knew we *had* to be friends."

Well...this is unexpected. At least it explained why she went from making fun of me to friendly on the first day. "I'm sorry that happened to you." Birds sang, their song somehow drowning out the city noises for a little while, but the clouds hung low, blocking the sunshine and causing a chill in the air. Rain threatened for the past few days but didn't fall. "So to start with, you honestly thought I tried to seduce my uncle."

She met my gaze, hers surprisingly steady. "Yeah, I can be a bitch when I'm threatened, according to my therapist. It's probably because my father left us when I was young then my mom married Eurotrash." She shrugged and took my hand, her grasp warm against my chilled fingers. "I feel threatened in that class. Honestly? I feel threatened in *all* of my classes. People here are rough."

They really are. I considered the kids playing again, while I processed her words.

Maybe I would answer faster when Bethany texted me about her hair moving forward. She hit pretty low on the nastiness scale to begin with, and her logic made sense to me. *Not to mention she ran out of the school and cut class for me.*

"Happy birthday," she said with a smile as she dropped my hand.

"Thanks." I glanced around the park again, still not sure what to do with myself. "Hey, Bethany? I've never cut school before. Should I go back? Or should I stay away, since I left?"

Her straight white teeth flashed when she laughed. "Do whatever you want. They won't bar you from the building, but you're already in trouble. Might as well make a full day of it. I gotta go back for a test in the afternoon." She rose and rolled her eyes. "But I'm glad you're okay. Collins is such a witch. She blackmails families, or so I heard. I don't know if it's true, but it's juicy, if it is."

As Bethany made her way back to Pullman, I contemplated how I would use my new bad girl streak. Curious, I pulled out my phone.

It erupted, overflowing with text messages.

Phoenix hadn't lost his phone, because he sent me a ton

of texts. Most told me he was very upset about what happened, which I knew before opening the phone. Half of them said he would cut school to come find me, since he could see on the app I went to the park.

Barrett encouraged him to stay in class and out of trouble, because he would come for me. The twins also texted, most of theirs seeming pretty upset because I didn't tell them it was my birthday.

I crossed my legs, leaning back on the bench until Barrett arrived. The gray sky threatened rain still, and everything about the situation suddenly struck me as really funny. I started to laugh, and I kept laughing until my sides hurt and tears rolled down my cheeks. *I stormed out of a classroom where the teacher accused me of trying to sleep with my uncle.* It sounded like something out of a melodrama, too theatrical for real life, even.

I laughed so hard, I doubled over and gasped for air as I tried to reply to the group thread. *I'm on a park bench. I'm okay. I'm...not sure what I just did. I didn't forget my birthday on purpose. I've never celebrated it before, so I honestly forgot. I planned to celebrate it, someday once I got away from my family and found friends.*

"Well," Barrett said as I still gasped and wheezed for air. "You have friends now. Happy Birthday, Sweetheart."

He offered his hand, and I fell into his arms with a sigh as the laughter finally subsided. "Shouldn't you be in class?"

"I am exactly where I should be." He grinned at me. "Do you hear that?"

The softest bit of music drifted to us over the other sounds of the park, the musician somewhere far away from us. I didn't really notice it until he pointed it out. "Sure. What is it?"

"I don't know. Dance with me anyway."

He spun me in a circle, twirling me and dipping me romantically. His smile sizzled down my spine, waking up a hunger for him I didn't expect. "I don't mean we're your friends, although we are. Still, we're more than that. Aside from us, you do have friends. Quite a few, it would seem. Phoenix said Bethany literally chased you out of class. Thanks for telling him to stay there. I don't want him to get sent away, but I barely convinced him I had this covered. I caught a fast ride share, so if you don't mind, I would like to spend the rest of my day with you."

I pressed my head against his shoulder, closing my eyes as I confessed, "Well, I guess I have a temper."

He grunted, a sound like a half laugh. "You do. It is coming out because you finally feel safe with us. That being said, maybe you shouldn't storm out of classrooms."

I sighed. "How much trouble am I in?" I wondered if I would meet the chipper principal under less than chipper circumstances, or if they would throw me out entirely.

He shook his head. "None. Your whole classroom witnessed that nightmare accusing you of trying to have sex with your uncle. The question is why did she think she could say something like that and get away with it? I looked into her on my way here. I didn't bother Kit, since he's working on other stuff for us, but his paralegal dug into her for me and found quite a history."

I snuggled further into his arms before confessing, "Bethany said she blackmails people."

He stopped spinning me, his gaze concerned instead of steady. "Well, that completes the picture. Her life looks pretty normal on paper until she gets dumped at the altar at the end of the 1980s. She was engaged to an investment banker, and she's been a problem ever since. Maybe a blackmailer, too, who knows? Regardless, it's time to get rid of her."

I widened my eyes. "What do you mean by that?"

Barrett laughed, spinning me again. "I'm not going to

have her killed, if that's what you're thinking. I'm not a hitman. No, I intend to have Stephen offer her a lot of money to go away. Otherwise, we'll expose some of her secrets to a lot of teenagers. Honestly, she must be abusing someone powerful to be so brave. If she attacked the crème de la crème, she'd be shit out of luck by now."

"Will Stephen pay her?" From what I knew, Kit usually handled that sort of thing.

"Kit's busy, and I think Granny probably berated him for putting you guys in harm's way. He'll probably avoid me for a while because of it, and Daniel was part of it. He is also *persona non grata* this week, but Stephen looked sad at Granny's the other night. He knows we're disappointed in him, so I think he'll do it."

I shook my head, wondering when Barrett learned how to handle his family like he played a chess game.

Finally, I said, "Listen, I don't know what's going to happen, Barrett. I think I might be gone in six months." I put up my hand to stop him before he could insist I wouldn't be going anywhere, since I wouldn't believe him anyway. "It's my birthday, so I get to say whatever I want without you arguing today. If I'm wrong and this is real, then someday, I hope our lives have as little drama as possible. Do you think we could manage drama-free?"

His smile became dreamy, so I dropped a quick kiss on his chin. He tugged on the end of my hair, boyish charm in his every cell. "Are you seriously going to try to use your birthday, even though you don't do birthdays? That was impressive. We'll make it our goal, life drama-free. We probably should live somewhere in the middle of the ocean, just the five of us, to ensure we don't have any outside drama, but we'll figure it out. In the meantime, what would you like to do today?"

I considered it, while he continued dancing me slowly

around in circles to distant notes captured on the breeze. "What's Coney Island like?" I finally asked.

"Honestly, I've never been there. It's after Labor Day, so I don't even know what's open, but let's go. Together."

Could it really be so simple?

With Barrett, sometimes yes, I learned.

He opened the door of the car he called for me, and as I ducked inside, he told me, "Reminder, the twins' birthday is in two weeks. Phoenix's is next month, while mine is in November. We're all fall babies."

"It might not be my birthday, for all I know. If I wasn't born in Colorado, maybe I wasn't born when I think, either."

He shrugged. "I don't mind an excuse to celebrate you again. We can have multiple Alatheia birthdays."

I pinched him, tossing him a fake scowl. "My mom celebrated it today, so this is the birthday I recognize, regardless of that fact. I don't honestly want more than one day."

"Then this will be it."

As we got in the car, the sky opened up, the promised rain finally falling all at once. I almost told him to cancel the plan, since nature said we shouldn't go to Coney Island. I didn't say it, though, and by the time we arrived, the rain had stopped.

The amusement park portion shut down after Labor Day, but we could still walk along the beach. I kicked off my shoes and held Barrett's hand, my toes sinking into the cool sand, while wondering if we were about to get soaked. The ocean appeared angry, churned up by the rain and capped with white peaks. As much as I appreciated the view, the scents, the breeze—*what a truly surprising treat*—I couldn't shake the urge to glance over my shoulder, certain eyes were on me. I couldn't see the PI anywhere but that didn't mean he couldn't see me.

"Little different from the Hamptons." Barrett said, capturing my attention as he kicked some sand at me. I shrieked, dodging easily. "Not better or worse, just different. What do you want to be when you grow up? We've talked about my dreams and goals, but I don't think we have discussed what you want out of life. So, what do you want?"

I used to just say *a life*. When I didn't even have a single friend, my goals were pretty simple overall. Could I honestly imagine something else? "I have no idea, honestly. You make me feel like I can do more than survive. I don't know what the rest looks like yet."

When his mouth met mine, I tasted his possession. It was different than how Barrett usually kissed me, but I hung on and gave myself to him as the sky opened up around us, the angry waves crashing to the beach at our feet.

❧ 15 ❧

My clothes continued to stick to me as though they were still soaked but I never felt happier. I ate a Nathan's hotdog and with my head on Barrett's also soggy shoulder, fell asleep in the rideshare on the way home.

"Alatheia," Barrett's gentle voice roused me about a block from home. For a birthday treat, I let myself call it my home, too. Tomorrow...would arrive soon enough.

I stretched and smiled at him. "Sorry, was I snoring?"

He adored me with his gaze, tracing his fingertips along the edge of my face in reverence. "No, Sweetheart, you weren't snoring, although I have caught you before. Not today." He kissed my lips gently. "But I figured I should warn you my brothers are likely to have a birthday surprise planned for you when we get back to the house. They've had hours to prepare."

"What time is it?" I asked and looked at my phone. *Almost five?* Normally, we wouldn't be home from school by then.

We got out of the car on sluggish feet and made our way inside. Barrett opened the door, and as I entered the three other Lent brothers cheered. I grinned, adrenaline hitting my system in a rush at their attention.

"Happy Birthday." Jeremy picked me up and spun me, despite my damp clothing. "I wish you'd told me sooner, but this way I get to surprise us both. First, we're going to dinner in a place I think you'll love. It goes really well with Julian's gift to you, which is..." He passed me to Julian, and I laughed.

"Baby," he said then kissed the end of my nose. "We are going to a Broadway show. It occurred to me you probably haven't ever seen one, and I think you will love it. I managed to get tickets to that musical no one can manage to see."

Of course he did. "What's the name of the musical? How do you know if we'll even like it?"

He kissed me, ignoring my question in favor of suspense. "Happy Birthday. I only wish you told me sooner so I could've done more."

More? Is he kidding? I was easy to impress, and a Broadway show was more than I would've thought to ask for if I had ages to plan.

He set me down in front of Phoenix, and I smiled at him. "The twins did their own thing, and I think you'll love it, but I have something else in mind. Every day when we walk to school, I've seen this in a store window and thought about buying it for you. So, today I got it on my way home. I bow to Jeremy's usual ability to be the gift giver, but I still hope you'll like this." He kissed my cheek then whispered, "I was so proud of how you yelled at her. She deserved it, and you did so great." He kissed my other cheek. "Here."

He placed something in my hand, but it took me a few seconds to look away from his handsome face. "What is it?" I asked, instead of looking.

"The thing about gifts, Red, is you have to open them. Go on." For Phoenix, I would almost describe his expression as sheepish.

I lifted the lid on the box then gasped in genuine surprise and pleasure. Sapphire earrings glittered up at me from a dark velvet bed. "Phoenix, these are gorgeous, but they're too much," I breathed, staring at them in awe.

"They're not nearly enough," he said, his voice low. I shivered as his words almost seemed to caress my skin. "I knew they would look beautiful with your hair. Go shower, Red. We'll leave in half an hour, and it would make me happy if you wear them. Please. I know you'll wear Jer's pearls, but wear these, too."

I grinned, stroking them with a fingertip. "I love them. I'll gladly wear them all the time."

"Good." He stepped back, gesturing toward the bedroom. "Go. We don't need ultra fancy, but probably not jeans. You can be casual, though. I hate to rush you, but hurry."

"Guys..." I began, but Barrett shook his head.

"Go," he suggested.

My first birthday since I was eleven years old. I almost bounced on my toes and squealed as I headed to the bedroom. I couldn't believe they did so much just for me.

Although I'd never done a tasting menu before, dinner was amazing. We all scarfed down the food, loving every bite. I finally managed to stop smiling enough to speak halfway through dessert.

I asked, "What do you all want for your birthdays? I doubt I can pull off something like this, but still..."

Julian took a bite of his tart, closing his eyes in pleasure before he answered. "Honestly? I just want to lie in bed and watch movies with you all day."

My brows popped up, since I could easily afford that, but it didn't seem like enough. "Really? I mean, I could use the card to get you an actual gift. They're already having me followed, so why not spend some of their money?"

He squeezed my fingertips across the table. "I have everything I want, Baby. If I don't have it, I can get it. I *want* time with you. Movies in bed, all day. That's my request."

Jeremy nodded. "Same, but I don't want movies all day. I only want your time. You can watch movies with him all day, just save up your energy because I get you at night. I don't know for what yet, but we'll do something, and it will be epic."

Julian pointed at his brother with a grin. "Bake us a cake?"

"Oh yes, bake us a cake, too. We failed there," Jeremy said then frowned. "You aren't getting a cake."

I shook my head, amused. "I don't need one."

My ears tingled, my new earrings a heavy and obvious weight against my neck. Big, gorgeous square studs, I thought, touching one in reverence. And I wore pearls around my neck—the Lents dressed me far better than I ever imagined.

"You're older than me now," Phoenix teased. "I always imagined dating an older woman. Cougar."

I held up one finger. "By one month. I'm older by one month."

"Right." He winked. "It counts, cougar."

Loopy was an incredibly funny musical. I laughed the duration, and even Phoenix—who didn't like musicals—laughed by the ending. The remodeled but ancient theatre gave the actors a brilliant stage, and overall, it took my breath away.

Our red velvet seats were comfortably situated, if a bit close together, reminiscent of an airplane. They packed as many people into the show as possible. The color reminded me of Dina's red walls, and I made a mental note to tell her all about it the next time I saw her. The color seemed so theatric, it fit Dina.

But up close, the walls seemed to be made of gold itself, which couldn't be possible in such a big space, yet the facsimile seemed strikingly effective. Chandeliers sparkled elegantly from the ceiling. Moldings. Trimmings. The very building dedicated to the art of theatre, taking the time to ensure a quality experience in the small details despite people only spending a couple of hours in the place.

I touched the seats reverently on our way out, the tiny brass placards on the back of each seat numbered for ease of use.

Julian frowned, seeming disappointed. "Next time, it'll be better."

"What? I thought it was fantastic." I couldn't imagine what he meant.

He shook his head. "It was so last minute. Our seats were terrible. We'll be closer next time."

We sat practically in the center of the orchestra. *How much closer can we get, onstage?* I blinked at him, utterly baffled. "They were perfect."

"Then why did you touch the seats like that when we left? You weren't thinking how shitty the seats were?" He tilted his head.

I sighed. "I didn't think you would even notice, but honestly? I made a memory of it. On purpose. I do it a lot when we're doing things together, Julian, and with all of you. I try to record everything in the moment I am happy, so I can remember it later, when things aren't so great."

We had made our way onto the street, since we weren't going to stop to meet the actors. Once we made it a block off Broadway, Julian hugged me. I loved his attention, but the suddenness startled me.

He finally pulled away. "I wanted to try to make a memory, like you said earlier. One of you and me hugging on the street, so I can pull it out the next time the world threatens to destroy something I love."

I nodded and touched his face gently. They often reminded me I wasn't the only one who had survived hell.

The more I knew them, the more I realized Phoenix getting kidnapped had damaged all of the brothers. Born in just under three years, they were close, which made sense. Barrett probably couldn't even remember a time before his brothers. They were a group, a team of sorts, but someone took Phoenix and hurt him. Because they were so connected, it hurt all of them, the damage almost reverberating down the threads that connected them.

By the time we got home, I held my abdomen because of the cramps. My period for sure started, so I groaned and headed into the bathroom. Never regular, I only had it once in the spring before this summer started. When it came, here and there, it seemed to have the enthusiasm from the time it missed.

"You okay?" Jer asked me when I exited the bathroom in my pajamas a while later.

"I got my little visitor," I admitted awkwardly.

He winced. "Sorry."

"Thanks," I said, climbing into the bed with concern about the waves of cramps no doubt on their way. It hurt, and there wasn't a pretty way to think about it. My aunt Amelia only shrugged at my irregular period, despite my concerns, since hers was similarly weird, which told me nothing. "I need to see a doctor. I have got to get health insurance. I am probably on someone's policy, but I have no idea who to ask."

The doorbell rang. We blinked at each other, startled at company at that hour, until Barrett went to answer it in his boxer shorts and a white t-shirt.

Phoenix's vacant gaze met mine, telling me he'd taken something while I cleaned up in the bathroom. He said, "It's obviously our parents. No one else would be here at this hour without getting announced by the doorman. Anyone else would have to wait downstairs until we permitted them upstairs."

Barrett reentered the bedroom, considering us all before admitting, "It's all of our parents. They want to see you, too, Alatheia. Are you up for it?"

I swallowed, because my cramps had started. Still, it wasn't like I usually catered to what I needed. I nodded. "Sure."

Jer stopped me, his hand on my arm. "You're in pain. If they start any bullshit, I'm throwing them out."

I sighed and stepped around him, since I didn't want him to kick his own family out of the apartment.

All five waited in the living room, and I considered them quietly from behind Phoenix. It was my first time seeing Rosalind since she threw me out of the Hamptons. With her hair pulled back in a high ponytail, she wore a pair of jeans and a white t-shirt, and for a second, I was struck by how young she looked. I never thought of the adults as young before.

She smiled at all five of us, while her husbands alternated between watching her and watching us.

Rosalind held a wrapped gift, and I stared at the elegant wrapping paper with awe. *Someone must've told her it was my birthday or she's very early for the twins.*

Her kind eyes regarded me. "Alatheia, I hear it is your birthday." She paused before she added, "Dina told me. I guess one of you probably told her."

Barrett raised his hand. "I thought she would want to know."

"She likely will have something planned for tomorrow. My mother-in-law won't be rushed when it comes to gifts. Anyway, this is for you. If I had known earlier, I would've done better, but I hope you like it. I won't forget it in the future. I'm actually good with dates."

I accepted the gift, thinking the entire interaction felt awkward with a capital A. "Thank you."

REBECCA ROYCE

With everyone staring at me, I managed to unwrap her present. My fingers became uncomfortably huge and unwieldy because of all the eyes, and it felt like it took an hour to get past the bow, but I found a stencil of my profile inside the box. She must have made it herself. "Did you do this? It's so beautiful."

"Yes, I made it today. Again, I wish I could've done better, if I'd known sooner. I honestly think you're lovely, so I wanted to capture you as you are now, at seventeen. You girls may take a lot of selfies, but I'm not sure you really see your actual beauty. I hope you like it."

The handmade gift touched me, and I swallowed hard, trying to find the right words. I felt her gift also gave me a statement of apology, and I would gladly take hers. "I'm not used to birthdays. I haven't had one in six years, but your sons spoiled me today, and this is beautiful. I don't take selfies, actually. I normally hate taking photos, but this is gorgeous. I'll treasure it."

She nodded then gestured at the couch. "You're welcome. May I sit?"

I startled when I realized she asked for my permission. *Really? Since when do I get to decide who is allowed in their apartment?* But I collected myself quickly and said, "Sure. Of course. Can I get you anything?"

I fumbled, not sure of the proper social niceties for the situation.

"No, thank you. We just ate." She glanced at her sons, her smile warm. "I'm glad to hear you celebrated her, but I can't believe you haven't taken photos with her. Always take photos, record your lives. It will preserve time."

The twins met each other's gazes before Jeremy confessed, "We've all taken candid photos of her."

They did? Heat blossomed on my cheeks again, my face an open book. "Really?"

208

"Yeah," Phoenix sat on the edge of my chair, playing with a lock of my hair idly. "I have some great ones. We got the vibe you wouldn't be into posing."

I never thought about it before, honestly. "If you want to take pictures, I don't have a problem with it, but I'd love to see the ones you took."

"We're already a little off track," Barrett said then sighed. "This was very nice, Mom, but how can we help you tonight?"

Her smile turned sad. "I thought we were having a nice little visit." She held up her hand. "I know, everything is my fault. *Our* fault. I came back a week early because Stephen said we should talk because Dina wanted to tell the story of the lake. Which, of course, includes my own story. He put her off, but he said we were out of time and should tell you now."

Phoenix sighed. "Although I'm personally invested in those answers, maybe Kit should tell Alatheia what the fuck was in that folder first? We can call it another birthday present, if you want."

"Language." Eric frowned as he stared him down. "Are you okay?"

He gave a quick thumbs up. "Sure."

"Many things," Kit admitted with a sigh. "I need a few more days before I'll have the answers for you, if you would trust me for that long? I get why you don't trust Stephen to tell you the truth, and it's fair if that goes for all of us. I don't want to lie, but I need a few days."

Barrett rocked back in his chair. "Next time you ask us to commit pseudo crimes, maybe you'll let us see what we steal before you disappear the information? Better yet, don't ever send them out to do your dirty work when I'm not home. That shit doesn't fly."

Rosalind furrowed her brow at her husband. "What did you do, Kit?"

He lifted his hands defensively. "It wasn't just me. Danny,

too, not that it matters right now. We'll know more soon. In the meantime, share our story, my love."

I sighed, irritated despite myself. Why couldn't I see the papers if my name was on them? But I felt arguing wasn't going to get me any more information anyway, so why bother?

Rosalind began, "Over the years, you believed I was the oldest child in my family, but I wasn't. I had an older sister, but she was murdered when she was twelve. We never found out who did it, but her throat was slit." She stared at the floor, her gaze vacant. "After Annette died, they put me in charge of the whole brood. You boys only met my mother about six times in your lives, but she worked around the clock. Birth control wasn't the same then, or who knows why, but she had so many babies. Then she would turn them over to her other children to raise and head back to work, so it landed on me." Her gaze traveled between Barrett and Jeremy. "Not an easy life by any means, especially since my fathers spent most of their time drunk. Wrong side of the lake, but darker than that, really. I accidentally met your fathers during a boat ride, and suddenly. . .it occurred to me that maybe I could leave there."

She said she didn't want anything to drink, but I rose to fetch her a water anyway. She appeared so brave to me in that moment, willing to tell her life story to her sons, the people most consistently angry and disappointed in her. It seemed the least I could do.

When I handed it to her, I could see the tremble of her fingers. She touched my wrist, and I saw the gratitude in her expression as she took a long sip.

Jules squeezed my knee as I passed him on my way back to my seat.

After she drank half the glass, she handed it to Daniel, who kissed her cheek. "How would you have known people left the lake when they used your disinformation to keep you there?"

She gave a small inelegant snort. "I should've. Everyone talked about those horrible Lents. I heard them saying how, if they ever came back, they would get it." She winced, as if guilty by association. "I figured it only meant you moved to the other side of the lake, never imagining anything further away. I didn't go to school, so I never had a formal education. Instead, we got homeschooled." Rosalind stood then paced to the window. "Except they never actually taught us anything, leaving us to mostly teach ourselves. Sometimes, I am so proud of where we can send you to school. Barrett attending an Ivy League University? It blows my mind. I am so very proud. But that's not important right now." She faced the room again, her shoulders stiff, as if readied for battle. She'd survived worse than telling her story, so she would get through it.

"Go ahead, Mom." Barrett said, offering her a small smile of encouragement.

She sighed, some of the starch leaving her shoulders as she said, "They were *so* handsome. I sat in some shitty boat, probably not seaworthy, and spotted four exceptionally hot guys in a sailboat. The Lents everyone talked about, but they looked like creatures from another dimension. So handsome, so crisp and clean. Older than me, but only by just a bit. They of course didn't notice me at *all*."

Kit laughed. "You were fourteen. Wouldn't it have been creepy if we did?"

"There was that. Eventually I met them, and they were funny, too. They mostly talked to the guys I hung out with, discussing fishing before they all went off together. Over the next few years, I would ask about them whenever I got the chance. Where did they live? I heard about their department stores, so I called their office and ordered a catalogue just to see what they offered. By the time I turned eighteen, things got dangerously bad for our family. We didn't have any money, so some nights we didn't eat. Then...my father lost me in a bet."

I sat forward, startled by her confession. "What?"

"Right? I wish I made it up, but that's what happened. He made a bet, and he lost. He traded me into marriage with my grandfather's best friend and his brothers." She visibly swallowed, shaking her head. "It would've helped the family, since they had some money. A lot of our debt could've been paid off." Her voice wobbled. "But I couldn't do it. I was only eighteen." Instead of rupturing into tears, she stood up straighter, her voice steadier. "I tried to get my head around doing it, but I couldn't. Instead, I ran away from home in the middle of the night. I'd saved some money for new shoes, so I used that little bit of money to get a bus ticket for as far away as I could go, which ended up being New York. I didn't know I planned a destination, but then I found myself in front of a department store. One of four in Manhattan, so I got lucky because their father, Ed, recognized me. He brought me home, and of course Dina fed me. She loves a lost stray."

I winced, feeling like her latest acquisition when all of the brothers glanced my way. I waved my hand at her in circles, hoping she would move it along past that point. I hated that word. My hand stilled, when I realized she called herself it, instead of me.

"None of us were home at the time. We went away to school." Stephen pulled her against his body, apparently no longer able to resist offering her his strength. "We wouldn't be home until winter break. When we heard she was staying with us, we certainly didn't feel the need to share it with anyone else in Louisiana. Mom said to keep it secret, so we were vaults. Once we met her and saw her...after we spent time with her, our plans to leave the Life and do things differently stopped. We only wanted your mother. She might've been young, but she wanted us, too."

She kissed his cheek, nuzzling into his arms. "You were young, too. We got lucky."

"We did," Dan agreed. "But we have a tendency in our family to fall for strong, smart, beautiful survivors." He met Barrett's gaze and shared a brief nod. "We might have a type."

Rosalind stepped out of his embrace, not finished with her story. "I thought I'd escaped them. All of them. I mean, I wanted to see my mom. She was cold and distant, but she was my mom. I wanted to check on the little ones, so I cheated and got in touch. I avoided my dad and some of the older boys, but honestly, I figured they were over it. I'd married the enemy, but they shouldn't have bet my life away. Things weren't easy for me at first, either. If they saw my social failures, they would have loved it. We still had some friends from down there, but they lived on the right side of the lake, and they visited us. You know them, by the way. When they took Phoenix, and River and Walt got killed, they actually never crossed my mind. I thought our money in this world, not that one, was what caused you to get kidnapped." She lifted her chin. "Dina never agreed. Not ever. I figured it was her prejudice, because she'd never liked the other side of the lake, but she didn't come from there. She didn't understand it and searched for any reason to hate everything about it, but I should have known better. Over time. . .it eventually sunk in she was right. Not that it meant I could do anything about it." She stared at Phoenix, but her gaze seemed to see the child again. "They took you and hurt you because of me."

Phoenix's eyes were glazed, but I didn't think it was from drugs. "Well, it at least explains some things. Thank you for telling us, finally."

"You're welcome." She practically whispered it, her husbands moving to her side as a unit.

"A lot of things happened that week that made no sense," Stephen defended and quickly looked at everyone. "Do you remember when you got sick, Barrett? You puked for forty-eight hours, and we all thought you just had a bug. Eric wasn't even worried."

He looked away, bunching his fists much like his son did when he tried to hold in frustration. "Kids get sick, so we'll never have any way of knowing for sure. I didn't have any reason to think otherwise at the time."

She nodded, saying, "I do wonder if they went after you first, in retrospect. You survived, so they failed. You got sick instead. Julian, you kept talking about seeing men in black jeans. You mentioned how it looked really ridiculous on the beach, and how hot they had to be, but we ignored you at the time. Too busy setting up for guests, so I didn't think about it."

Kit nodded. "Jeremy had nightmares all week. He said there were people in the house, creeping around in the night. He would come and sleep in the bed with Mom and whoever was with her. Maybe it all meant nothing. Coincidence? Maybe. Or it could be correlation. Regardless, it ended with Phoenix getting taken. Now everything has meaning, whether we want it or not."

I hated whoever did this to them. I hated it for all of them, and I wished I could make it right somehow.

❧ 16 ❧

Their parents prepared to leave as if they hadn't just dropped an emotional bomb on the room. Their own relatives possibly had helped with Phoenix's kidnapping. They went after the kids, maybe all of them. *It's so awful.*

"Kit," Barrett said, catching his arm. "I get that you don't want to talk about Alatheia's stuff tonight. I mean, if I'm honest, I don't get it, and I don't like it, but fine."

Phoenix interrupted, pointing out, "I could go steal the folder again."

Kit glared at him. "Don't."

"I didn't say I *would*, I just said I could." He scowled, crossing his arms rebelliously.

Barrett continued. "She needs health insurance, so could you put a rush on that bit? What if she gets sick or needs to go to the hospital or something?"

Eric stood quickly, hyper focused on me suddenly. "Are you feeling okay, Alatheia?"

"I'm good, thanks." No way would I discuss my cramps or the weirdness of my cycle with Phoenix's dad. *Too weird, I can't do it.* Everything in our world might be weird, but that somehow crossed a line.

"I don't think that's their point." Kit shook his head. "Regardless, I'll put her on one of our policies, which is easy on paper since she is an employee for Granny. We'll have her a card by the end of the week, if not sooner."

I opened and closed my mouth, surprised it went so easily. "Thank you."

"You're welcome." Kit headed for the door, brushing his hands against each other as if to shake off the conversation. "We've given you guys a lot of information to process, so that's probably enough for tonight. Happy Birthday, Alatheia. We'll see you all soon, maybe for dinner? Upstairs, next week if you're available?"

No one answered. I didn't know about them, but I still couldn't find my voice.

Once they left, Phoenix disappeared into his room, but I expected him to need something after the encounter. The other Lents remained quiet, so I left them to their thoughts. I focused all my worry toward Phoenix, and gathered all my bravery to knock on his door, despite him leaving it part way open.

"Hey," I said then leaned against the frame, hoping I looked casual. "You okay?"

He stared out the window, sitting in the window seat with his arms around one bent leg. "I'm foggy in the head, but they killed my buzz. That leaves me just foggy."

I couldn't pretend to understand what he meant. I joked, "Maybe some time, I'll try it so I know what you mean."

He spun to face me, his face intense. "I'm not a violent man, but I would destroy anyone who gave you drugs."

I shouldn't like him going all protective, but it warmed me up inside. "Okay," I said simply then walked over to drape my arms around his neck. "It's late."

"Give me a little while to think? I think I need to go to the lake this summer. I'm not a kid anymore. If I look them in the eyes, maybe I'll remember something. Will you come with me?"

I usually would remind them I might have to leave, and tell them how I didn't have any control over the situation, but I recognized it wasn't the time for that. "Anywhere you go, I'll go. You're going to the lake? I'm there, too."

"Thank you."

We rocked, almost slow dancing without music, there in his bedroom. Finally, he spoke against my hair. "If I knew how much I would love you, I wouldn't have taken so long to find you."

I shook my head. "Your brother only beat you to me by a few days."

"Too many," he said and closed his eyes. "I think we should head to Barrett's room before I fall asleep standing up. Thank you for bringing back my high." He laughed, his smile a bit goofy. "The Alatheia high."

We walked arm in arm, then dropped together onto Barrett's bed . I heard water running, which meant Barrett would be in the shower, and the twins weren't in the bedroom yet. By the time he came out of the bathroom, Phoenix snored as he held me close.

His oldest brother remained silhouetted as he considered us for long moments before he said softly, "If I could go back, I would get kidnapped instead of him."

I stroked Phoenix's hair. "Sounds like they tried to take you."

"I don't remember the puking. I only remember him being taken. Then again, I always have to ask myself, could I have survived it like he did? You see him now, and he's about a million different things. He's brilliant, smart, kind, funny... but totally out of it most days. All of that remains true, but the other kids didn't get away alive. Phoenix did. He made it. Would I have made it? Could any of us, if we were in his place?"

I offered my hand, so he came to me and took it. I tugged him closer, trying to ignore the way my stomach cramped and the headache was forming in my temples. For the moment, I could ignore it. "That's quite a heavy load of guilt you're carrying around, Barrett Lent."

"Guilt and gratitude. As fucked up as we are, we're all still here."

I smiled. "For that, I am grateful, too."

My sketch from their mother rested on Barrett's desk, since I didn't really have anywhere else to put it. He shared everything with me, including his bathroom. I got out of the bed then moved past him to quickly take care of my unfortunate period needs. When I came back, he was reading cross legged on the floor. The twins still didn't make an appearance, which wasn't like them, so I frowned.

I hoped they weren't guilt tripping themselves like Barrett... "Be right back," I whispered to him.

He nodded. "Don't let Jeremy make any big plans that can blow up."

I blew out a breath, since it proved Barrett knew exactly what I was thinking. He was thinking it, too. I followed the sound of their voices to Jer's room, where they stood shirtless and ready for bed. The sight of them honestly took my breath away for a few seconds, so it took me a minute to catch onto their low voices arguing.

"They're going to have to deal with it. I'm not going to college until we get this sorted. It's time they told us specifically who took Phoenix. They have to give us answers. I'm sick of them trying to bury it and hope it goes away. They managed it before for twelve years and things still blew up on them. No, this has to be handled." Jeremy punched his fist into his opened hand then propped his hands on his hips.

Julian nodded. "Okay, so we graduate then go down there. We don't leave until someone responsible pays for fucking with our family and hurting our little brother."

I knocked, so they would realize I'd heard their plan. "Phoenix intends to visit this summer, too. I didn't ask Barrett, but I would guess it's the general consensus. No Hamptons until after the lake, because I told Phoenix I would go, too."

Jer's shoulders sagged, but instead of looking relieved, he seemed to take on more weight. "It makes things easier, at least. They never manage to stop us or even slow us down when we move collectively."

He slipped an arm around me, tugging me close with a sigh. "I wish it had been me."

I knew it. Obsessing. Even if they all suffered trauma, they knew only Phoenix suffered forever.

Julian joined us, sliding into my other side as if he belonged there. "I'm glad you're coming, but you're wrong, Jer. It should've been me."

They argued the whole way to Barrett's bedroom about which one of them should've been kidnapped. The sounds of New York City pressed into my consciousness, horns in the distance and the hum of it all like white noise to me, making me sigh in pleasure. In fact, between the city and the twins snoring, I wasn't sure I would ever sleep well in true quiet again.

My period cramps woke me at dawn, despite Jer's comforting arm around me and the steady way Phoenix breathed. I moaned as I woke, and Barrett mumbled to himself. Julian snored, deeply asleep on his mattress.

I snuck out of bed, making my way toward the living room so I wouldn't wake anyone else. I checked my phone,

REBECCA ROYCE

surprised when I saw Tiffany had pushed off our coffee by an hour. At three a.m. , which struck me as even weirder, because she knew she probably wouldn't be up in time. *Late night, good for her.*

A message from Bethany offered to reserve me for a spa day. I answered her quickly, panicking briefly because I wasn't sure how to pay for it and because I'd never had one before. The guys would likely pay for it, but I wasn't going to ask them. I would rather use my own information, so Phoenix could open me a bank account. Then *Poor Relation* could take care of some of my needs.

I asked for a rain check then blamed my period. Hopefully, she wouldn't feel blown off. I might not have initially been excited about her friendship, but she'd really grown on me.

The third message made me groan a little bit louder, but partially out of social panic. It simply read—*This is Murial. I missed your birthday. Meet me at the Met tomorrow at five. Don't be late. Bring a Lent, if you must. They're your shadows lately, so I don't care which one. But only bring one, because I don't want to be a parade.*

My heart thudded and my hand shook, but the message didn't vanish. *Shit.* I wondered if I could get out of it for cramps, too.

Then again, Murial probably could afford to have a team massage her ovaries until any pain vanished as if it never began.

I wouldn't even be surprised. Not with how weird everything else seemed to be lately.

Jeremy entered the room, his jaw stretched with a yawn. "The room gets colder when you leave it. I notice it even when I'm not the one next to you. Currently, it's freezing in there."

I held my waist, as if I could hold my intestines inside

despite the fact it felt the muscles of my abdomen tried to make them come outside. "Hurting a little bit, so I thought I would wait it out here. Murial summoned me to the Met tonight, and she said I could bring one of you. Could she have bugged the apartment?" I made a mental note to keep the plot in mind for *Poor Relation.*

"If she bugged the apartment, we would've been fucked over a long time ago." He slid to my side on the couch. "Art tonight, then. I'll tag along. Don't worry, she'll get tired of torturing you sooner or later. Right now, you're new, a curiosity and interesting to her, but she'll move on eventually. Before you know it, she'll be trying to intimidate or show off to someone else. She was always like this. We've all known each other a long time, so I remember when she used to wear braids to school. Two of them. Long after a lot of the other girls stopped, she still wore them. One of the girls said something to her about it once, then she just looked at them and they withered. Still, she stopped wearing braids. She's human like the rest of us. In her strange Murial way, she might actually be trying to be friends."

I groaned. "I don't want to be her friend. She frightens me. I already have Bethany to figure out. I don't need a possible psychotic as a buddy, too."

"Phoenix said Bethany chased you from class, which means we may like her. Marco might have a thing for her. Maybe we should try to see if we can set that up."

I lifted my head to stare at him. "Jeremy Lent, you are a romantic at heart."

"Only since I met you. Okay, this is stupid, but I was online last night when I couldn't sleep, and there might be something I can do to help with the cramps. First up, you should take an anti-inflammatory." He jumped off the couch and returned quickly with two pills, which I swallowed. "Roll onto your back and pull up your shirt. I want to rub your stomach."

He wants to what? I didn't argue, though, because I trusted Jeremy implicitly. I blinked, surprised at the realization and the truth of it. *I trust Jeremy Lent.*

"Jeremy, I was just thinking..." My voice trailed off, and I chickened out before I said the words.

"Hmm?" He placed a gentle hand on my abdomen, his touch warm. "You were thinking what?"

"That I can trust you with anything and everything."

He met my gaze, staring back at me for weighted moments. We didn't speak, both of us breathing hard. When he answered, it was in a low voice, almost a whisper. "Thank you. I know what that means for you. I love that you told me."

He placed his hands on my stomach, their warmth soothing. "I watched a video. If this gets uncomfortable or doesn't work, tell me to stop. It's just something I saw."

"You couldn't sleep? Did I keep you up?"

He shook his head, a piece of his blond hair falling into his eyes, the only blond of the brothers. I thought he looked like a surfer dude when I met him, and I could still see it.

Jer dropped to his knees and started to rub circles on my abs. I closed my eyes, sighing and relaxing into his touch. It felt magnificent.

"This circular motion is supposed to help. No, you didn't keep me awake. You're the best cuddle ever. I was thinking about last night's revelations. I didn't realize I know so little about my family, but I could list it all on one hand. Our great-grandparents made money logging. They died doing it. That's one. Grandfathers and Granny made money on department stores, but they died in a car crash. Granny sold the business, and she made a ton of money. Secondly, the fathers used their money from working to invest in themselves. They became huge, then stuck some of it in ever growing trust funds for us. That's three. I know *three* things about my family's history. I don't know anything about my mom's family, other than what she told us last night, and we haven't figured anything out about you."

I tried to focus on his summary, but his touch made that difficult. I moaned in pleasure and closed my eyes. "Don't stop doing that."

"I won't." He chuckled, a soft rumble of sound. "I'm glad it's real and not just an internet thing."

Me too. Finally, I could think again. With my thoughts in order, I said, "You'll find the answers. You accomplish everything you set out to do, so this won't be any different."

"I love that you see me that way." He shook his head. "Most of the time I feel like I'm barely getting by, never quite living up to my potential. Either that or, conversely, I'm being overlooked."

For real? I blinked, surprised at how different his description was from reality. "I don't see you that way at all. I am so sorry if you've felt that way." I wouldn't call him a liar, even if it didn't match with my mental image.

He replaced his hands with his lips, kissing my stomach. "Thank you."

۞

TIFFANY LOOKED hungover on our coffee meetup. I sipped my chai and tried to pretend it didn't bother me. I'd never had friend time with another girl before, so I tried to focus on the high points instead of my frustration.

"How do you do it?" she asked as she leaned back in her chair. "How do you hang out with Phoenix and stay sober?"

"It's not really an option for me, " I answered honestly without thinking, and then I wished I'd said anything else.

She perked up, radar focused on my confession. "Why, are you some kind of addict? Dating Phoenix will be hard."

Wow. She is tricky. First impressions can be so wrong. She struck me as the nice one, and Phoenix had suggested our friendship. She might have more in common with her snake boyfriend than I initially thought. Not to mention, she knew Murial had summoned me upstairs, didn't come with me, and didn't even think to tell Phoenix what happened to me. This despite her being supposedly convinced we were together and desperate for news about him.

I wished now that I hadn't come to coffee.

The Poor Relation would have seen through her act sooner, but I sometimes seemed slower on the uptake.

Aloud, I said, "I'm not an addict, but I don't trust people. You heard about my aunt's boyfriend. If I wasn't sober, I don't know how that would've turned out. As for Phoenix, who said I'm dating just him?"

She laughed. "Can you imagine someone trying to take on more than just Phoenix Lent? Alone, he has got to take a ton of energy to maintain. He's probably like my Hal."

A ton of energy to maintain? I wondered if she wasn't mean or manipulative but instead just overwrought.

I'd based my opinions on first impressions for years, thinking shoes told the stories. Despite my theory, I'd read Tiffany wrong. I'd read Bethany wrong. Murial...I didn't think I had read her wrong. Maybe I didn't understand shoes in New York City? Maybe shoes were different in San Francisco and Chicago.

Or maybe I'm just not as smart and clever as I pretend.

I decided to be blunt. "Did Hal ask you to get information on Phoenix? Let's just lay the cards on the table."

She winced. "I'm not very subtle, am I?"

"Nope." I sipped my drink, enjoying the way the chai's spices filled up my tastebuds.

"Sure, Hal wants to know about Phoenix. He misses him. I know he thinks he fucked up, but I don't even know what he did. He won't tell me or talk about it." I kept my expression blank, so she wouldn't guess I knew. I could and would keep Phoenix's private life private, his secrets safe with me. "But he got excited when Phoenix said we should be friends. He figured it was an olive branch."

I shrugged. "I think Phoenix figured we had something in common. He didn't think you participated in a lot of the bullshit, and he wouldn't use me in some secret conversation with Hal. If Hal wants to talk to Phoenix, he should do that instead of trying to send you through me." I pushed back my chair. "I hope you feel better, Tiffany. I'll see you at school."

Her face crumpled, and she reached for my arm. "Listen, I do want to be friends. I mean, I don't really have any friends, I guess. It's been a long time for me. I'm semi popular, so I'm invited places, but then again I'm with Hal. Hal brings the drugs."

"I won't ever tell you anything about Phoenix Lent. Not one thing. If you still want to be my friend despite that, let me know. Otherwise, we tried. No harm, no foul." I smiled, but I could feel the lack of warmth in my expression, more for the act than any genuine emotion.

I'd never had something to protect besides myself before. But I would protect what was mine.

"Do you think I'm dressed okay?" I asked Jeremy as we walked toward the side entrance of the Met.

I had visited the museum twice over the summer, but I didn't know Murial's plan. I had no idea how to dress, or even what she might want.

So I opted for a black dress, simple cotton. I pulled on a

khaki overcoat to keep warm on the walk home. Other than that, I wore black tights and black slip-on shoes and left my hair straight and down. It probably wouldn't stay that way, likely to frizz at the humidity. I added Jeremy's pearls and Phoenix's sapphires, my secret confidence boosters.

"You look beautiful." He squeezed my fingertips, dropping a quick kiss on my temple. "Don't let her make you nervous. If she's shitty, we'll leave."

He wore khakis, a blue business type shirt and a darker navy blazer—surfer dude turned finance bro by just a wardrobe change.

I asked, "Meaning she can't hold me prisoner?"

He laughed. "No one will ever hold you prisoner."

Curious, I asked, "Hey, have you ever surfed?"

He snorted. "Random, but yes, badly. The fathers all tried to bond with us for a little while after Phoenix came home from the hospital after the kidnapping. Eric took us to Hawaii, but Barrett hated it. He stayed in the room the whole time. Julian broke his finger slipping on something wet and complained the whole time, while Phoenix seemed practically catatonic. Prescription drugs, because of his trauma, so it left me to pretend I was happy. I tried to surf. It wasn't pretty."

Wow. He gave me a lot more than I asked for, so I quirked a brow at him. "That sounds awful."

"It was. Particularly for Eric, who honestly believed he could heal us all by flying to Maui. It didn't help that we had to call him Uncle Eric the whole time." He shook his head. "But that was nothing compared to the disaster of Kit taking us to a dude ranch. Oh wow. No. Stephen thought we needed to hike? Patagonia."

I stared at him. "And Daniel?"

"His was the best of the bunch, actually. He chose dirt bikes. We rode dirt bikes for a week, after Phoenix started talking again, too. He said shitty things mostly, but still...he spoke. Our vacations usually suck, if I'm honest."

I lifted a hand, waving at Murial who I spotted up ahead. "I sometimes got brought on attempts at family vacations with my aunts and uncles. I usually tried to be as invisible as possible. The Hamptons was sort of a vacation. For a couple of days, at least."

"Let's go on a real vacation."

I laughed. "Could we go right now? We have school."

Murial wore a nondescript khaki dress and a pair of black heels I didn't recognize. Her perfect ponytail and mascara made me think of a porcelain doll. Next to her, Davis wore almost the same outfit as Jer, but his shirt was white.

All in all, we modeled a page from some catalog for rich kids on the Upper East Side—*proceed with caution*. I didn't know if I should be amused or ashamed for becoming part of the cliché.

"Lent." Davis said then nodded to Jeremy. "Alatheia, you look lovely."

There it is. The creep factor worked its way up my spine as his gaze traced up and down my body. His expression said if he got me alone, he wouldn't let me leave if I said no. Maybe, like Tiffany, I read him wrong. I didn't think so.

"Davis," Jeremy replied, and I turned my attention to Murial.

"Thanks for inviting us to do..." I let my voice trail off, gesturing vaguely toward her.

"One of my uncles is investigating whether or not a painting he purchased was stolen from a Jewish family during the Holocaust. It would be bad taste to keep it, if it was, and he'll return it. I expect press, but it might be a forgery. They're in there now to make the determination. Fake? Or the *real deal*. I thought you might like to see it happen."

The real deal? My hands went cold. *Does she know?*

I met Jeremy's gaze, and he raised his eyebrows. I didn't know if it comforted me or not that he seemed as confused as me.

I nodded, glancing back to Murial with a smile I hoped reached my eyes. "Certainly seems interesting, but I'm not sure I'll be of much use."

"Come," she said simply then waved her hand. "Let's go."

I followed her through a private entrance where the guard nodded at us. Jeremy hung behind me while Davis stayed on my left. I wished I could ask him for space or insist he take two steps away, but Murial led all of us, and I followed. Her heels clicked on the floor, resounding like she owned the place. I glanced around at various patrons considering displays in the museum, and tried to pick out the important ones in the room.

"Is it your father?" I asked Davis, because I had to say something. Social pressure weighed on me like a brick to the chest. "The guy who is having the painting evaluated?"

He shook his head, releasing a half chuckle. "No, my father is a drunk and a buffoon, and he's probably somewhere—who knows where—doing drunken things and buffoonery."

I jerked in surprise at his harsh judgement, especially since it took me a long time to be able to speak about my aunts and uncles with any kind of censure. I'd never heard someone talk about their parent in such a way.

Murial stopped abruptly, and we all also came to a halt, lest we plow into her.

"Here is the situation with my family, since you haven't been informed." She rolled her eyes at Jeremy, as if he failed her completely.

He shrugged. "I'm not sure I know anything about your family, Murial. If I know it, Alatheia knows it, too. Your mother was a super model who married your father, a billionaire. No one has seen either of them in years, and you don't summer in the Hamptons. What am I missing? Oh, Davis is your cousin. What else?"

She sighed loudly. "Yes, to all of that, except for my parents being missing. I've seen them, and I promise, they're not missing. My mother is an only child, while my father had three brothers. He's the oldest. Davis's awful father is in Tokyo, isn't he, darling?" she asked Davis, but plowed onward before he could respond. "Last I heard, anyway. Davis lives with me, and is more like my brother than my cousin. Then there were two other brothers, one of whom is looking into the painting. He stands to make a lot of money if we can keep it. The baby disappeared years ago, and no one knows anything about him. Maybe he is living on an Ashram? Or lost in Alaska? Or married to a shrew in Oklahoma? We have no idea, and we don't care. Granny wrote him off years ago, and we all do what Granny says."

She turned and started walking again, but I stared at Jeremy. I might be new to friendships, but the exchange still struck me as wildly bizarre.

The very rich in New York City are odd people. Not necessarily in a bad way, but very different from people in other places.

Finally, we reached our destination. Murial tapped on the door, hand on her hip.

"Do you just refer to your father as a drunk and buffoon all the time?" Jeremy asked then lifted an eyebrow. "If I said that about mine, I might get punched."

"Yes, well, I wouldn't trifle with Kit Lent, either. Everyone knows not to mess with him." Davis rolled his eyes. "Most people know not to even ask, but pretty Alatheia doesn't know the story. My granny dubbed him that, by the way. Pretty much whatever Granny says is what goes."

They're so strange. I didn't have any grandmothers myself. My maternal ones died, and my mother always said my paternal ones croaked, too. Jeremy had a wonderful granny, even if his mother's parents sounded like they left something to be desired. Despite that, I knew he wouldn't publicly call them names.

The door swung open and a man with red hair stared at us before finally smiling. "Murial, Davis, these are your friends?"

She smiled at him warmly. "Yes, this is Alatheia Winder and Jeremy Lent."

Friends? Stretching it, but okay. I didn't want to get on her bad side, that was it.

Regardless, it seemed to satisfy him. He didn't introduce himself, but we followed him inside. For a place as well laid out as the Met, the room seemed like a lesson in austere chaos. The people who worked there had cluttered the wide space with various art pieces, easels, and lamps casting light, while the walls were lined with shelves holding art reference books. Several magnifying glasses and microscopes were scattered across the tables, and the air smelled faintly of oil paint and varnish. Experts in lab coats didn't acknowledge our presence or even look up from their work when we entered, too focused on their work perhaps.

In that room, masterpieces could either be validated or debunked, the fate of each canvas hanging in the balance.

"How often do they do this?" I whispered to Murial because it seemed appropriate.

She answered me in her full blast voice, which seemed oddly loud in the otherwise quiet room. "I don't know. Uncle Taylor? How often do they do this?"

"Once a month or more, I would think. Not only the Holocaust pieces—although there are at least ten thousand of them still missing, maybe more. I don't claim to be an expert, but there are all sorts of ownership claims." He shook his head. "I don't have a specific number, so I admit, I fabricated that one. I don't want to distract them." Uncle Taylor's gaze fell on me, and he squinted a bit. "You remind me of someone. I can't put my finger on it. Have we met?"

I didn't remember him, but anything was possible. "Have you spent much time in Chicago or San Francisco?"

Jeremy touched the small of my back, the warmth strangely comforting. He said, "I'm sure you haven't met her. When would you have met a teenage girl?"

Taylor narrowed his gaze again but then went back to his consideration of the painting. I had to admit, I was really interested in their process, since it wasn't something I either expected to see nor was it something I thought many got to see in their lifetimes. Jeremy, having delivered that little jab at Taylor, turned his attention to the exam as well. Davis seemed bored, scrolling on his phone. Murial, though, seemed equally rapt.

"What painting is it, or do you know? Or who it might be, if it's not a fake?" I asked her.

Murial smiled. "I *knew* you would like this. It could be a

painting by Maurycy Gottlieb. Are you familiar with his work?"

I'd never heard the name that I remembered. "My art knowledge may be limited. You seem to know a lot more art history than me. I'm sorry I'm so..ignorant about this stuff."

Her slow, perfect grin rewarded me for my honesty. "You are the first person to come to my house and know it was a Rembrandt on sight. I'll update your knowledge about important things, Alatheia. Don't you worry about that."

Oh boy. I realized she officially considered me her project.

I took a deep breath. "Thank you?"

In a storytelling voice, Murial continued. "Maurycy Gottlieb was very popular in Jewish, particularly Polish Jewish, homes right before World War Two. If this is real, my uncle will lose potentially eight hundred thousand dollars in sales, because it technically needs to be returned to the rightful owner. If it's not real, he's out anyway. Still, if it's real, at least he gets to have some good PR when he turns it over."

She sparkled as she spoke. Murial, for whatever reason, lived for the art. "He knows he's lost money either way, but he wants to make up for it in publicity, if he can. Everything and everyone has worth, if you can find it, because everyone wants something." She side-eyed me. "What do you want, Alatheia?"

I pinched my lips closed. No way I would answer that. *Not to her.*

Jeremy touched my hand, reminding me he was there, even if he couldn't hold my hand. I still sensed him, a warmth next to me, as if I glowed brighter due to his proximity.

The curator, a tall man with a groomed beard, held a magnifying glass up to the artwork to squint through the lens. He set the glass down then nodded, not saying a word. Beside him, a female researcher with short black hair carefully adjusted the light shining down on the painting. She spoke into her phone, and I thought she took notes about what she saw.

"They have really interesting jobs," I whispered to Jeremy.

"They do."

❦

IN THE END, they had some more testing to do, but they were pretty sure it was real.

We all exited the room together, with Taylor dashing by us to talk to his publicist. Murial smiled brightly at me. "I knew you would like that."

"I did. I'm still not really clear why you thought I would, but I did." The *real deal* comment from earlier echoed through my thoughts like a ghost, but nothing else she did indicated she meant anything by it. *Maybe she watches the show and picked up the lingo?*

"I read people really well. For example, my cousin likes you a lot, Alatheia, but you don't like him, which only makes Davis like you more. Right, Davis?"

I sucked in my breath, surprised at her bluntness and afraid to steal a glance toward Davis. *Oh boy. So embarrassing. Why is she doing this?* When I finally got the courage to peek at Davis, I noticed his smile showed all his straight teeth. Whatever else he was, Davis wasn't embarrassed in the least.

"True," he agreed easily with a careless shrug.

"That said, I can't figure out you and the Lents. You say you aren't dating, and I believe you. Yet they remain really interested in you in a way that just doesn't feel platonic."

Jer rocked back on his feet, hands tucked in his pockets as he smiled at her. "Well, she's a really interesting person. You've obviously taken a strong interest in her, too."

I hoped he wouldn't trigger her temper. They might be part of her world, as she said, but I wasn't. The only one who could get hurt in the situation was me, which felt like a really important factor for him to remember. I decided it might be safer to ignore her comment about Davis liking me, since I didn't know how to define my relationship with the Lents either, beyond that I loved them. Instead, we could focus on safer topics.

So I said, "I am their granny's companion, but you knew that. It's a little old fashioned, but have you ever read that book. . ."

She interrupted me and said, "I guarantee I haven't. I don't read if it isn't required by school. Art is my thing. Why bother with reading?"

Does she really want me to answer? "There are all kinds of art. Everything speaks to us in different ways. Think about art, or reading... I like music and plays, too."

"Boring." She sighed and her gaze swiveled to Jeremy. "You what? Met her at your granny's?"

He shook his head. "Why are you so interested, anyway?"

"I like stories." She smiled at me. "Maybe I *should* read."

I preferred her focus on me rather than Jeremy. I couldn't believe we just chatted in a random hallway of the Met. "I met Julian at his granny's, and later on, I met Jeremy through Julian. Eventually, I met Barrett and Phoenix the same way."

She tapped her foot then started walking. I didn't know where she was headed, but I followed her. "Not very interesting, actually. But I do find it sort of curious how you brought Jeremy today. Barrett is usually right and proper all the time, while Julian is nice to everyone. God knows if Phoenix even knows what's going on most of the time, but you brought Jeremy. The one who already made his way through all of my friends."

He jolted next to me, instantly going stiff at the mention of his former hookups. It didn't bother me, but it clearly bothered him. "I have done no such thing."

"You know you have," she practically purred, her tone saccharine sweet, but it came across just gross. "I mean, Maggie didn't lose her shit like that over nothing, and I think we both know better."

He sighed. "Maggie is always losing her shit. It's why she got suspended sophomore year. She set the bathrooms on fire."

She did what? I opened and closed my mouth. Why would he hook up with someone like her in the first place? I didn't ask aloud though, making a mental note to ask when we were alone.

"And Greer..."

He interrupted. "Hooks up with everyone, which you know. She thought she hooked up with Julian. She didn't even know it was me."

"That *is* true." She nodded, tapping her chin with one elegant finger. "I guess my point here, Alatheia, is that you want to be careful with this one. He has no regard for the hearts he leaves shattered in his wake."

She couldn't have been more wrong about Jeremy, but I didn't argue. He felt things so deeply, so acutely. He kept so much of his life hidden from the world, so she would never be able to truly understand how hard life could be for him. The guys each found a way to cope. Barrett walked a line so nobody questioned him about his family. Julian people-pleased, kissing asses with a charm that could make their head spin. He charmed them so well, in fact, that they stopped wondering about the scandal with Phoenix. Their youngest brother took substances to avoid the realm and the rest of us most of the time, preferring a world without his trauma, dulled by narcotics. Meanwhile, Jeremy ran around trying to protect everyone else. I got lucky and saw him in the moments when he could lose himself for a while.

Although lately, they seemed to be switching it up. Julian

was getting angry and into fights while Phoenix tried to get off the drugs. And Jeremy remained romantic and there for me whenever I needed him.

But to Murial, I simply said, "I don't want to talk about their family. Not ever, I mean it. They're very good people and my friends." She didn't need to know how precisely close I got to the brothers. I tapped my lip with my own finger, mimicking her motion from earlier. "But I do have an idea. How about if we go see the two Michiel Sweerts paintings? I've been reading about him, so I know they have two of his works here. I looked him up online after you pointed him out next to the Rembrandt. I mean, how cool is it that you have one of his one hundred paintings, when some sources say it could be as low as forty or fifty?"

She brightened immediately. "Oh, Alatheia, you did! You listened and researched. *Yes*, there are so few of them. My uncle found one when I wanted it then Daddy bought it for me." It just blew my mind, but I didn't say it aloud. If I had that kind of money, I would do something charitable with it. I wouldn't line my walls with paintings, not even treasured ones, but I wasn't there to judge. *Okay, maybe I am a little bit. She certainly judges everyone else around her.* "Yes, maybe only half of his work is in private collections. It's hard to verify, because people don't like to talk too much about what they have in their own homes."

Well...she does.

I smiled anyway, and let her lead us toward the Sweerts paintings. I distracted her for the moment, but I still didn't understand her objectives, nor did I know what she wanted from me. I was really unimportant to her level of life, less important than an insect. *So why bother with me at all?*

Finally, she turned back to face Jer. He lifted his eyebrows, stiffening like he was ready to take a blow. She explained, "You're not my type. Your friend Alatheia is over there. As beautiful as she is, she's actually not who I want to be with. But I'm not done with you all, either."

He cleared his throat. "You really must be bored."

"Aren't we all? It's the nature of things. Everyone wants things, but there's so little we can't have, right? Perhaps we want Alatheia for a while. I don't know if you're taking pity on her because of your granny—"

He interrupted. "You're nowhere close."

"I know I need new friends, because Greer is stupid and Maggie is crazy. They might have become that way because of you, so you could take responsibility. Alatheia won't tell me what she wants, so I'm likely to be frustrated until I figure it out."

Davis grinned as he joined us. "Me. She wants me. She just doesn't know it yet."

I tried to keep my expression blank, but I frowned in response. *Not in the slightest. Ew, actually.* It was one of the few things I knew for sure.

☙❦❧

MURIAL AND DAVIS left in a waiting black car before Jer pulled me into a tight hug.

"I love you, " he whispered in my ear before he shuddered against me.

I held on tightly, as if I could ground him in the present with me. "I don't care what she said about you. She doesn't know you."

"I care what you hear, though. I shouldn't have done some of that shit, but I never pretended to have long-term feelings for anyone before you. I didn't, regardless of what they might say. Could you even imagine explaining my family to Maggie?"

I giggled at the thought then put my head on his shoulder.

He smelled so warm and safe. "Jer, why Maggie? I mean, she's nuts. Clearly. It seems like you knew that, so why her?"

"I don't know, actually." He kissed the top of my head. "I did a lot of stupid shit. Maybe I wanted to avoid things I can't control and didn't know how to handle? I'm sorry that isn't much of an answer." A car horn sounded near us, and I jumped, which made him laugh gently in my ear. "I've got you, Princess. There's no one else for me. Nothing meaningless, just you. Forever."

"I don't care who you were with before, I really don't. I understand people will throw them in my face at Pullman , partially because they want to see if they get a response, since they don't know what we're doing. Maybe she tried to warn me off?" I still didn't understand her, and I shook my head, not sure if I should ever understand her. "Anyway, hopefully she'll move on to something new. Everything you said was incredibly sweet. I'm trying. Okay? I think you know how I feel about you, but it's hard to let myself relax. We can blame trauma, if you like. If I don't get sent away, I'll calm down a lot. Be patient with me."

He kissed my temple, and I practically sagged against him. I loved melting into him, until he basically held us both upright.

"Always. Always. What do you want? I mean, you won't tell her, but will you tell me?"

I lifted my head to kiss him on the lips, which made him smile. "For now? I want that. Thank you for coming with me."

❦

"SOMETHING'S WRONG WITH PHOENIX, and I don't know...I just *know*." Julian chewed on his lip then ran a hand through his hair, pacing back and forth as if he couldn't stay still. I blew out a breath, realizing his stress meant my movie plan wouldn't happen. We kept saying we would take an afternoon off, maybe go see a movie, but it didn't seem to be in the cards for us.

Jer crossed his arms over his chest, considering his brother carefully. "What do you mean?"

Barrett entered from the kitchen, his expression also creased with worry. "I think he took something else. Not the regular K-hole, I think he took something else. Seems really off."

I widened my eyes, glancing between the brothers quickly. "Should we call an ambulance? Call Eric? What do we do?"

Julian shook his head. "I don't know. They threatened him, so if he gets in trouble again, he's gone. I'm not calling our parents unless we lose his pulse."

I decided I wouldn't know more until I saw Phoenix, who was in his room. I found him pacing from one end of it to the other in large, measured strides, his head down as he seemed to talk to himself. "Phoenix? You okay?"

He couldn't seem to hear me past the voices in his mind, still muttering to himself.

"See?" Julian and Jeremy said from behind me.

I ignored them, focused on their brother. I grabbed his arm. "Phoenix? Are you okay?"

His eyes focused on my face, but he didn't seem to see me. "I have to find Alatheia before they take her to the dark place."

He wants to find me? "I'm right here. I'm talking to you. We're together right now."

Jer whistled through his teeth. "He's on a dark trip somewhere. Did he go anywhere while we were out?"

"To Joe's. I can text him, see if he knows what he took. Good call. Don't bother trying, since he won't answer you and will probably hide for days because he's terrified of you."

Jules left the room, phone in hand. I wasn't nearly as worried about the drugs as the fact Phoenix genuinely seemed afraid. My heart turned over, and I gripped his hands, tempted to weep for him. I'd seen him freaked out about rainstorms, and sometimes in his sleep he said he needed to find his way home. *This is different.* He might have been afraid then, but he knew where he was in the storm. His dreams evaporated if I stroked his head or kissed him gently. In this case, I didn't know how to find him, but I knew he was lost in a dark place.

I wrapped my arms around him to stop his frenetic motion. He struggled a bit against me, saying, "They're going to take her to the dark place. I can't let them take her, you don't understand. I'll find her, if they take her. Somehow."

"Yeah," Julian said, and I realized he talked to someone on the phone in the other room. Hopefully Joe, and he had answers. "What?"

I rocked back and forth with Phoenix, still holding his wiry frame against me. "Come on. Let's go sit in the living room. On the couch. We're home. I am with you, and neither of us are in a dark place."

With Jer's help, I led him into the living room. Phoenix dropped to the couch then took his head in his hands, rocking back and forth.

Julian whirled around, holding the phone away from his mouth. "It's just THZ, but he said, and I quote, *everyone is going dark with it, man.* Including his boy Avery, apparently."

Barrett grabbed the phone, aggression so clear in his motions that Julian actually backed up a step. "This is Barrett. Listen, dipshit, don't you ever fucking give my brother anything that takes him dark again. I don't blame you for his choices, but I can judge you for what you chose to sell to him. I get that if you're not his dealer, it would be someone else, and we both know you like the money. But let me make myself *very* clear. If you ever give him anything, and I mean *any*thing, that takes him dark again, it won't be Jeremy you should be scared of anymore."

When he hung up, he was panting, his eyes wild when they turned to me and his pupils huge. With a slow, slightly shaking hand, he handed the phone back to Julian. I held Phoenix and stared at Barrett. *Prim and proper?* Wasn't that how Murial described Barrett? *Yeah...she doesn't know them at all.*

❧ 18 ❧

Phoenix rocked back and forth on the couch, his head in his hands, despite my best efforts. Sometimes he muttered about a dark place, swatting at invisible hands reaching for him. I stroked his back. I wanted to scream, since there wasn't much else I could do for him, other than be with him until it ended.

Barrett said, "This is THC, a kind of marijuana. It shouldn't be doing this to him."

I knew very little about drugs, so I shrugged, useless in the conversation.

Jeremy stared out the window as if he might see the answers on the street below. "It's synthetic, so it can happen, unfortunately."

"Didn't he tell us once that Joe was *quote unquote safe?*" Julian sat on the floor in front of Phoenix, touching his brother's knees gently. "Isn't that what he told us years ago? That's why he went to him for his stuff? Wasn't that the whole point? No bad mixtures? No fentanyl. All of it was supposed to be *fine.*"

Barrett drummed on the piano, turning to music to try to soothe his nerves. I didn't know the song, but the melody was sad, and it matched my mood. We all stayed with Phoenix right then, and he was lost in the dark alone.

"How would Phoenix know it would go bad?" Jeremy didn't turn around, gaze locked on the lawn. "I mean I ate it up, just like you all did. He fed us a line, and it was exactly what we wanted to hear. As if we could pretend there were *safe* drugs or a *safe* drug dealer when we all knew it was bullshit."

Barrett's hands faltered and he missed a note. For a few seconds, he stilled his hands, breathing deeply through his nose before his fingers started rolling over the keys again.

Julian grabbed his brother's knee, demanding his attention. "K2 is illegal. If we call Eric, it's over."

"Give it more time. It's probably almost over." Jeremy still stared outside, but suddenly I wondered if it only was because he didn't want to look at Phoenix.

I grabbed Dina's journal off the table, deciding I would read while we waited for him to ride out the drug's dark place. I needed something—anything—to distract me from reality. I kept my hand on Phoenix's back while I began to read.

ॐ

SEPTEMBER 1ST, 1966

Marriage is an adjustment? I knew it would be true before I married them, but, boy, is it a hard lesson to learn in reality. Once we were away from my mother-in-law's and her rules, we decided to invent our own rules. One of them is they don't seem to think that I should work. I find it particularly funny, because I always assumed I would be working. Even when I attended boarding school, I expected to have to get a job someday.

Then again, I didn't get to finish school, which made things complicated. Still, I am quite capable. Money is tight, the men preparing to launch the first store—which is fine, as I am not one to spend much money, usually. But I could help them. They disagree, claiming I should be setting up our house. We set up the damn house already. Oh, did I mention we moved? Did I forget to mention that? We moved to Riverdale, in the Bronx. We could afford a little more space and two other families like ours live in the area nearby. I intend to meet them shortly, perhaps I'll bring along a gift from one of the stores?

They aren't close friends of the Lents, because they moved away from the lake before the Lents made their wealth. However, after a few overtures by Victor, we got invited to a dinner. I'll let you know how it goes.

Our house is a brick row house, which means one of our walls attaches to that of our neighbor. They are perfect for us, though, since he can't hear, is always shouting, and she can't see very well. They haven't even looked strangely at our four-bedroom paradise in the Bronx.

But the house is dull when they work all day and leave me here. I cook for them, which takes up some time, and they compliment my efforts at length. Perhaps they hope I'll just get pregnant soon, thereby distracting myself with something to do at home. Perhaps I hope for that, as well. . . It would fill the time. I can imagine a child with their faces, their eyes, running down the halls and laughing. I also discovered I prefer to fill my time and become desperately bored without occupation.

But I do love them so.

I think I shall paint all the downstairs walls red today.

They might hate it, but they probably won't tell me, because they want me to be happy. I'll know if they hate it, though. If they suddenly all get busy doing other things, refusing to sit in the rooms. . . Yes, I need activity, so for now, I'll paint the walls red. Tomorrow? Who knows?

DL

I THOUGHT of the red walls in her beautiful apartment on the Upper East Side, the same building where my aunt lived. Julian warned me within seconds of meeting him that they didn't like it if people made fun of their granny's wall color. Personally, I loved it—so warm and vivid all at the same time. In our current home, trees crawled up the walls, a fantasy forest painted by their mother for them. *Painting the walls must be a Lent woman thing.* I smiled at the thought. If I ever painted the walls in my own home, I would paint them red, too. *For Dina, the first woman to be nice to me in five years. Half a decade of time, holy cow.*

"What is Granny doing?" Julian asked. "What is she up to in there, anyway? Can you tell me any of it?"

I could be vague, but I wasn't going to share a story she wanted to tell in her own words. It warmed me that she'd been shocked I kept her secrets already.

"They moved to the Bronx," I said and smiled at him. "I've never been there. Have you?"

He lifted his eyebrows. Jeremy joined us, crossing his legs to sit next to Jules. He said, "I forgot she lived there. I never think of her as living anywhere except her apartment, but that's just because she's lived there my whole memorable life."

Barrett stopped playing and joined us, sitting on the other

side of Julian. "The pictures in her bedroom are all from their time in the Bronx. I never ask her much about them, or about our grandfathers. I feel terrible about that, but all I honestly know is they had a better relationship with their parents than we have with ours."

Phoenix lifted his head and raised his hand, as if getting attention in a class. "That is probably because of me." He grimaced. "Sorry. For that and this."

I kissed his cheek. "Are you okay? Are you *you*? Are you thirsty? Need anything?"

"No." He sighed. "I'm sorry. What was I doing? You all look like someone died."

Barrett got to his feet and clenched his fists, his caged fury reminding me of his more temperamental brothers. "Probably because all four of us feared you were going to die. You might still die." He repeated it. "And you fucking scared us, okay?"

He stormed from the room, and Phoenix caught his breath then gulped. For a second, I wondered if he would cry. Instead, he leaned back against the couch, staring at the ceiling. "I fucked up again, when this time, I was actually trying to see if I could make things better."

Barrett reentered the room carrying a leather backpack he used for school. "I'm going to the library."

Phoenix managed to stumble to his feet. "Barrett, I'm sorry. I am so sorry I scared you. All of you."

His brother breathed heavily, his knuckles still white because his hands were bunched into tense fists. "You kept saying you needed to get to Alatheia. You were afraid they would take her to the dark place. What is the dark place?"

Phoenix ran a hand through his hair, closing his eyes as if trying to remember. "It's the only thing I can describe about where they took me. I guess. . .I thought they were going to take Alatheia?"

Julian stood. "Who are *they*?"

Phoenix shrugged, blowing out a frustrated breath. "No idea, just a general sense of *them*. A *they*. I can't describe it better, and I've tried in therapy." Usually, he ran away by that point in discussing his issues. If we challenged Phoenix on anything, he tended to bolt. Instead, he told his brother, "It was a dark place, but that's all I know. I can't..." He took a deep breath. "I really can't come up with anything else about it. But I can't have them taking you, Red. I can't. What would I do if they came for you?"

I wrapped my arms around him again, surprised at how damp his tee shirt felt, drenched in sweat. "No one is taking me anywhere. Especially not like that. If anyone makes me go any place, you can come with me. You told me that, that you would find me anywhere. I believe you."

He kissed my head. "Thank you. Yes, I would. I...I thought maybe I could just do weed. People are stoned all day every day, so I could take gummies. Smoke it. Eat it. Whatever. I could just spend all day a little bit stoned, blur everything away, and no one would notice. I figured it would be better than what I've been doing, anyway."

Jeremy stared at him, his face blank with shock. "You thought you could just stop and swap drugs? Like a replacement drug?"

Phoenix gave a one-armed shrug, his expression sheepish. "I read something about it, thought it might work. Leave it to Joe to give me some kind of dark weed the first time I tried it. I didn't intend to semi relive the worst time of my life, especially not with a special guest from the future, so I lost my girl, too."

Barrett dropped his backpack with a thud, the fight drooping out of him. "We can get you help. We can talk to Eric—"

"They'll send me away. I don't mean to rehab and back,

like half of our classmates. I know them, and they will send me away from here. They will make me leave you guys. Leave Alatheia. By the time I get back, it'll be too late for me with her, and you know it. You'll all be cemented into your roles in the relationship and I'll be gone. I know I said I didn't want to do this, before I met her, but I do. I don't want to be on the outside. I can't leave. Do you understand?"

Barrett hugged his brother, which meant I had to let go, but I didn't mind. I sniffled, glad they shared the moment.

"I let you down. I let them take you," Barrett said, tears running down his cheeks as he wept into his brother's neck. Julian audibly sucked in a breath.

The moment charged with electricity, intense emotions filling the room in a way that never happened. I rubbed my arms, feeling part of something, too.

"No," Phoenix said roughly and gripped him back like his life depended on it.

"You don't get it. We all had friends in that group. From the lake, among the people who came up every year."

His younger brother wept, too. "Yeah, I know. Mine died. Walter and River died."

"Yes, they did, but it wasn't your fault. It's mine. I wanted to be alone with my friends, and I didn't let you all hang out with me. I tried to look cool, because one of my so-called friends called me a rich loser. Tess? Anyway, I heard our fathers talking about Tess possibly being the girl for all of us, and I hated her. But, still, fuck, if I had to marry her, she should at least find me cool. So to impress her, I told you to get away, hoping for alone time with Tess and Gordan. Instead, someone took you."

"No!" Julian's shout caught all of our attention, and we stared as tears ran down his face. "We were ten, eleven, and twelve. We never should've been allowed on the beach at midnight alone. You were *twelve*. You weren't responsible for us. You were a kid, but that's not what you tell yourself, is it, Barrett? Even now. For years, you handled things, leaving us alone in the apartment because you thought you should take care of us since you were about fifteen. No, I won't let you spend one more day taking responsibility for what happened. Some sick bad person or people took our brother, but he lived. We don't know why yet, but thank you to the universe or god or whatever for it. Beyond that, every single *adult* was responsible for what happened. Every single one."

We all breathed hard, emotion riding us as if we ran a race. Julian continued, saying, "Phoenix, I wouldn't ever move on without you. If they sent you somewhere, we would just wait for you to come home. Otherwise, I go with you. Okay? Hell, we'll all go with you. We don't do this without you anymore. It's all of us or nothing." He smacked down his fist, and his brothers covered it with their own, making a stack until they broke with laughter.

He wiped at his face, staring at me. "Thank you. I love you."

"Don't thank me," I said, but my voice wavered.

"Well, this is a lot of emotion for people who pretend we feel nothing but disdain." Jeremy squeezed Phoenix's arm. "You don't know they would send you away, but we can't guarantee they wouldn't. None of us will ever really know what they would or wouldn't do. Let's get out of here."

His abrupt shift must have hit all of us strangely, because the room fell silent. Finally, Barrett laughed. "Where do you propose we go?"

Jeremy shrugged, stuffing his hands in his pockets. "Dinner in Riverdale. In honor of Granny. Makes sense to me."

Actually, I loved the idea. "Should we invite her?"

"She's away," Barrett answered. It didn't surprise me in the least that he would know. "She is in Westport with friends."

"Then in her honor without her." Phoenix grinned. He must have liked the idea. "But why are we going to the Bronx for Dina?"

Barrett laughed and patted him on the back. "Still a little bit out of it?"

"Yeah, but not in a dark way. Kind of what I was hoping for in general." He shrugged. "So, why the Bronx?"

"She used to live there, back when she first got married."

He nodded. "Okay, sounds good. Let's move. You learn about it from the journal?"

"I did."

Julian sighed. "He gave you dark weed, let's call it that. Darkweed, like it's one word."

"Look at the writer, coming up with creative names." He pounded on Julian's shoulder, and he outright laughed.

The darkness vanished, banished from the apartment by their laughter. I glanced at Jeremy, realizing he liked to take care of everyone else. He fixed, so I hugged him. He startled, then squeezed me against his body. Once I spun out of his arms, I hugged Julian for his eloquent ability to address the elephant in the room. He wasn't wrong; the adults had fucked up the situation, and we were left with the fallout.

He kissed my forehead. "Love you, Baby."

Finally, I hugged Barrett, breathing his steady scent deep into my lungs. "I wasn't there, but I know for a fact it wasn't your fault. Also, can I just point out how gross it is if they were matchmaking you at twelve?"

He shook his head. "Right? It's probably always going to feel like it was my fault, but thank you, Sweetheart. I love you. I love having you here."

Finally, I hugged Phoenix again, sighing my way back into his arms. "You scared me. I'm so glad you were trying for a change you hoped would help. I mean it. If they sent you away, it would leave a gaping hole in our lives. There's no moving on without you, so don't ever worry about that."

He kissed the end of my nose. "Okay, I believe you. Thank you. I love you."

I sighed, relaxing into his touch. They felt like home, and if I was honest, I felt safe. As if for once the world might not rip me away from where I wanted to be...

He blinked. "How was the Met with Murial?

I laughed. "*So* weird. I mean so, so weird." I stepped away, grinning up at him. "I don't think I can express how weird."

Jeremy patted Phoenix on the back. "Davis is in love with her."

Phoenix growled. "I hate that fucker."

I grinned. *Okay. Phoenix is back.*

๑๑๑

THEY PICKED an Irish Pub for dinner, but none of them bothered to pull out fake IDs. They ordered sodas and water, but I wasn't sure if it was because of the scary bartender or for my sake.

Dina lived there with her husbands once, and she painted her downstairs red. *Mostly because she was bored.* I tried to imagine Dina bored, and couldn't imagine her sitting still long enough to get bored. She always seemed to be in motion, going somewhere or doing something, thinking about things, and helping in some way. I tried to imagine leaving her home to tend the house, and I giggled.

"You're thinking about something?" Julian asked and tapped my foot.

Barrett grinned. "I noticed, too, but I'm less rude."

"I would share, but it's meant to be a surprise from Dina to all of you, so I can't. I was thinking about her life, that's all."

I glanced out the window then, just turning my head, and the flash of glass caught my eye. That's when I spotted the figure outside with a camera. I groaned and pointed with my thumb. "It's the PI. He's out there right now."

"Really?" Barrett leaned across the table to try to spot him. "That's him?"

I forgot only Phoenix and I had ever seen him before, so I pointed and clarified. "That's him. The last time we saw him, Phoenix gave him the finger."

Jeremy snorted. "You did?"

"Yeah, totally. Watch, I'll do it again." He sat forward and extended his middle finger so that the PI could snap pictures through the window. All three of the guys did the same and I cracked up. I didn't bother to give him the finger. I wouldn't risk doing anything that could get me sent away. They couldn't stop the Lents from being profane, but I would be in serious trouble..maybe. I honestly didn't know any of the rules or where my barriers might actually be.

I chewed on my bottom lip. "I hope Kit can get me some answers this week."

I would love to know why they're having a high school student followed.

I turned away from the window, though, refusing to worry about it. Let them take pictures of us eating dinner and walking through parks. We didn't say anything incriminating or even so much as hold hands. Overall, probably the most benign day ever, once we left the apartment. Luckily, they couldn't get pictures of us at home, because I wouldn't want ones for Phoenix's sake. I didn't know what my family would do to him out of spite and meanness.

Or to fuck with me, because they know it would hurt me if they hurt him.

"I think we should try to get some Knicks tickets. I want

to see them in the Garden," Jeremy said and played with his straw. "You know you all want to go with me."

I tried to focus on the moment, on the conversation, and the company of the men around me. *Knicks are...basketball?*

❧

OUR LIVES FELL into a routine again, which I loved. The explosion of feelings over Phoenix's darkweed experience cooled down the world around us, like a thunderstorm leading into cooler autumnal temperatures. Kit promised to talk to me at the twin s' birthday dinner about some things he found out. In the meantime, I at least had a health insurance card for my medical needs, which was a huge relief.

I got texts every morning from Murial—usually pictures of paintings she thought I should learn about. Sometimes, I did her homework, but only if I liked the look of them. Bethany's morning texts usually were about her OOTD—I was so bad at social media, I didn't know it meant *outfit of the day* until Julian kissed me and explained it. I didn't expect her sense of humor, but I appreciated it. Tiffany still sent me texts here and there, also about artwork. If I had to have one consistent conversation with her, I wasn't upset it turned out to be about art.

We would be losing a water polo match at the end of the week. Sarah was stressed about it, so if I could magically become a better player just to perk her up, I would. Unfortunately, I had pretty much plateaued. The twins were still ranked number one in New York after their beating in California, which was nice.

Then Julian had to stay home in the mornings, not going in early anymore because of a shoulder injury. Jeremy sometimes faked it to get extra time at home, but Julian really got hurt, so it worried me.

I pressed the ice to his shoulder while he leaned against the counter, my legs bracketing him as I sat there. Being Jules, he remained cheerfully pleasant despite his pain.

"Just think, maybe it's a real permanent issue. Maybe something with a growth plate or something. Then, I won't have to play the rest of the season."

I shook my head, rolling my eyes at his theatrics. "You would still go cheer and advise. You're the captain. Besides, if it is serious, it might mean surgery. That would suck."

"It would." He sighed. "But I love *this*. Not the ice, but leaning between your legs in the kitchen is sort of heaven."

Phoenix thumped around the kitchen, uncharacteristically grumpy. He woke up that way, so he noisily clattered coffee cups and grumbled as he went to get coffee.

"Something wrong?" I asked. He hadn't slept well since the darkweed incident, bad dreams plaguing him each night. I usually awoke to him gasping, trying to protect me, so I held him when I noticed.

He shook his head. "Honestly? I'm kind of pissed because Julian is home right now."

I blinked, surprised. "Really?"

Jules sighed. "Why is that?"

"Because this is *my* alone time with her. Every morning, before school. We have a routine, and you're breaking it."

He poured coffee into his cup, scowling the entire time. He handed me a coffee, but he ignored his brother—*intentionally not getting him one*, I thought.

"You have alone time with her all day long. We can't even see her in the hallway. Not to mention, you sleep next to her every night. I hurt my fucking shoulder, so I am not going to feel bad because I get a few extra minutes with Alatheia for the next couple of days."

Phoenix glared at him. "Don't act like you wouldn't be feeling the same way if I infringed on your time with her."

"I *have* no solo time with her. Actually, I intend to take some tomorrow, and thanks for the reminder."

He didn't lie, since it was their birthday. They said what they wanted from me was one-on-one time. Their plan? I would stay in bed to watch movies with Jules all day then go out with Jeremy in the evening. That would be after their family dinner, but nobody bothered to fill me in on the specifics of what they considered that to mean.

I also had to make a cake.

I didn't know how to respond to them fighting for my time, so I got tense, because anxiety was my coping mechanism. I decided to ask Dina, since she had experience being an outsider then marrying into a close-knit group of brothers.

For the moment, I should at least say something. "When you get like this over me, it makes me nervous inside. I worry I'm not giving you sufficient attention, and things will explode. Regardless, the only logical solution will be to get rid of me."

Only a few weeks ago, I wouldn't have found the courage to admit it to them, but I wasn't sure it meant an improvement that I did.

I rushed to add, "I know you'll say it's not true, that you would never, but I needed to tell you how I feel. You guys can believe what you want, okay?"

Julian moved to stand shoulder-to-shoulder with Phoenix. "You already know what we will say? You just told us you do, and I never knew you were psychic. It must come in handy. Meanwhile, Phoenix and I have been swiping at each other verbally since we were old enough to talk. He's the baby who made me give up my pacifier."

He scrunched up his face at his brother, nudging him with his shoulder. "What the fuck are you talking about?"

"You were born, and they decided I was too old for a pacifier. At a mere thirteen months of age, yet they ripped it away. . .because of you."

Phoenix stared in bafflement at Julian. "You can't possibly remember that."

"No, but Granny told me about it." He smiled. "She wanted to make sure I didn't forget, so I could hold my resentment forever."

Phoenix actually laughed then poured Julian a cup of coffee.

I took a deep breath, because somehow, it all still worked.

✣ 19 ✣

"How's the baking going?" Barrett whispered in my ear. I almost jumped out of my skin. He'd been at school, one of his late nights, so I was alone in the kitchen making a homemade cake for the twins. Or trying. It was ridiculous. They had a Michelin starred chef cook their birthday dinner before, and with my lack of experience, I was attempting to follow a recipe from a cookbook. It likely would be a disaster.

I glanced at their older brother, who I adored so much, and confessed, "This may not be my thing."

"Can I help?" He squeezed me from behind, nuzzling into my neck, and I decided I enjoyed his brand of assistance. He so rarely showed easy affection. I turned in his arms to note his loose muscles and easy expression..*totally relaxed.*

"Good day?" I asked.

"Good now."

He hoisted me up onto the counter next to the bowl where I was trying to make icing. I scooped some of the chocolate out of the bowl onto my finger and offered it to him with a wink. "Want to taste?"

Holding eye contact the whole time, he bent over and licked it off my finger, wrapping his tongue around the digit and sizzling my nerve endings. I gasped, heat rising in my body as my heartbeat raced. I wanted him. . .and them. When should I tell them we could try more than just kissing?

I figured if I got brave enough to say it aloud, it meant I would be brave enough to do it.

I dipped my finger back into the bowl, reveling in his reaction. He did it again, closing his eyes and moaning as he laved my finger and then bit the end.

Practically transfixed, I watched him with hot cheeks. The twins were at water polo—I had skipped their game to bake—and Phoenix was at Joe's, leaving us utterly alone in the apartment. For some reason, the knowledge we were alone made me brave, so I took what I needed from him.

I wrapped my arms around him and drew him closer to me, pulling him between my legs so his hardness bumped up against me. Without hesitating, I kissed him, my lips hungry for his mouth and my tongue bold.

He responded with equal enthusiasm, pushing me back at first, but when he tried to pull away to give us time to breathe, I didn't let him. Instead, I twined my legs around his waist and ground up against him. Barrett took the hint.

He kissed and *kissed* me, his hand fondling my breast until I gasped for him. His whiskers scraped at my cheek and neck as he dragged open mouthed kisses over my skin until I sizzled with heat for him.

Barrett picked me up and carried me over to the couch. Once he lay on top of me, he picked up where he had left off. As he dragged my shirt lower, revealing my shoulder blades, I couldn't get enough of him.

I kissed him, my mouth hungry for whatever tastes I could find. I memorized his flavor, knowing I would be addicted to it. He tugged on my shirt and then stopped, meeting my gaze with concern. "This okay?"

I nodded. "Yes, I want your hands on me."

He kissed my lips again. Once. Then twice. "You always set the rules. I get to be here with you. It's amazing."

I didn't want to set rules, but I couldn't lose my head until I got some kind of birth control from the doctor. *Not just yet.* He pulled my shirt over my head and his gaze traveled over my chest, taking in my black bra. My cheeks heated, the hunger in his gaze so obvious. I wanted him to touch me so much but did he. . .*think I am pretty like this?*

He met my gaze, whispering reverently, "You're so beautiful." His voice sounded hoarse. "Can I?" He motioned toward my bra. "We could be skin-to-skin."

Since it meant he would take his shirt off too, I nodded. "Sure."

"Pants still on." I didn't know if he said it to reassure me or to remind himself. Either way, I wasn't worried in the least.

Then again, maybe he was reminding me, too.

I tugged at his shirt while he fiddled with my bra. Both went flying, and I gasped as his body was revealed to me. Barrett was strong, with defined muscles. I ran my hands over his abs, amazed when his skin seemed to jolt where I touched him.

"Just in case you wonder what you do to me," he said, and placed my hand lower. He felt very hard under my hand.

I bit down on my bottom lip. "You know I have no experience, and you have some so..."

He shook his head. "Everything is new with you. Everything."

Barrett pressed his body into me, touching our chests together, skin to skin, heartbeat to heartbeat. He licked his tongue over my bottom lip before he kissed me again. Over and over, until I felt drunk on the taste of him. I kissed him back, my enthusiasm and curiosity making up for my inexperience for the most part. Sometimes I led, sometimes he did, until we both squirmed with needs building inside. I could feel the hard press of him practically pulsing against me with promise. My body was hot, maybe hotter than ever before, so I jerked against him, seeking some relief. My nipples hardened, and he reached between us to stroke my breasts.

His body seemed to vibrate, and the sounds he made deepened. I ground against him while pressure surged inside of me. I needed...something. I wasn't sure how to reach for it. But it was *so close*. I dug my fingernails into his back, gasping with the unexplained need.

He stopped moving to stare down at me, and I practically mewled in complaint. "I love you. I'm never going to forget this." He kissed my chin, pinning my wandering hands above my head. "We need to stop."

"Why?" I asked with a pout, jerking my hips into him again so we both moaned. I really didn't want to stop. I wanted him to kiss me again, hungry for more of him.

He thumbed my lips. "Because I'm getting too excited. I've got to take a breath, Baby. Believe me, it's not lack of interest."

I growled at him, even if it made sense. He kissed me one more time, as if he couldn't resist one last taste. "And you have icing to make, right?"

Shit. Yes, I did.

BARRETT HELPED WITH THE ICING, and since he was good at absolutely everything, of course it came out perfect. We cleaned up together, still touching as much as possible. I put the cake in the oven, crossing my fingers it came out okay.

"Come on," he said and jerked his head for me to follow. *Where are we going?*

He sat on the piano bench then patted the seat so I would sit next to him. He kissed my cheek when I sat, lingering for a second while electricity charged the air between us. Things had changed a little bit between us, although I couldn't define it. *Can he?*

"Do you play?" he asked, his voice low.

"No. Piano lessons never came up when I was young, and since Mom died, well. . .nobody really bothered with stuff like that." I smiled. "I like hearing you play. It makes this place feel like home, because wherever you go, there is music."

"You mean me stumbling through songs?" He shook his head. "I like to play, but I am by no means very good." He touched a key. "This is middle C."

The city lights touched his profile, carving out his face as if from ivory. I considered his handsome face carefully as he watched me, and finally I asked, "Are you going to teach me to play?"

"I am."

The door swung open as the twins got home from school, Jer coming to an abrupt halt as soon as he spotted us. "Why does it smell like something is baking?"

He dropped his bag on the floor and Barrett laughed. "Because something *is* baking. She's making your cake."

"Well, I am trying at least. It will probably be awful," I confessed, and Julian dropped a kiss on my cheek.

"Nothing you've made has been awful."

I shook my head. "You lie or you have an iron stomach."

Jeremy slid down on the couch as Phoenix got home, flopping onto the chair as soon as he arrived. "Hey, something smells good. I'm hungry."

Barrett kissed my cheek again, whispering in my ear, "Another time."

I shivered because he was right, wasn't he? *More times.* The idea made me hot, suddenly, in the way his kisses made me hot.

Julian yawned. "You guys look awful cozy."

Phoenix held up his phone and wiggled it. "I'm ordering food. Anyone want something?"

Jeremy sunk into the couch. "Depends. What are you getting?"

I love my life.

❦

THE SUN WOKE me from my heavy, dreamy state, pulling me into consciousness as if through mud. Some nights, I slept harder than others, as if exhaustion sometimes just won. *But other days aren't the twins' birthday.* I grinned. Phoenix surrendered his side of the bed and slept on his own mattress in the room—a good sign for his recovery—but it gave the twins the space for their special day.

I worried a little bit about having Jer and Jules both snoring in my ears at the same time. Usually, it was one or the other, but since I slept like the dead, it didn't matter.

I glanced at the light, deciding it was later morning sun before I even checked my phone for the time. The room was quiet, only the sounds of breathing around me. *Everyone is still asleep.* Usually, one or another of them had to be up early to leave, so I never got to be the first one up.

I hated to wake anyone, but I had to pee, so I wiggled myself free from entanglement. As quickly and with as little movement as possible, I climbed out of bed. Jer rolled toward Julian when I left, but didn't touch him, completely dead to the world. *Birthday snoozes.* They were eighteen years old, and therefore legally adults. I wondered if it felt different? *I should ask them. Maybe*

Barrett will remember. I used the bathroom to clean up a little bit. Getting ready for my day of movie watching in bed with Jules did not require me to dress up, but I also didn't want to be disgusting.

When I came out of the bathroom, they were all awake, which meant I failed at stealth.

"Happy Birthday," I said and smiled at the twins. "You're eighteen."

"Yes." Jer shoved Julian. "Eighteen years of sharing space with him. Literally *every* second of my existence."

Julian laughed. "You wouldn't know what to do without me."

"So, the plan, if I remember correctly..." Phoenix rubbed his eyes. "Is Jules gets Alatheia all day, right? Afterward, we have dinner with the parents and Granny. Then Jeremy gets her all night. Right?"

Jeremy nodded. "That's the plan."

Phoenix rose and stretched. "Happy Birthday, brothers-of-mine. I will see you at dinner, then. I'm going skating."

"Thanks," Julian said then grinned at him. "Be safe."

"Nah. Where is the fun in that?" He squeezed my arm on his way out the door.

Barrett groaned. "I actually have to go to the library. so I'm going to be gone most of the day, too. I let the parents know we're having dessert here, so I'll clean up before you all arrive."

I gawked at him. *My cake? They are all going to eat my cake.* I didn't mind baking for us, since failures could be laughed off. It was a different story if we were feeding their whole family. "Guys, we need to supplement the cake. I don't think it's very good. I mean, I tried, I really did, but I can't feed your mother that cake. Barrett, could you bring home a pie or something? Do they sell tiramisu at the grocery store? Can we order one?"

He laughed. "She'll eat the cake. It'll be wonderful, don't stress. See you at dinner."

Julian rolled out of bed then walked over to me. "Movies in my room. That way, if Barrett needs his room, he won't interrupt."

At least one of us planned ahead. I wouldn't have thought to worry about Barrett, but he remembered.

Jeremy kissed my cheek. "You hardly moved last night, the best snuggle ever. I'll see you at dinner. Don't forget, I get you all night, so try to take a nap today in the midst of your movies. I intend to keep you out *all* night." He paused, seeming to notice my expression. "You know I'm just kidding, right? I know you would hate that...but I scared you for a second, right?"

I laughed, because my social anxiety would've hated every moment of it. I followed him to his bedroom, where he ducked into the bathroom quickly. When he came back out, he wore pajama pants from the night before and I licked my lips at his body.

Julian climbed in next to me, and I tried to keep my hands to myself. "Are you hungry?"

"It's your birthday. Shouldn't I be asking you that? What do you want?" I ran my hand through his soft air as he rested his head in my lap and wrapped his arms around my waist.

He lifted his blue-eyed gaze to meet my own. "I want food delivery," he admitted. He rolled to a sitting position and started scrolling on his phone. "Let's eat in bed together. Pancakes?"

Pancakes in bed? "Maybe we could eat on the floor? It could get...sticky."

"That's probably a good call. Okay, let's order."

JULIAN ACTUALLY WANTED to spend the whole day watching movies in his bed. We ate pancakes on the floor and then cuddled up in bed watching his choice of movies. He liked plays made into movies, which wasn't surprising considering his life goals.

I needed to get to work on *Poor Relation*. I had left her and her potential love interest in a bit of a precarious situation...and therefore the readers hung on the cliffhanger, too. They might or might not get caught making out on the train on their way back to the city, which would be a problem for him. He wasn't meant for her, since his aunt wanted him to date and marry a girl with status. Being with him would pull her out of Poor Relation status. The guys hated the plot altogether. No matter how much I told him that the character wasn't any more them than Gretchen was me, they refused to believe they didn't play a role in my writing.

By contrast, I never felt better in terms of our relationship. I wished we had more time for more movies normally, honestly. So far we'd watched *A Streetcar Named Desire*, *Amadeus,* and *Fences*.

He kissed my neck, bringing my senses to life and making my bones melt. "This was my dream," he said against my skin. Barrett came and left the apartment a while ago, and I could see sunlight waning out the window. Phoenix hadn't returned yet, and I didn't know where Jeremy went for the day.

"Watching movies with me..." I said as I lifted my eyes to his. "Seems more like I am the one who got the present."

"Not true," he replied, shaking his head. "Can we do this every year? For my birthday, unless I have to work and can't come home that day. In those cases, we can just do it on a Saturday. Or a Sunday. So can we?"

I grinned at him, stroking my fingers through his hair again. "Yes."

"Awesome. Even more awesome because you just said yes instead of telling me *unless I get sent away*."

I swallowed and looked away, but I told myself I wasn't getting too relaxed, and nothing would bite me in the ass at any second. Other than the PI, my family hadn't bothered me in quite some time. I still didn't know what my aunt had meant by *handled*. But later Kit planned to share what he found in the folder, which should give me a lot of answers. Still, it was hard for me to imagine them wanting to send me away. For the first time ever I had good grades and didn't get in any trouble. Even the day I stormed out of the classroom didn't cause so much as a ripple. Then again, Collins seemed downright subdued the next day and every day since. Her class practically became a study hall.

If my family kept a tail on me 24/7, they would know I had made friends, but none of them were particularly nefarious. I even played a sport.

I spent no money and didn't even live in their apartment.

So why bother to send me away? It seemed like less trouble overall for them to continue to ignore my presence altogether.

Or so I could hope.

I showered then met Julian in the hallway. No other brothers lingered in the apartment since they all said they would meet us for dinner. The twins didn't pick a fancy place, so likely wouldn't come home to change first. Still, I slipped into a black skirt that clung to my rear a little bit more than I liked and a white tank top—an outfit I noticed they all seemed to really like on me.

"It's getting a little chilly at night." Julian said from where he leaned against his doorframe. "Grab a sweater."

I nodded. *Good call.* I should remember summer had ended so things could get chilly at dusk. I put in my sapphire earrings then slipped my pearls around my neck before I grabbed a white sweater. When Dina bought me clothes, she really thought about almost everything.

I wanted to pay it forward, so to speak. If I got the chance later in life, I wanted to help someone like she helped me. I didn't put on the sweater but stared at myself in the mirror for a few long moments, considering my profile and how much I had changed with age. My appearance overall would do, but I doubted I'd ever see the day where I stopped worrying about what their parents thought of me.

I sighed. *Okay. I shouldn't say never.* Nothing in my life had ever made sense, and I couldn't have predicted any of it, no matter how perfect it felt.

Julian moved behind me, wrapping his arms around me as he dropped a kiss on my temple. He was dressed in jeans and a black t-shirt, and his blue eyes met my own in the mirror.

"You look really good," I whispered to him, because he looked hot, like some actor or something.

He kissed my shoulder, and his gaze seemed hungry. "You look better."

I blurted my curiosity. "Does it feel different to be eighteen? Like, is there suddenly a sense you're an adult?"

He laughed. "No, not at all. I think I felt different when I turned seventeen? There was a sense of, okay, Barrett is going to be graduating soon. We knew soon we would need to step up and be grownups, but I don't know. The answer is no, I don't feel different, anyway."

I smiled at him. "Happy Birthday."

"Thank you. I love you." He took my hand to lead me from the apartment.

"Do you miss sleeping in your room?" I asked, honestly curious. We headed toward the elevator together.

He shook his head. "I never think about it, and I mean *never*. It's just a place to store my things. We do really need another bedroom, so you could have your own space, too.

That way, you could kick us out if you wanted space. And it would give all of us more one- on-one time with you, since that's how my parents do it."

I really never thought about it. "I would miss us all being together. I sleep so well knowing you're all nearby."

"Me too. It does feel like it's supposed to be." He paused. "But there will come a time we will all want *some* alone time at night."

I didn't misunderstand him. "Right."

"Given that we are unlikely to move to different apartments for a very long time, you'll be stuck sharing Barrett's closet. Actually, you can spread out your clothes, if you want. You're welcome to some of my closet."

I shook my head, thinking it would get confusing. I struggled to remember where I put things already, so leaving them all over the house would make it worse. Still, Barrett might prefer it. "Let me ask your brother if he wants some more space."

"He won't." Jules laughed. "Just if you want to."

We said hello to the doormen. They treated me like a resident lately. I didn't even notice it anymore, which in and of itself was bizarre but good.

I put my head on Julian's shoulder, and he sighed. "Thank you for today."

"No need to ever thank me for anything." I kissed his hand.

Ten minutes later, we made it to the restaurant, a cozy place with soft, golden lanterns hanging from the ceiling. Red walls featured gold tapestries adorned with dragons and phoenixes. The red was different from Dina's apartment, brighter. Each table was set with porcelain plates and bowls, and the scent of stir-fried vegetables and meat immediately made my stomach growl.

Julian squeezed my fingers. "We'll have a table in the back.

It's always the same one. Nothing changes here, which I love. We used to come once a week with Granny when we were little, then it became our birthday spot. She still comes a lot with her friends."

He led me toward the back, where a large table waited for us. We were last to arrive, so I glanced at my phone to make sure we weren't late only to see we were right on time. Everyone stood to greet us. Julian hugged Jeremy, saying something I couldn't hear. Jer grinned at him and patted him on the back.

There was a seat empty next to Dina, so I took it. Jeremy sat on my other side and kissed my cheek. "Have a good day?"

"It was fun," I admitted with a grin. "I'd never seen any of the movies we watched before, and they were all just amazing."

"Yeah. . .you made Jules' day." He grinned. "He can't get any of us to watch that many of his favorite movies in one sitting."

I shook my head. "I guess the question now is...what are we doing tonight?"

"You'll see." He winked at me, so I focused on dinner and let him surprise me.

Conversation flowed easily, and even Phoenix seemed alert. He hadn't hurt himself skating, which was great since a few times he came back with bad road rash. They teased each other and talked, but I did notice they engaged more with their granny than their parents.

Rosalind leaned forward at one point to admit, "This is great. I really can't remember the last time none of them got unhappy and stormed away from the table."

Barrett shook his head. "Still early. Anything can happen."

She rolled her eyes but laughed. "No, seriously, I was hoping, Alatheia, you might be available for lunch next weekend."

Everyone went eerily silent, waiting for my answer as if it mattered, but Phoenix turned to her before I could summon my voice.

"Is this a good lunch or a bad lunch? I don't want her to have lunch with you if you're just going to complain or say mean things."

Rosalind held up her hands, her smile genuine. "A good lunch. I owe your girlfriend a lot of apologies. I was certainly not at my best this summer, so I would really like to properly apologize and get to know her."

"I would like that," I lied. I really wouldn't, but that seemed like the right answer. She scared me more than a little, but I wouldn't get over it if I didn't try.

The conversation perked back up, as if the glitch never happened, and I looked at Dina. "Can I ask you a question?"

I noticed her skin seemed a little off, paler than normal, but not so much that I wanted to mention it in front of everyone. Still, I wondered if she wasn't sleeping. "Absolutely. Always. You look so pretty tonight."

"Thank you. I was wondering...since you came from somewhere else, too, you weren't raised in the Life. Is it possible you have advice about how to handle something? A situation?"

She nodded. "I honestly would be more shocked if you *didn't* have a million questions. Go ahead. What got you wondering?"

I sighed. "How do you handle it when they argue?"

She lifted an eyebrow. "Specifically? Like about what?"

"About *me*. About how to divide the time evenly, and make sure everyone's needs are met, but there is only one me. It doesn't come up a lot, because mostly it all evens out. But sometimes...I don't know what to do."

Dina lifted one shoulder, her expression distant. "Nothing. Do nothing. When it comes to balance, they were brothers before they were yours. Their rivalry practically started in the womb. They compete, but they will adjust over time. If one of them gets really upset, you'll know they need you. Leave it unless it explodes."

I nodded. Her practical advice actually made sense to me. Watching them together, it was easy to see. They were always brothers, and they always would be. I found their connection beautiful.

"I'm telling you, these people are strange." Jeremy shook his head. "And that is coming from *me*, and we are *strange*."

Stephen pursed his lips. "I wouldn't say we're overtly strange. I mean, you have to know us to notice the weird. We hide our oddness, our secret creature we keep in the closet."

Kit drummed his fingers on the table and I sort of followed the conversation, but I mostly watched Dina. She seemed really quiet, only answered when they spoke to her, and her skin had gone even paler than before.

"Are you okay?" I finally asked, and she met my question with kind eyes.

"I am always fine, my darling. Yes, I'm good. Thank you for checking. I'm just taking everything in tonight."

Rosalind glanced our way and frowned, but otherwise, as we waited for the bill, the conversation flowed as normal. My stomach practically hurt, I ate so much, but the food was amazing. I particularly enjoyed my chicken, but the soup was a little bit spicy for me. I didn't dare complain even a little, though, knowing it was a magical place to the brothers—the place of birthdays, and no fighting.

"Who was it again?" Kit asked as he handed the bill to Daniel, who pulled out his wallet.

Jeremy rolled his eyes. "Thanks for listening."

"I have a million things on my mind right now, Birthday Boy."

"Fine." Jer laughed. "Murial Monk. You must know the family. They are exactly the people you all want to know all the time."

The oldest of their fathers lifted his eyebrows. "Murial Monk took you and Alatheia on a backstage tour of the Met?" Daniel and Stephen both shot him a look, then laser focused on me. Even Eric seemed to pay attention, and he was the quietest of all of them.

Jer squeezed my fingers. "She did. They're weird."

"You need to be careful around them." He stared at me as he said it, as if to impart some hidden meaning I totally didn't get.

Phoenix cleared his throat. "Is there some reason Alatheia should warrant more caution or are you worried in general, because of the type of people Murial's family is?

He didn't clarify, leaving it at, "Just be careful."

I'd never seen Kit squirm before, but bringing up the Monks left him positively twitching in his seat.

We all left together, and my fists clenched by my sides. The thought of my silly cake made my stomach clench, too, so I turned around to address all of them.

"I've never made a cake before. I...I hope it's not terrible," I admitted, thinking at least I warned them.

Rosalind slipped her arm around me, giving my shoulders a comforting squeeze. "Don't be silly, it'll be wonderful. Thank you for baking for the boys."

Dina smiled. "I'm tired tonight. I didn't sleep well last night, so I'll stop by tomorrow for a piece. I'll say goodnight for now, my darlings." She waved her hand as a car pulled up next to her, but she regularly had that kind of timing. I loved it for her.

They all waved their goodbyes, but I stood back and watched them. I couldn't believe no one said anything about how pale she looked, or worried because she got tired so easily. She was in her seventies, and she said she was tired. Maybe it was normal? I didn't know, and I wasn't a doctor, but she looked off to me.

Not that I could check on her. Rosalind kept her arm around me, so I forgot about Dina in favor of my fears of Rosalind.

❧

ULTIMATELY, the cake turned out fine. The guys liked it, wolfing down their slices in a couple of bites. Julian grinned the whole time, while Jeremy ate two pieces, which was great. I wanted them to enjoy their birthday. Everyone sang to them and a memory rushed through me of when I was young. My mom used to make me a cake then light candles and sing. I remembered her, so joyful about me being her daughter and a year older, and I couldn't help but smile. But the smile faded slowly, because I realized how long it had been since I'd thought of her at all.

Funny, memories and how they worked.

But the cake was just okay, not great. I thought I could do better, and already had ideas for my second attempt.

After we ate, Kit indicated we would talk in the living room, so people grabbed drinks and headed that direction. I sat down, my palms sweaty, and tried to stuff them in my lap so no one would notice how my hands shook. I could play denial with the best of them, but Kit would—finally—reveal what was in that folder.

Rosalind sat on the arm of his chair, her hand on his shoulder obviously meant as a comfort to him. I wondered abruptly if it would be really bad, and a spike of fear iced my veins.

Phoenix jumped up then snuggled close next to me. I hugged him back wondering if he somehow sensed I was starting to panic? I would bet he noticed somehow. Phoenix, like me, was accustomed to receiving bad news.

"I'll get right to it. The birth certificate they have for you is a fraud. It's not your birth certificate, or anyone's legal record."

Kit steepled his hands as if it was a business meeting and he hadn't just crushed my world.

"What?" I sputtered.

He nodded. "I know this probably sounds shocking and odd. On their document, it names you, Alatheia Winder, daughter of Delphine Stapleton Winder and Peter Lucas Winder. The thing is, the document doesn't exist. The certificate number is fabricated, even the seal on it is faked. We searched for your real birth certificate, but so far, we came up empty."

I shook my head. I couldn't even focus on what anyone else was saying right then, my gaze glued to Kit. "But I exist. I'm here."

He nodded. "I understand it's shocking news. But we do know you're here."

"Kit. " Rosalind squeezed his shoulder. "Gentle. She isn't a client. She is their love. Come on—less lawyer, more father."

He took a deep breath, blowing it out while looking into her eyes. "Sorry, bad habit. You're right, you are here, but you weren't born in Colorado, at least not on that day or where they said it happened. There's no record of it. You could have been a home birth, which they never recorded, but why bother to create the fake? I don't know, like I said, and we're still looking into it. I can't think of anyone who would benefit from your birth certificate being falsified."

I caught my breath. "My mother's maiden name wasn't Stapleton. I mean...that is my Uncle's last name, but she always said her maiden name was Faust. Why didn't I ever think about this before?"

Barrett met my gaze. "Because you were eleven when she died, and how would you have even researched it on your own?"

"I'm not eleven anymore," I pointed out, jerking my chin up in false bravado. "I must be wrong. Stapleton is the family name."

Kit shook his head. "Don't worry so much about names. You've been through a lot. If you weren't interesting, that file would've been thin and boring. Old grades. Vaccine records. Did you know they have a picture of your mom and her sister together smiling? Do you want it?"

My mother, yes. My aunt? *No.* I nodded. "Sure. Thank you."

"I'll bring it down tomorrow. I know this is a lot. We will get to the bottom of it. The situation is just going to take some work. I'm hiring an investigator to look into your past. He'll start in Colorado and go from there. We'll get ahead of this. In the meantime, I have the fake. It's good enough for you to open a bank account or whatever with it. I doubt very much anyone else is going to do this close of a look-see."

Jer winced. "Look-see."

"What's wrong with that?" Kit blinked.

"Little cringe, Kit. Little cringe."

Phoenix kissed my temple and whispered, "We can make

the *Poor Relation* pay for you now. A bank account. Get you some independence that we don't care about you needing but you do."

He was right. I smiled at him.

"Why would they do this?" I asked, hoping anyone could miraculously pull the answer out of the air.

Kit shook his head. "I don't want to speculate."

"I think your family was hiding you, " Stephen answered. "I mean obviously I don't know but I asked myself, why would I procure a birth certificate for you that was obviously fake? I think that the one that you really have out there somewhere is fake too. I think your mother used another name. Your father called himself Winder. That's not his real name either. And when your family got ahold of you it was important they have something to make it clear you were who they wanted you to be. That's what I think."

That made the most sense of anything. I had nothing but questions, but the Lents were good at managing my expectations. They spent six years not knowing who took Phoenix and killed the other kids. So...I didn't know, and they didn't know, and together we were just a bunch of unanswered questions.

JEREMY STAYED QUIET. I glanced up at him, asking, "Are you okay? Are we getting on a boat? What's happening?"

"Yes and yes. I'm more concerned about you than anything else. I hope you find it fun and distracting, as that's the goal."

He nodded toward a man who stood by a boat ramp and we stepped together onto the yacht. "Is this yours?"

"Eric's," he replied and smiled. "But tonight, it's ours. A nighttime cruise on the Hudson, a ride up and down the river.

We can be alone out here on the water. I'm glad you brought your sweater, but I'll give you my sweatshirt, if you need it."

As he spoke, the boat started to move. I glanced around, but they remained an invisible captain and a crew. Jeremy took my hand and led me up the stairs, so we stood on the top deck of a boat. "If you drank, I would give you some champagne, but for tonight, we'll stick with lemonade."

A pitcher wet with condensation waited in front of us on a table. He poured us both a glass, the ice clinking cheerfully. I defended my choices, pointing out, "Someday, I'll drink. I will." A lot of things that used to be hard nos for me had become maybes, but it would be a process in my mind of getting used to things and feeling safe again.

"We'll have a glass together when that day comes, but don't feel pressured by me."

I sat on one of the couches and after a second, Jer joined me. He smelled clean, like soap, so I breathed him in and closed my eyes.

"Was this really what you wanted to do for your birthday, or did you do it for me because you thought it was what I would want and you always get what you want, Jeremy Lent?"

His sigh moved through me, making me shiver with awakened needs. "I wouldn't want to do this alone or just with my brothers. Or my friends or teammates. Actually, I even find boating with my family tedious. Eric always decides he is Captain of the Ocean then starts overusing marine terms... It's a whole thing. But, I want this with you. For my birthday? Sure, and also I loved the cake."

I laughed. "No, you didn't. It was barely edible, but you made a real effort and I appreciate that. Maybe I'll get better at baking. . .or maybe I am not meant to bake."

He pinched me jokingly. "I *did* like it. You read me wrong."

Then he leaned over and kissed me. I responded eagerly,

right there on the Hudson River, on a yacht. I could never have imagined any of it, especially under the stars with the Manhattan skyline as our only witness.

"I don't care where you were born or about your name. It is my intention, in three years..." He held up that many fingers and wiggled them at me. "To give you my last name. We'll be young, but if I could, I would marry you today. Instead, we'll wait until I'm twenty-one and you'll be twenty. Then take my last name and have one I gave you gladly."

I caught my breath, cupping his face in my hands. "Jeremy, what a beautiful dream."

"I'll make this one come true."

In that moment, I believed him.

WE WENT BACK TO WASH, rinse, repeat, which I loved, since the ease of routine soothed my soul. Rosalind caught the flu, and apparently it got pretty bad, delaying our lunch together —which was fine by me. At some point, I knew it would catch up with me, but I could obsess about it then. Dina showed up smiling again, fit as a fiddle, proving I worried for nothing. I sighed a little, because I wasn't sure if my fears about her were real or just a reflection of my abandonment issues.

Regardless, routines were my happy place, my idea of heaven. Or maybe the guys were heaven? Leaves started changing in October, red peeking out here and there to hint at what would come. I reveled in it, and in having a place to belong.

Maybe tomorrow, I would go on a nature walk in the park, just to look at the leaves?

Better to think about that than about how hard I tried not to drown. I shouldn't be daydreaming during a game, but it was all I could manage as I continued my egg beaters. Someone from the other team threatened to scratch up my back with her should-have-been-cut fingernails, or what felt like cartoonishly long claws. I swam left and she backed off, thankfully, but my back ached from her attack.

I scanned the pool, trying to think about more than not drowning. Which made me think about *Poor Relation*, which I needed to make another episode for, possibly tonight? *I could be eating pizza*, I realized bitterly as the claw girl caught up to me again. *I could be planning how to make Phoenix's birthday cake even better than the one I made for the twins.*

I swam backwards and—*oh, fuck*—managed to get my hands on the ball. What was Sarah thinking? Why would she pass to me? I couldn't ask, so I swam for all I was worth. The crowd started to shout as I sliced through the water, keeping hold of the ball in a combination of luck and skill. My opponent tried to take it from me, but she didn't get close. I shot past her, surprised to be faster in the water than before. Not fast enough, maybe, but faster than when I started. I focused on the goalie, moving as if locked on target. People shouted, but I didn't hear a whistle. The whistles seemed constant during the boys' games, but our refs apparently wanted to let us drown.

Me? Bitter? Never. As I approached her, the goalie's eyes were wide, but if I had breath, I would've told her not to worry. I *never* scored. Not in practice. Not ever, so I knew I didn't have a snowball's chance in hell when I lifted my arm and aimed for the left side of the goal.

As the ball soared through the air, I held my breath. I watched it like a miracle happening before my very eyes. The goalie tried to stop it, but she missed. The ball went into the goal, and the crowd went wild. I must have yelped? The bell clamored loudly, chiming over the noise. *The end-of-game bell. What?* I stared blankly at my teammates as they started to

shout and punch their fists in the air. *Why? What happened?*
My gaze flew to the scoreboard—oh! We tied. We *tied. Wait,
because of me?* I blinked in shock, but I realized my shot got us
the tie.

I swam for the side, surprised I somehow stayed above
water despite my utter shock. I practically pulled myself out
of the water next to Sarah, who immediately started hugging
me. Valerie hugged me, too, while my teeth clattered a bit
from shock. Everyone looked so happy, so I grinned back
despite my shaking hands. I didn't have to say anything—*I
tied the game. 'Nuff said.*

It didn't mesh with my mental picture of myself. *Who
would've thought it?* Not me, not me ever.

Sometime later, after I showered, I collected hugs from
the three high- school- age Lents who waited outside our
locker rooms. Even Phoenix, who hated the pool, attended to
see me play. Barrett had a class late tonight, including a test,
which made him grumpy because he couldn't skip. He'd
barely grunted goodbye as he rushed out the door with his
shoulders hunched that morning.

I couldn't help my big silly grin at the available Lents.
"Yeah, I *did* that. Did you see me? I mean, it's probably a one
and done, but still!"

"Maybe it's the beginning of a streak," Julian said and
hugged me again, taking advantage of my win to hold me
close against him for a moment. "I'm trying so hard not to
kiss you. I *want* to kiss you. More than anything."

Sarah rushed past us, smacking my back as she passed.
"Party at my house. Right now, and don't bother saying no,
Al. I *will* come get you. We're having a big party to celebrate.
Huge."

Jeremy called out to her, "She doesn't go to parties
without us."

I don't? I could've argued for my independence or something, but I didn't bother since I didn't really want to go to any parties without them.

She sighed. "Then I guess you can come, Lent. Come on. Bring your friends. We just fucking *tied.*"

I cleared my throat, focusing on the Lents. "We don't have to go, if you guys don't want to, so don't feel pressured on my account."

"You deserve to celebrate. Besides, I haven't ever been to Sarah's house, so I'm curious." Julian shrugged. "I'll text the guy s' team. Let's make it water polo night."

A water polo night. I pulled out my own phone, texting Murial impulsively. She knew where everything happened anywhere, but I would invite her, since we were friends or something.

Then I took Phoenix's hand, allowing a goofy grin to spread across my face. "I just scored."

"I know," he said and laughed. "I am *so* fucking proud of you. For a second, I was sure you zoned out, your brain on something other than the game, and I wasn't sure you would even see the ball coming."

I nodded. "I was. You nailed it. It was pure luck my brain clicked on at the right second."

He tapped his nose. "I knew it."

☙❧

SARAH'S HOME was huge and a good distance from the school in Morningside Heights. I'd never visited Morningside Heights before, but it all looked very historic and like it should be said with capital letters. Jeremy told me some of the history while I took in the beautiful architecture and gardening. Her family lived in a building without a doorman, which seemed novel to me after living with the Lents for so long. So far, it seemed true of a lot of locations chosen for parties, though. *Easier for everyone to just get in and out.* I suddenly wondered about Murial's doorman or security. *Maybe she had let them leave for the night?* I doubted she kept a Rembrandt without the very best security available.

I thought about her most recent text—she'd moved to designers from painters, educating me on a wider range of subjects—and I wondered if she would show up.

Considering the party was planned the moment we tied, it came together almost weirdly well. I spotted alcohol everywhere, almost every hand holding a bottle or red plastic cup. Music thumped through the space, filling it while allowing for conversation at the same time. A ton of people showed up, the press of bodies nearly claustrophobic. I remembered my last party, the night I met Murial. As someone dumped part of their drink on my arm, I grimaced and realized it probably was a good choice—parties might not be my thing.

I honestly didn't like crowds, not even when they were filled with people I knew. After a few weeks at the school and a while on the team, I recognized almost everyone there. Even the seniors, who mostly stayed in their own hallways, started to look familiar to me.

"You with me?" Phoenix asked and held out his hand. "I'm not leaving you alone at this one."

Jeremy slipped his arm around my waist, trying to tug me free from Phoenix's hold. "Or you could come with us. You pick. Regardless, text me if you need anything."

"She'll stay with me," Phoenix said, swinging me back to him like a yo-yo. A very sexy yo-yo who nuzzled at my neck, making my pulse race, before telling his brother, "You go do senior things or water polo things, and leave us lowly underclassmen alone."

Jer laughed. "Looks like Jules has me covered. I'll be over there." He pointed. "Don't leave without one of us this time, okay? We can leave anytime. I'm gonna go find a beer."

Phoenix managed to find a quiet corner and tugged me into it, giving us a moment of privacy and stillness. He pulled a bag out of his pocket, and glanced up as Hal appeared around the corner. I noticed Phoenix wasn't talking to him and quirked a brow.

"Thirsty?" he asked me instead of explaining.

"I can give you a minute and go find you a beer. Stay near here, I'll be back," I promised, then slipped back into the bustling crowd. I found soda in the kitchen, so I poured myself a glass. By the time I returned to Phoenix holding one for me and him, he stared into a bag of white powder.

I'd never seen him do drugs, and I couldn't tell them apart if I tried. *Is that ketamine? Marijuana?* He frowned and threw a weighted look at Joe, standing to his left.

"Why do I have so much?"

Joe shrugged then glanced at someone who touched his elbow. I set down my drink near Phoenix, considering the bag carefully. "Do you usually have less?"

"This is like a week's worth of drugs." He put a little on the table then pulled a straw out of his pocket. In a second, he snorted it up his nose, holding his nostrils closed while I stared in shock. He closed his eyes for a second and then sniffed.

Abject fascination? I wondered. *Or am I watching in horror?* Regardless of what I called the emotion, or whether or not I watched, it happened all the time. He used drugs like that all the time. He casually sniffed white powder up his nose. I held my fist against my stomach as if in physical pain, because I found it awful. *Am I purposefully pretending he isn't doing this by not seeing it happen to make myself feel better about it?*

I took a sip of my soda, trying to swallow down the bile rising in my throat. I gulped more, hardly tasting it. His eyes —that strange removed look he got when he was in a k-hole —which I now understood he achieved by snorting things up his nose—took away his gaze. Okay. I downed my diet soda, closing my eyes as if I could erase it all, but it replayed in my memory crystal clear.

I looked up to see Hal nod toward Phoenix. "Hey, Lent."

Even in his state, he glared toward Hal. "What the hell you want?"

"Thought you might like to know Maggie stuck something in your girl's drink. And she just drank it."

What? I glanced into my cup as Phoenix whirled unsteadily to grab my elbows. "What? What did she put in it?" he asked me.

I sure as hell didn't know. *Maggie?* I scanned the room, hoping to see her face, but realizing the colors blurred a bit, lights turning to stars. My heart rate kicked up just as Phoenix stuck the bag of white powder back in his coat pocket.

Whatever, I couldn't spot her, but then again I didn't see her when I grabbed my drink, either. My phone dinged, and I reached for it in annoyance. I felt fine. *Maybe Hal is full of shit?* The twins sent a text saying they went on a beer run—wasn't there enough already in the building?

Phoenix slid his arm around me. "Are you...are you okay?"

Wow. His gaze seemed so blank as to be nearly vacant, like a sleepwalker. "Yeah, I think so. I don't feel weird or anything. I also don't see Maggie, but I haven't seen her all night." I shrugged.

"Hal, are you full of shit?" Phoenix called out, but Hal vanished into the crowd. I spotted Murial, though, and waved.

"Hi," she said and smiled. "What a random party this is."

"Is it?" I looked around, the lights still going blurry, the way I saw online they did when people had astigmatism. I wondered if I could be abruptly developing astigmatism. Aloud, I told her, "Hal just said Maggie put something in my drink. I don't see her, and I feel fine, so we were discussing whether or not he's full of shit."

She put her hands on her hips, her eyes narrowing in a way that sent a chill down my spine. "She did *what*, now? Stay here. I'll find out if she did and what it was."

Phoenix turned me to face him again, and I remembered how lovely he really was. Truly handsome, with his carved features and shiny hair. "You sure you're okay?"

I should panic but everyone always seemed so strange to me. Who would make up a story like a drugged drink, though? I wondered abruptly if I could use it for *Poor Relation*. If it was drugged, the drink tasted fine.

Phoenix started to kind of turn...glowy. In fact, everyone did, but their shades varied. Everyone in the room glowed, their dancing or moving bodies wreathed with dimly bright color. It was kind of...awesome. Usually, people at Pullman might seem so full of themselves, but why wouldn't they be? *They are gorgeous. Bathed in light. Huh.*

"Hey," Phoenix said again. He took my cheeks in his hands, turning my face to his. "Look at me."

I tried, but I honestly wanted to look at something more interesting. My body was hot, so I tugged at my collar. Oh, I liked how it felt to have his hands on my cheeks. I liked it...*a lot*. I nuzzled into his touch, turning my head to bite at the pad of his hand.

"Keep doing that," I said and grinned at him, sliding into his touch. "Forever. I can feel you everywhere."

Phoenix lifted his lids, his gaze unfocused, but his brows furrowed as if he tried to fight it. "Would love to, but you're not okay, Red. Your pupils are huge."

Murial returned. "It's ecstasy. I am so done with her. Her obsession with you is ridiculous."

Phoenix sighed. "Well, this will be fun, but it will wear off.

Eventually. Why would she give her ecstasy? It's not painful—just the opposite."

"Who knows why she does anything? Maybe she thinks that she'll fuck you then Jeremy won't like it? I don't know. I am not going to pretend to understand how a crazy person thinks."

She patted my arm, and I jolted at her touch. Murial glittered brightly gold, almost too bright. It didn't feel good against my light, like Phoenix's touch. I didn't want her to touch me at all, so I frowned at her. She stared into my vacant gaze then shrugged. "Yeah, she's gone. See you later. Let's go to the Whitney tomorrow."

I couldn't be bothered to think about her, especially since she took her gold light away, leaving me alone with the much preferable Phoenix. I told him, "You are so gorgeous. You always are. Have I told you that? How completely beautiful you are to me?" Tears came to my eyes. "Or how much I love being part of your life? Because I really do. I mean, I love you, Phoenix. I don't usually say it, because I am such a superstitious scaredy cat, but I love you."

He shook his head, his lips thinned. "Say that to me again tomorrow."

The twins arrived, and Jeremy held a beer. "How's it going?"

"She got drugged by Maggie. She slipped something in her soda, and now she's high as a kite on ecstasy." Phoenix passed me to Jeremy, as if I were baggage or something. Luckily, I liked his glow and scent, too, so I burrowed into his arms. "I am not in any condition to know what to do here. Should we call Barrett?"

"What?" Jeremy shouted as his arms came around me gently. I shuddered at his warmth, nuzzling into his neck where his scent somehow smelled warmer. I could really get used to the sensations, especially the lovely glows.

I held onto him, my nails digging a little into his back. "I love you, Jeremy. I love you *so* much."

He shook his head, and his voice sounded rough when he said, "Hush. Not here. We need to get you home."

A loud bang resounded through the house, and everyone went still and silent for a second.

"Fuck," someone shouted. "It's the cops."

✵ 2 1 ✵

The what? The word *cop* didn't really translate to anything in my glowy state. Instead of worrying about it, I focused on the colors, reaching for a pretty one near Jules' ear.

"Time to go." Jer said and tugged on me but Jules stopped him.

"We're too late. All the exits and entrances are blocked. They'll let us go, so we just need to wait. We're fine."

Jeremy shook his head. "No, Phoenix *isn't* fine, and Maggie drugged our girl with ecstasy."

Julian took a deep breath, his eyes huge. "We'll handle it."

"I love you." I told Julian, sliding my hand down his cheek and loving the slight stubble of his face. "I really want you to know that."

He winced. "I love you, too, but I cannot believe this happened to you."

The police were everywhere, people shouting as they tried to escape their capture. Phoenix stumbled, and I bumped into him as I saw the bag begin to fall out of his jacket. *Oh fuck.* I remembered his parents saying they would send him away if he got in trouble again, and that amount of drugs... No way would he get away with it.

I slipped the bag free of his pocket, intending to turn around and throw it away in a garbage can or something.

"Hey," a shout said near my ear, and I turned around into the arms of the police officer. "What do you have there?"

I can't honestly say I remember exactly what happened then. Everything got so blurry, glows blending and lights swirling in my vision while sound went a bit distorted. Something in my hand? Shouting, and Jeremy shouting. Julian, too. *What is happening?* I held my hands over my ears as if I could block away the barrage of noise. Phoenix's face looked scared, his glow dim and vaguely red as he reached for me. *Red is for danger,* I thought. I would love for him to touch me again. I would give anything for his arms, and I reached out a hand toward him—

But he wasn't the one touching me. A very tall, red-headed police officer grabbed the bag from my clenched fist then put handcuffs on me. I gasped, startled at the cold weight of them on my arms, which suddenly looked awfully small. When he yanked my arms back, it hurt, so I cried out in response. His voice droned on at me, but it was like those adults in that one old cartoon—none of it made sense, just weird distorted noises. I managed to hear part of it...

"You have the right to remain silent..."

Jeremy shouted still, but he was too far away, the sound of his voice vanishing into the distance. "Don't say anything. Kit will come for you. Do you understand? Kit or someone from his office will come. Don't you say *any*thing."

It wasn't my first time in a police car, but usually they didn't help me duck to get inside. The last time was when my mother died. *This is different.* I blurred out for a while, not really paying attention or focused on what happened to my body until the flashing light of the PI taking my photo made me want to gag, turning my stomach with the painful brightness. I wished I could give him the finger.

Am I...being arrested?

◈✦◈

HOURS PASSED SLOWLY, and I dozed off and on sideways on a bench. They told me they called my aunt, my guardian, but I didn't know if she would come. A lawyer came, and he told me she sent him. The only thing I remember about him was he was young. I could hardly think, though and everything hurt. They wanted a sample of my blood, but the young lawyer said he gave my guardian's permission for it to be taken.

I held out my arm, allowing the draw, not even in control of the blood in my own body. Why would I be? As a minor, we didn't have control over anything. I lay sideways again on the hard bench, and tears leaked out of my eyes when I closed them. *Alone.* The lawyer left, but I was still there. I rubbed my eyes, angry at the tears, but tempted to rupture into heartbroken sobs. Then again, my mouth was so dry, and nausea kept rolling through me. I pressed my head against my knees, pinching my eyes closed, but it didn't help. I wanted one of my guys to hold me in their arms. *Just be held. Where are the Lents?*

It probably was ridiculous for me to wait for a knight in shining armor when life already proved happily ever afters weren't real, but some part of me hoped anyway.

The door swung open suddenly, and a woman in a pants suit stared at me. Her hair hung short, angling inward toward her high cheekbones, and almost sharpening her serious expression. "Alatheia, come with me."

I followed her, since they let me. *Am I going home now? Where is home?* No, she led me to a room with a buzzing light.

It buzzed and buzzed, the noise grating on my nerves immediately. Before I even sat, I knew I wouldn't be able to focus past that noise.

I rubbed at my eyes, as if I could press the pain out of them with my fingertips.

"So, we know what you're on," she began.

I swallowed, which wasn't useful since my mouth still felt so dry. I didn't remember exactly what they said she put in my drink, so it turned out suit lady had one up on me. "I don't know, so would you tell me?"

She frowned. "Ecstasy."

"I didn't mean to take it," I confessed, despite the brothers telling me to say nothing. I could tell them that much, right? I could be honest.

The lawyer sat down across from me, next to the woman. She opened a file folder.

"This is your attorney. He is here on behalf of your family to represent you. I have spoken to your aunt, who told me about your deeply troubled past and history of this kind of thing. I don't know how this is the first time you got caught." She frowned at me, her expression stern.

Tricia said what? It didn't even make sense, so I shook my head. "I'm not *deeply troubled*, and I certainly don't have any *history*. I'm not like that at all. I am a...well- behaved, normal person. Honestly, I don't feel very well, and I just want to go home now."

She shook her head, tapping the folder with one long fingertip. "I'm afraid I don't believe you, Alatheia. We have multiple reports on file from your aunt. She had to resort to hiring a PI just to keep track of your location. I also know how you ran away from home, moved in with a known drug addict, and had his family threaten your aunt. Did I miss anything?"

I opened and closed my mouth, stunned beyond words as

I tried to process what she was saying. She told them I was a runaway? When did she file police reports? Terror iced my veins, but I still just wanted to go home. I didn't want to have the conversation with them. I didn't want anything other than a bed and a pillow.

Where are the Lents? I needed to pull it together, to come up with some kind of response to their claims other than *nuh-uh*. The Lents weren't there, and I was on my own—again.

I stared down my lawyer, supposedly representing me or there on my behalf. "Shouldn't you be doing something to help me?"

"He has, or as much as can be done in your case," she snapped then frowned. "You had a bag with an excess of 500 milligrams of ketamine on your person. Do you have any idea the consequences of your mistake, or know what the penalty would be if you were tried as an adult?"

I shook my head, but I vaguely remembered stealing the bag from Phoenix so he didn't get caught with it. "No," since I honestly didn't know the consequences, just that they would've been worse for him.

"It's a felony. Normally, one that would result in very serious jail time; however, your family, much to my chagrin, has made other arrangements." She stood, closing the folder and tapping it on the table once for emphasis. "I would like for you to tell us, who is your dealer? That is a huge amount of ketamine. Where did you get it, Alatheia? If you tell us, things will go a bit better for you."

I swallowed, but no one ever offered me a drink, so my mouth was still bone dry. I knew where Phoenix got his drugs, and even where Joe lived, but I knew better than to say anything. Phoenix didn't respect Hal because he tattled. I wouldn't do the same. Besides, I didn't buy any drugs; Maggie drugged me. I stole the bag from Phoenix.

I pinched my lips together, making it obvious I didn't intend to answer before I said, "I don't remember."

She sighed and slammed the door on her way out of the room.

The lawyer cleared his throat. "We spoke to Judge Kent." I nodded, although I didn't know any judges, not to mention ones named Kent. "He knew your family for a long time, so since this is your first offense, we made special arrangements for you. You will be going away to a school specifically intended for rehabilitation for your bad behavior."

My what? I finally found my voice. "I don't have bad behavior."

He sighed, opening his own folder and pointing at a page as if it mattered. "I could go down the list, if you like. We have the ruckus at Pullman, both in the locker room and in the classroom of a much beloved teacher."

A ruckus? "Are you talking about Collins?"

He sighed, standing. "We're not getting anywhere with this conversation. Follow me. The school awaits you, and this is your second chance. Do you understand what I'm telling you? If you screw this up, you're going to jail for a felony. Your life will be *over*."

I rose slowly, my hands shaking. "I don't feel well, and I want to speak to Kit Lent."

"Not an option." He shook his head. "As I said, follow me, Alatheia."

This can't be happening. I stopped at the garbage can, where thankfully I puked instead of on my shoes. The lawyer awkwardly waited, not even offering me a drink or a paper towel when I finished retching.

I followed him, because I wasn't sure what else to even do. I was being sent away, and I couldn't stop them. It might be awful but as a minor, I knew I wouldn't be able to stop them. I thought about the promises they made, how they said they would come for me if I got taken away, and my heart thudded in my throat. *They promised. Barrett. Julian. Jeremy. Phoenix. They said they would come.*

The nameless lawyer practically dragged me from the room, since I apparently dawdled along too slowly. Soon I stood outside in the cold, the wind biting at my arms and warn ing of winter.

Two men waited, their arms crossed as they stared me down. A gray haired guy and a younger, dark haired one, both huge and burly, like linebackers.

"Your family arranged for us to escort you to school. We can do this the easy way or the hard way. You won't like the hard way, but I might," said the gray haired one with an oily grin.

I swallowed. "I'm not trouble."

"You are, but you won't be soon." The door to the van opened and they shoved me inside. The older man stuck a needle in my arm. I cried out, not sure what was happening, then held my arm in shock. The world tilted right, everything slanting before going black. I closed my eyes, thinking, *This can't be good.*

I HAVEN'T WRITTEN in a month. Not since the diagnosis, but I have to today. My heart is breaking, but not because of my own worries. No, I weep for my dear Alatheia. She went missing, and no one has been able to find her. Kit's partner tried to get to her, but he got turned away, everything locked in juvenile records. Her family prepared for the opportunity, as if they were just biding their time.

It is awful. I was there when Kit told the boys she was gone—and that we don't yet know where. My sons will find her. They are such good men. But the boys—my hearts—

they're devastated. Phoenix completely fell apart, but perhaps in the long run that will be a good thing. He actually asked Eric for help—a first since he was tiny. Thank the Lord, perhaps he will be off drugs soon. They'll send him to the lake, to the clinic that helped so many of us over the years.

The other side of the lake won't be able to touch him.

But it isn't just Phoenix who fell apart when she went missing. They've all collapsed. I don't know what will happen until we get her back, but I know I don't want to shift the attention to me right now. After they get Alatheia back, I will tell them.

Until then, they need me strong, so I will be strong. Robert always said I was good in a crisis, but I feel so helpless now. Kit told me not to interfere just yet. If he needs me, he'll tell me. My loves are calling me home, but I can't come yet, Boys. Not yet. The children still need me.

DL

UNTITLED

Thank you so much for reading! If you liked Dahlias, please go grab Lilies which is next up in the series and is either available for pre-order right now or to read right away depending on when you are reading this book! I appreciate every reader. These days I pretty much hide from social media (it is scary out there!) but you can email me at BeccaGrim79@gmail.com and I am a wonderful pen-pal!

--RR